TWO FAMILIES AT WAR

David Lowther

Sacristy
Press

Sacristy Press
PO Box 612, Durham, DH1 9HT

www.sacristy.co.uk

First published in 2015 by Sacristy Press, Durham

Sacristy Limited, registered in England & Wales, number 7565667

British Library Cataloguing-in-Publication Data
A catalogue record for the book is available from the British Library

ISBN 978-1-908381-16-3

PART ONE

Persecution: June 1938

"Fear is the parent of cruelty"
JAMES ANTHONY FRONDE, 1877

CHAPTER ONE

Jonathan lay prostrate on his stomach. Still in the same position, he slowly opened his eyes and looked at the pavement, his cheek resting on the ground. He saw a mixture of water from the rain that had recently fallen and blood, his own blood, pouring from his nose and leaking from a cut on his lip. Cautiously, he looked up from the pavement that stretched away from him towards the entrance to the park. A group of four boys who, until a couple of years ago, had been amongst his closest friends at his local school, the gymnasium, stood there. They were looking back towards him, laughing loudly and throwing insults before they turned into the park.

Gingerly, Jonathan pushed himself into a kneeling position and stood up. Several people passed by, but totally ignored him. He inspected the damage. His shirt was torn and covered in blood and his trousers were damp and filthy. The contents of his school bag were strewn across the pavement. The bag itself he found in the gutter. He collected his belongings and fastened them into the bag. His nose was still bleeding, but not too much. He'd had a bloody nose before, playing football, and he remembered how his teacher had dealt with it, so he tipped his head back and pinched the bridge of his nose with his thumb and first finger. After a moment or so that seemed to do the trick and he slowly set off towards his home in Grünewald Strasse. It was a bit of a struggle. Apart from being punched in the face, he'd received several kicks to his legs and a couple of particularly nasty ones to his stomach. He knew he'd feel bruised for a while.

Jonathan completed the short walk in a little less than ten minutes and wearily made his way up the steps to the family apartment in the five storey building. He let himself in and found his mother waiting for him

"My god Jonathan! What's happened?" his mother Ruth asked.

"I got beaten up by four of my former friends."

"Are you all right? You look terrible."

"I probably look a lot worse than I feel. I'll be fine," Jonathan replied.

"But why now?"

"I got kicked out of the gymnasium today," referring to the school where he had been a pupil for almost five years. "I suppose those brave members of the master race thought they'd celebrate by giving me a going over."

Ruth led Jonathan to the kitchen, bathed his nose and mouth and rubbed butter onto his forehead where a large lump had appeared. Then she told him to run a bath and lie in the warm water to soothe his wounds. By the time he'd finished, she said, his father would be home for the evening meal.

Jonathan, his mother and his father Benjamin had lived in Grünewald Strasse for almost fifteen years. The boy was now fifteen and tall, broad shouldered and muscular with the same straight light brown hair he'd inherited from his parents, although flecks of grey were now beginning to appear in his father's sideboards. Both parents were tall and Ruth looked like the athlete she once was during her childhood in Potsdam. She had the tough wiry frame of a sprinter and hurdler. She had once been beautiful and still, as she approached early middle age, much of that beauty was in evidence. Her strong personality meant that she often led the family decision-making process, although Benjamin was a partner, not a meek follower.

There were just the three of them, the Gerber family. They were hard working and, until recently, fairly wealthy. They did, however, have one huge disadvantage in the "new" Germany of Adolf Hitler: they were Jewish, although none were orthodox. As a family, they'd frequently attended the Berlin Reform Congregation, a very liberal place of worship where services were conducted entirely in German. Of course, the Nazis had begun to persecute the Jews soon after they came to power in 1933. As a result Jonathan had not had a bar mitzvah. Some members of the Congregation had converted to Protestantism but this was not enough to save them from the hatred of the Nazis. Ruth had grown up with her brother Klaus east of the capital. Both her parents, who were now dead, had been teachers. Neither had forced traditional Jewish religious behaviour on their children. The Gerber family did not altogether shun Jewish life. From time to time, they took part in social events based at the local synagogue and sometimes worshipped on Holy Days like Yom Kippur and Passover, but Saturday was a working day for Benjamin so he ignored the Sabbath. Klaus had seen the writing on the wall for Germany's Jews soon after Hitler became Chancellor in early 1933 and had taken his family to re-settle in America. Benjamin had inherited his busy store from his father and had managed, until recently, to keep the business expanding. The two had met when Ruth had applied for a job there as an office assistant.

None of the Gerbers looked Jewish. They attended the synagogue infrequently and they didn't have a Jewish name, although their first names were Old Testament, but so were many German names. They had always celebrated Christmas and Easter, though not in church with the other Berliners. They loved the German Christmas and enjoyed it with millions of others. Being Jewish in Berlin had only begun to really trouble them after the Olympic Games two years before. People thought that eventually Hitler would be overthrown and things would return to normal. But, after the Olympic truce, when the Nazis did all they could to cover up their anti-Semitic activities for fear of offending visiting athletes, officials and spectators, they began to attack the Jews with even greater hostility. Soon afterwards their friends began to avoid them, Benjamin's general store began to lose customers, and Jonathan became the victim of bullying and insults at school. It was astonishing that he'd kept his place at the gymnasium for so long since the Nazis had told the Jews to set up their own schools in 1936. It was only the support of his teacher, Herr Drezner, that had prevented the axe from falling earlier. The kindly teacher had seen in the Jewish boy great potential, both as a scholar and a sportsman, and had helped him all he could. But neither his sporting prowess nor his bright intelligence had saved him from the wave of anti-Semitic hatred that had swept across the country's schools and all sections of society. Inevitably, Drezner had been denounced by several of the pupils as a Jew lover and had promptly vanished to heaven knows where. Jonathan's time was up.

◆   ◆   ◆

While Jonathan was soaking in the bath, Ruth was preparing the evening meal. The kitchen, like the rest of the apartment, was clean and spacious. As well as the sparkling kitchen and bathroom, there were two good-sized bedrooms and a beautiful large living area, tastefully furnished with light oak dining chairs, table and sideboard. A three-seat settee in off-white leather and three matching easy chairs and low tables for coffee and drinks provided comfortable accommodation for the family and their visitors, who by now had become few and far between. The drapes were soft yellow and the walls brilliant white, making the whole room appear light and happy.

The Gerbers were the only Jewish family in the building. Immediately below them lived the Friedmans; Axel and Julia, with their two girls Erika and Wander. Ruth had been very friendly with Julia until a couple of years ago when the Nazi menace began to grow. Jonathan had been a close friend with fifteen year old Erika since both were young children, but that relationship was now a distant memory.

Above the Gerbers lived the Bergs; Dieter and Marlise with their young daughter Elizabeth. They had kept themselves to themselves since moving in a little over a year ago, rather like the Kellers on the top floor, Joseph and Greta, with their infant children Johannes and Nadine.

Although the Gerbers' friendship with the Friedmans had cooled in recent years, there was no animosity between them. Nor was there with the Kellers or the Bergs, but the same couldn't be said of the Kaufmanns who lived in the ground floor apartment. These two, Hans and Karen, were childless and poured all their energies into being totally committed and fanatical Nazis. Hans was a March Violet, one of the hundreds of thousands who had become members of the party after Hitler's accession to power in 1933. He had made up for lost time by joining the local Brownshirts and had even used his apartment to interrogate so-called enemies of the state from time to time. Both husband and wife stared with hatred at the Gerbers every time their paths crossed. All other families in the apartment building were extremely wary of the Kaufmanns who excelled at eavesdropping and denouncing. Any loose word or suspicious action could lead to a visit from the Gestapo. Jonathan was sure that it was their threat to the Friedmans that had ended his friendship with Erika.

◆　　　◆　　　◆

Benjamin had closed up his store and strode into the apartment wearing hat and coat and clutching his briefcase while Jonathan was still in the bath. He was a tall, handsome man who usually called out a cheerful "hello" as soon as he entered. His wife's expression, however, stopped him in his tracks and, after Ruth had greeted him with a kiss, she recounted the tale of their son's beating and expulsion from the gymnasium.

"Is he badly hurt?" asked Benjamin, his face creased with worry.

"Just cuts and bruises. You know how tough he is. The wounds will heal but I'm not sure how long he'll tolerate being treated worse than an animal."

"Do you think he'll strike back one day?"

"I'm certain of it. There were four of them today but one day there may only be one or two and he'll go for them and end up in the hands of the Gestapo. Then we'll all be locked up."

"You're right," Benjamin replied. "It's time we gave some serious thought to our future, especially for Jonathan's sake."

Benjamin slumped into a chair and leant forward with his head in his hands. His mind drifted back to earlier days when his small family shared happy evenings at the cinema, theatre or music hall following a meal at one of the many fine cafés on the Ku'damm. He thought of Jonathan, the star footballer at his gymnasium, and lovely summer afternoon walks in the Tiergarten. His store, which sold clothes, shoes, pots and pans, cutlery, small items of furniture, cloth and sweets, once had five serving counters but the slump in trade meant there were now only two. The family doctor and dentist had struck them from their patients' lists. The Nazi laws now forbade all things like entertainments for Jews, except for visits to the Tiergarten, where poorly located benches were painted yellow for their exclusive use. The best seats were reserved for everyone else.

"Pull yourself together Benjamin," Ruth snapped, shaking her husband from his day-dreaming. "We need to do something about this, not sit about moping and sighing. And we need to involve Jonathan in these discussions. He's nearly sixteen and has a right to say what he thinks and feels."

"I'm sorry. You're quite right."

◆   ◆   ◆

At this point Jonathan walked into the room. He had on a clean shirt and trousers and tried to appear cheerful.

"Hi Dad."

"Hello son. Your mother tells me you've been in the wars. How are you?"

"Alright. There were too many for me. If there'd just been three of them, I'd have left them in the gutter."

Benjamin laughed. "I'm sure of that but after dinner I think the three of us need to sit down and chat about the future. There's more to this than just the odd beating up."

"I know that, Dad."

CHAPTER TWO

The evening meal passed quietly. Little was said. A mood of desolation seemed to envelop all three. Ruth cleared the table, assisted by Jonathan who then did the washing up while his mother prepared the coffee. Eventually they settled down with their drinks. Jonathan slouched back on the settee while his parents took an easy chair each.

Ruth began. "Benjamin, you should tell us what's happening. Jonathan and I can add things that we consider important."

"Right," said Benjamin who then described everything that had happened to his family and most of the rest of Berlin's Jews over the past five and a half years and especially the last couple of years when the pressure had greatly increased.

He told Jonathan about the boycott of Jewish shops in April 1933, although that hadn't amounted to much, and then said that things had worsened from 1935 onwards by which time Hitler had removed most of his political opponents, especially the Communists.

"It was almost as if he was working to a timetable; get rid of the Communists then turn on the Jews," Benjamin continued.

He then explained the growing number of attacks on Jews, especially from the Brownshirts, and told his son about the devastating effects of the passing of the Nuremberg Laws in 1935.

"Before those laws we were full citizens, with the same rights as every other German. Now we're just subjects, with no rights at all, like in a conquered country. I was proud to be German. I fought for my country in the war. For a while we war veterans were protected from the worst behaviour of the Nazis. Now I'm just like every other Jew, a pariah. Even if I'd won the Iron Cross First Class in France, I'd still be treated like a dog."

"Why does Hitler hate the Jews so much?" asked Jonathan.

Ruth spoke for the first time. "There're about a million Jews in Germany, a tiny fraction of the population, yet many of our leading scientists, artists, writers, doctors, musicians, lawyers, bankers and even some former politicians, are Jewish. I'm sure Hitler's jealous of that. And don't forget that before 1933 things were pretty dreadful with millions of poor people out of work after we'd lost the war. The Jews are blamed for all of that."

Benjamin then talked about the decline in his business due to the boycott of Jewish shops. He'd made a lot of money supplying work clothing, tools and cooking utensils in bulk to town and city councils, but now such contracts were forbidden to be given to Jews by the government.

"How has all this affected you, Jonathan?" asked Ruth.

"Apart from being beaten up and insulted, I've been banned from swimming and all sports, listened at school while some of the teachers described the Jews as vermin, refused entry to the public library and lost all of my friends."

"And what's more," said Ruth "films are censored, newspapers that speak out against the government have been closed down, the radio is controlled by the Nazis, music by some of our greatest composers has been banned and I can't even have a cup of coffee in the Romanisches Café in the Ku'damm, or anywhere else, come to that."

Benjamin then told his son about the disappearance of many Jews and Communists into the concentration camps. Their "local" one was north of the city in Oranienburg and several of his acquaintances had been taken there, never to be seen again.

"It's terrible," said Jonathan. "What can we do about it?"

"The same as many other Jews: emigrate," said Ruth.

There was a moment's silence. Jonathan quietly spoke. "There's no other choice really. How do we go about it and how soon can we go?"

"Tomorrow if we could, but there are a lot of fences to jump. It could take as long as a year," sighed Benjamin.

"A year!" exclaimed Jonathan. "How can we survive till then?"

"With difficulty," said Ruth, "and things may get worse until we escape. But we will survive and we will get out."

Benjamin then went through the difficulties of emigrating from Germany. They had to be issued with an exit visa, but not before obtaining a visa from the country to which they wished to emigrate.

"Not all countries welcome Jewish refugees," Benjamin explained. "There are lots of people all over the world without employment, so they won't want thousands of refugees pouring into their country to compete for what jobs there are. We need to go to a country where someone will speak up for us and help us to settle down. It's no good us turning up at some foreign port expecting to be welcomed with open arms. Someone has to sponsor us."

Benjamin then told Jonathan how he would be forbidden to take up employment in most countries and that some countries like the USA had quotas of the number of refugees they would allow into their country each year. All countries had waiting lists, so the sooner they got on these lists the better.

"So who will sponsor us and where?" asked Jonathan.

"Your father and I have thought about this and we've come up with two possibilities; your uncle Klaus and his family in Detroit in America and your father's business friend Richard Walker in England."

"Who's Richard Walker? I've never heard of him."

Benjamin then told him about the Englishman who had left Germany with his Jewish wife and two boys after the Nuremberg Laws had been passed. They now lived in Kingston in south-west London where Richard had an important job in a department store.

"Richard and I had many business dealings together and we became very close friends. I'm sure he'd try to help."

"And so would my brother Klaus in Detroit," added Ruth.

"Either of those sounds good to me," said Jonathan. "It's a good job I learned English at the gymnasium. That's something I got from the place, at least."

Ruth smiled. "I'm sure your father and I will cope with the language as well. If we have any problems, we can always turn to you to act as interpreter."

Jonathan laughed then stopped abruptly as another thought flashed through his mind. "How will we pay for all this if you can't work Dad? And what about school?"

"You'll go to school and probably university wherever we end up. As for money, there will be difficulties, but we'll manage .Your father and I have already talked about money. Tell him, Benjamin."

Benjamin went through the problems they'd face. The government would force them to sell their apartment, furniture, possessions as well as his business and goods at a ridiculous knock-down price. No chance that the Nazis would allow any Jew to make a profit or break-even when they disposed of their assets. Any valuables like jewellery would have to be given to the authorities before their departure. Each person was allowed to take ten Reichmarks in cash out of the country. In America that was worth about four dollars and in England about one-and-a-half of their pounds.

"That won't get us far," said Jonathan. "What will you do?"

"Your father has an idea about that."

Jonathan sat silently in thought for a moment then his face lit up.

"I've got it Dad! Your stamps."

Benjamin had been a keen stamp collector since he was a boy and his collection, now worth more than two hundred thousand Reichmarks, was safely locked up in the bedroom. Jonathan had never taken much interest in stamp collecting and preferred to spend his time swimming and playing football. Now he saw the wisdom of his father's hobby.

"You're right, son. The problem is that, if I sell them in Germany, we'll not be able to take the cash out with us. If we try to take them with us, I'll be arrested as we try to leave. If we post them to someone overseas, there's a good chance that the snooping Nazis will open the mail and hang on to them. I'll have to think of something, but we'll have to be very careful. Remember Goering's new law a couple of years back? Any Jew caught smuggling his possessions out of the country will be arrested, tried and, if found guilty, executed."

"What about mum's jewels?"

"Not worth much," said Ruth. "I sold all of the decent stuff ages ago and your father used the cash to buy more stamps."

"You've worked all of this out brilliantly," Jonathan said to his parents.

"Not quite," said his father. "I still need to find a way of getting the stamps out."

It was almost time for bed by now and all three were feeling tired. They were worn out by the events of the day and the long discussion they'd had which had led them to deciding to leave the country in which they'd been born and lived all of their lives.

"Before we go to bed, we need to agree on a plan of action," suggested Ruth, as methodical as ever.

"Agreed," replied Benjamin. "You map it out please, Ruth."

"First I must write to Klaus in Detroit and you must write to Richard in England. We have to be careful with what we say. Don't forget, there's good chance they'll open the mail before it leaves Germany."

"You shouldn't have a problem in writing to your brother in Detroit. That's not a difficulty now that the Nazis know that everyone has to have a sponsor before being given a visa. They'll be glad to see the back of us. In fact, they'll be glad to see Germany totally free of Jews."

"What about Richard?" Ruth asked.

"That's a bit trickier. I think I'll write to him and invite him to Berlin to discuss business. He's not a relative after all. They might be a bit suspicious if I invite him to sponsor us. The Nazis won't know he doesn't sell goods anymore and Richard will know that I know that. So when he reads the letter, he'll smell a rat and sense we're in trouble. I'm sure he'll come. He likes a bit of intrigue."

Ruth then outlined the rest of the plan. Without arousing too much suspicion amongst the skeleton staff at his declining business, Benjamin would begin to dispose of what goods he could and convert the cash into stamps. Ruth would visit the US and British Embassies and collect the necessary immigration forms. They'd put together the cash needed to emigrate; cost of passage by ship, visa fee, the Nazis' emigration tax as well as money to live on in the time between selling the business and actually leaving the country. Everything else would be converted to stamps to pay for their new lives overseas. Meanwhile, they'd live on an austerity budget; plain food and no entertainments.

"What can I do?" asked Jonathan.

"You can look after your mother. Go with her to the Embassies and on all other errands. Neither of you look like Jews, so you shouldn't be bothered by the uniformed brigades. Somehow force your arms up and give the wretched German greeting. Strut about confidently as if you own the place, like the Nazis do. If by any chance you are insulted, turn the other cheek. I don't want you beating up any Brownshirts or Hitler Youths."

"What about school?"

"Forget it. You'll easily catch up when we get to our new country."

"One last thing," said Ruth. "Keep all this totally secret and don't say anything within earshot of those horrible Kaufmanns."

CHAPTER THREE

June passed into July. Most of the Nazis were getting excited about the rumblings in Czechoslovakia. Hitler was demanding that Germans living in that part of Czechoslovakia known as the Sudetenland be given self-rule and was making numerous threats to make sure this happened.

The Gerber family paid this little attention. They'd agreed on a plan and now set about putting it into action. Ruth wrote to her brother Klaus in Detroit and Benjamin wrote a straightforward letter to Richard Walker in England inviting him to Berlin to discuss business.

Jonathan, for the time being, stayed at home, reading and doing some strange looking exercises designed to keep up his strength and fitness. His parents felt it was better that he remain indoors until his cuts and bruises healed so that questions wouldn't be raised about his appearance.

Eventually, he set out with his mother to the US Embassy to register their interest in emigrating to Detroit and collect the application forms for visas. They had planned to follow this up with a visit to the British Embassy on the same day, but, when they arrived at the American Embassy, they found a huge queue, stretching back more than one hundred metres to the Brandenburg Gate.

It was almost six when they arrived home, so it was a late dinner and early night before heading out to the British Embassy the following morning.

The British Embassy was on Wilhelmstrasse, uncomfortably close to the heart of the Nazi government. The previous day's pattern was repeated; endless queues with hundreds of hopeful Jewish emigrants waiting patiently in line. It was another long day that ended with the documentation they needed safely in their hands. At both embassies, Ruth had been closely questioned about where they were planning to go, who would be looking after them, whether they'd be a financial burden on their new country, and so on.

It was all rather mundane, yet necessary, and when they arrived home there was some good news waiting for them. Klaus had replied from Detroit saying that he and his family would be delighted to welcome them into their home and advised them to complete their visa applications as quickly as possible.

Pleased as they were about this, they knew that this was only a first step in a long process. They had to deliver the applications, wait for replies, and, if they were positive, book passage to America and then go through the tortuous process of getting official permission to leave Germany. The application forms were completed and, one day in late August, they again joined the queue at the American Embassy.

The official who dealt with them checked their papers, said he was satisfied with the way in which they had been completed and then warned them that it would be some time before they received a reply and, in any case, the US Government operated a quota system and there was no guarantee that they would be granted visas.

International tension grew throughout September and it seemed possible that Germany might be at war with France, Britain, Russia and Czechoslovakia over the Sudeten business. The German people were on tenterhooks. In the middle of September, international meetings were held in the hope that the situation might be resolved without bloodshed.

Jonathan began to venture into the city, mostly to buy English books at second-hand shops to help him master the language. On these trips he noticed that few ordinary Berliners wanted war, but the arrogant Nazis were spoiling for a fight.

In the midst of the shuttle diplomacy, involving the British Prime Minister Chamberlain and Hitler, a reply came from Richard Walker. He was pleased to hear from his old friend and, of course, he would visit him in Berlin to discuss business. He gave his date and time of arrival at Berlin's Anhalter Station and asked if Benjamin would meet him there. Benjamin replied that he would. He knew full well that the delay in their correspondence was caused by snooping from the authorities. It was a time of great nervousness, both in the Gerber household and outside in the wider world. Jonathan secretly hoped that Britain and her allies would declare war on Germany and mercilessly overthrow the Nazi regime. His hopes were dashed, however, when the rather feeble looking Chamberlain and his French counterpart Daladier signed a treaty in Munich at the end of September, in which they meekly agreed to Hitler's demands and three million Sudeten Germans became part of Hitler's Reich.

◆　◆　◆

About a week after Munich, while the Germans were marching into the Sudetenland, Richard Walker arrived in Berlin. The whole family greeted him at the station. Richard, like Benjamin, walked with purpose, and Jonathan watched as a man of a little over medium height strode towards them. He was carrying a suitcase in one hand and his fawn raincoat over the other arm. A brown trilby with a light grey band was perched on the back of his head, giving him a somewhat easy-going air. He took his hat off to kiss Ruth on the cheek, revealing a full head of curly brown hair, which made him look more like thirty than the forty-five he actually was. They set off by U-Bahn, after shaking hands, to Grünewald Strasse, making one change en route. On the way across the city, they talked of little but Richard's journey, which he said was fine, and the weather.

It was a cloudy and cool autumn day when they let Richard into the apartment. As far as he could remember, Jonathan had never met Richard before but he was impressed by what he saw; a bright and cheerful man who seemed to be both intelligent and kind and had a face that inspired confidence. The two took an instant liking to one another and Jonathan quickly realised that the Englishman was more than the happy-go-lucky man they'd met off the train.

As soon as they were in the apartment, a rather curious incident took place. Richard put his finger to his lips, warning everyone to keep quiet. He then proceeded to examine every light fitting, peered behind the furniture and a couple of pictures on the wall, and then looked behind the curtains. He then left the living room and repeated the process in both bedrooms, the bathroom and the kitchen, watched by a dumbfounded Gerber family. After he'd finished, he beckoned the three of them to follow him into the kitchen. He turned the cold tap on at full blast and, with the noise of the rushing water creating a fair old din, he asked Benjamin for a screwdriver. Benjamin reached down and took the tool from the cupboard under the sink. Richard nodded his thanks and, with the tap still running, left the kitchen and dismantled and closely inspected the telephone. Satisfied, he re-assembled it, returned to the kitchen, handed the screwdriver back to Benjamin and asked how thick the walls and ceilings were. Having been assured that they were very thick indeed, he turned the tap off, smiled and said, "Sorry about that but the Nazis are masters at eavesdropping. They bug phones, install hidden microphones and use sympathetic tenants to listen in on conversations. Is there anyone in the building you don't trust?"

"The Kaufmanns on the ground floor," replied Ruth. "They're both rabid Nazis and he's a Brownshirt."

"I don't suppose for one minute that even the Nazis would have the resources to bug the home of every Jew in Berlin but, having read our correspondence, they could have easily tipped off the apartment block spy to keep an eye on us. They gave me a hard time at the border, which suggests they were on the look-out for me. Still, it all seems clear and we're safe to talk in here. Outdoors is another matter. Small talk only. I know I'm sounding a bit melodramatic but you can't be sure of anything. We're in the surveillance state after all."

Ruth then left for the kitchen to make coffee and returned with four steaming mugs and a plate of cakes.

As they ate and drank their way through the snacks, Ruth said. "I've put you in Jonathan's room. He can sleep in here on our camp bed. It's only for a couple of days after all."

Jonathan gave a wry grin. Richard smiled at him and said, "I suggest that after you and I have finished our coffees, Benjamin, we head off to your store. It would raise suspicion with your spies downstairs if we stayed closeted in here for two days. Besides, we're here to talk about business. What better place to do that than at your store? After dinner tonight you can tell me how I can help you. There's obviously something out of the ordinary or else why didn't you spell it all out in a letter?"

Benjamin saw the sense of this and instantly agreed, at the same time realising that his prolonged absence from the store might raise suspicion.

"And tomorrow," Richard continued, "Ruth and Jonathan can give me a quick tour of your wonderful city while you're at work Benjamin. We can tie up any loose ends after dinner tomorrow evening before I return home the following morning."

After Benjamin and Richard left the apartment, mother and son sat down and, for a moment, just looked at each other. They realised they'd hit the jackpot. If anyone could help them, Richard could and, despite the fact that their acquaintance was brief, they already knew they could trust him.

Ruth spent the rest of the afternoon cleaning the apartment and preparing dinner. She settled on a pot roast with cream sauce, mashed potatoes and green vegetables followed by apfelstrudel with whipped cream. Two bottles of German white wine were chilled for this special occasion.

Jonathan's afternoon was spent reading, exercising and thinking about Richard. In times of such uncertainty, he felt himself fortunate to be in the hands of such reliable people.

◆　　◆　　◆

Richard and Benjamin returned a little after six and, after a quick wash and brush up, the four of them settled down to what proved to be an excellent dinner, washed down by the first class white wine. Once the dishes were cleared and the washing up done, they relaxed with their coffees and their guest signalled the start of the real business of the day. "How can I help you?"

Benjamin outlined the problems of being a Jew in Berlin and the family's urgent need to emigrate. He told him that they had applied for US visas and were hoping to do the same for Great Britain. Richard immediately guaranteed his total support and said he would do all he could to see they received visas, but he warned them it wouldn't be easy.

"Rather like America, the UK government is being careful about how many refugees they admit. Unemployment is still high and there just aren't enough jobs to go round. If you were an eminent scientist, they'd grab you like a shot. Many people in England think that war is inevitable, even if Chamberlain doesn't. Those preparing for war need all the expertise they can find which is why German scientists would be so welcome."

"Does that mean we've little chance, Richard?" Ruth asked.

"Not at all. It'll just take longer. Where do you plan to live?"

Cautiously, and with slight embarrassment, Benjamin looked at Richard.

"Well, we'd hoped that you might find us something temporary until we can get a place of our own."

"Consider it done. You'll stay with me to begin with. It'll be a bit crowded but I've some friends who might help."

"Thank you, Richard," said Benjamin.

"What about money. How will you live?"

Benjamin said that they would be bringing hardly any cash with them. Richard already knew about the restrictions and Ruth explained that whatever paltry sums of money they raised by selling their assets in Berlin would be swallowed up by emigration and travel costs. Then Benjamin told Richard about the stamps.

Richard, who seemed to have a nose for subterfuge, jumped at this straightaway.

"So you've got the stamps, they're worth a small fortune, but getting them out could be tricky. I can't think of an immediate solution, but there must be one. Let me sleep on it and I'll see if I can come up with a plan and we'll talk again after dinner tomorrow."

The rest of the evening passed quietly, with Richard talking about his family's new life in England, how well his boys were doing at school, the excellent job which his boss Reg had found him. He spoke of Reg's family, his courageous son who was an anti-appeasement journalist and his other son who was a brilliant scientist in the making. But most of all he said how happy his Jewish wife Inge was at being out of Berlin.

"So I know how you feel and, if you come to England, we'll look after you. If you go to America, I'm sure you'll be equally happy there. Now

I'll think about how to smuggle those stamps out. If you'll excuse me, I'm going to turn in early. Thank you, Ruth, for a wonderful meal."

◆　　◆　　◆

Benjamin set off for work early the next morning. After a leisurely breakfast, Ruth, Jonathan and Richard started out for a day in the city. They caught the U-Bahn to Zoo Garden Bahnhof, strolled around the world famous zoo, wandered in and out of the shops on the Ku'damm, ate a traditional German sausage lunch, then walked through the Tiergarten to the Brandenburg Gate. Then they caught the S-Bahn back to Zoo and finished the journey home underground. All of them had seen these sights before but they behaved like enthusiastic tourists with smiles on their faces and even gave the dreaded German greeting on a couple of occasions. By the time they got home, Benjamin had returned from the store. Ruth hurriedly prepared their evening meal which they ate quickly before settling down to listen to Richard.

Richard told them what he proposed to do about the stamp smuggling.

"A friend of mine has got an excellent contact in the British Foreign Office. I propose to ask my pal to see if he can arrange, through his Foreign Office man, to have the stamps collected from you in Berlin then taken by courier to England. It's no use mailing them from the Berlin Embassy or even sending them via diplomatic bag. The Nazis seem to have their noses into everything. It would mean one of you taking the stamps to the Embassy in a suitably disguised package and handing them only to the person whom my contact says is totally reliable. I hope the same person will then take them to England. He won't be searched because he'll be carrying diplomatic papers. However he chooses to travel to England, he'll be under strict instructions to hand them over personally to me at Liverpool Street Station or wherever. I'll then deposit the stamps in a bank."

"Sounds good, Richard," said Benjamin. "How will we know it's all going ahead?"

"I've thought about that too. As soon as I've set it up, I'll write to you about nothing in particular but the letter will include the phrase thank you for your hospitality. If that phrase isn't there, it's not going ahead. At my end I'll suggest that our reliable courier writes to you about your visa applications. You might have other letters about those, of course, but the one about the stamp smuggling will include the phrase please bring the appropriate documentation to me and then he'll name a date, time and room. When I've safely received them, I'll write to you again and include the phrase let's hope there's no war this year. That'll tell you the stamps are safely tucked away. If you end up in America, I'll get them to you there, I promise."

Jonathan was busily writing these phrases down when Benjamin said, "That should work. Thank you, Richard."

"I know it all sounds a bit cloak and dagger but we've got to get this right. Your whole future is at stake. Oh, and one last thing, don't deal with anyone else at the Embassy except the writer of the letter. Ambassador Henderson is a close friend of Chamberlain and seems to like the Nazis, and he's got plenty of colleagues who feel the same way."

The next day Ruth and Jonathan accompanied Richard to the Bahnhof and saw him on his way back home. Both were very envious of their friend but tried not to show it, and were even more delighted when Richard promised to do what he could about speeding up their visa application, although he warned them it would be more difficult than the stamp smuggling. Things were definitely looking up for the Gerbers and, for a while, they faced the future with some optimism.

◆   ◆   ◆

Two weeks later a young Polish Jew shot a Nazi diplomat in Paris.

CHAPTER FOUR

Benjamin sensed a great tension when he went to work on 9 November. The compulsory National Radio in his store gave constant updates on the health of the Nazi diplomat who was called von Rath. It announced that the criminal was a seventeen year old Jew named Herschel Grynszpan, and called for revenge on all Jews. A couple of his remaining employees looked at him with hatred, others averted their gaze, and one even viewed him with sympathy. More updates on von Rath's condition followed; Hitler's personal physician was now looking after him.

Benjamin felt like a marked man as he quickly made his way home at the end of the day. He let himself into the apartment and locked and bolted the door. A terrified Ruth and Jonathan jumped up from their seats and embraced him, relieved that he had reached home unharmed. The three could hardly touch their food and, after the table was cleared, sat down with their nerves stretched to breaking point, keeping themselves up-to-date with events from the radio. An announcement of von Rath's death came in the early evening, describing it as an attack by world Jewry on the Third Reich and calling for the party faithful to take revenge.

Just after nine o'clock the front door of the apartment building slammed shut. Peering through the curtains, Ruth told the others that Kaufmann was marching away from the building in his ordinary clothes. They settled down and waited.

◆ ◆ ◆

The family sat and chatted nervously. They discussed how the Nazis were enacting new anti-Jewish measures every day. Jewish doctors and dentists had been struck off medical registers, and Jews now had to carry ID cards with the names Israel or Sara added to their existing names. Anti-Semitic demonstrations had been reported from all parts of the country. Signs such as "Jews not welcome here" and "whoever buys from a Jew is a traitor to their country" were appearing everywhere. A professor in Munich had identified Jewish traits such as cruelty, hatred, violent emotions and Asiatic eyes. The Gerbers knew that they were not identifiable as Jews but they were well aware at the risks of covering this up.

◆   ◆   ◆

Kaufmann headed for the nearest bar where he found half-a-dozen of his Brownshirt mates drinking. They were all well on the way to being drunk. All the talk was of what they were going to do to the Jews tonight. Conversation became louder and more violent as the evening went on.

Just after eleven their commander appeared with more Brownshirts. The newcomers, like everyone else, were in ordinary clothes. The boss told them to collect cans of petrol, axes and hammers from the wagon outside and then go out and take revenge on the Jews.

The bellowing mob strutted towards the Zoo Garden Bahnhof. They passed a synagogue and, with a huge roar, marched in. Seizing several religious artefacts, including an ancient-looking copy of the Old Testament, the Torah and the altar cloth, they threw them into the street. Returning to the building and smashing everything they could find into a pile of rubble, they finally poured petrol over the wreckage of the house of worship. They put a match to the bonfire before dashing into the street and starting a second fire of the stuff they'd thrown out of the synagogue. Smoke and then flames came from the building and soon the street fire was ablaze. Almost immediately afterwards, with a huge cheer from the Brownshirts, a roaring inferno was rushing towards the dark November night sky. The inebriated rabble celebrated long and loudly before setting off for more sport.

Soon they were in the Ku'damm where they found many fine Jewish shops. These they systematically destroyed. Starting with the windows, they demolished everything. The brutish Brownshirts stepped through the mess into the shops and, despite being given strict orders not to loot, grabbed everything they could; jewellery, cameras, watches, clothes, cosmetics, clothes and shoes. Every window of every Jewish shop was smashed and the pavement soon became coated with a thick carpet of glass. Anything they couldn't steal, they destroyed. Furniture was reduced to sawdust and curtains were set on fire.

◆　　◆　　◆

There were several groups of Brownshirts spread throughout the Ku'damm and the adjoining streets. Having totally obliterated many of the premises of one of the world's most luxurious shopping areas to their satisfaction, Kaufmann and his associates turned their attention towards the residential areas.

They marched purposefully, still fuelled by alcohol, towards Chalottenburg where many wealthy Jews lived. The boss pointed them towards a large villa which, he told them, was home to a rich Jew and his family. They broke in through the front door with axes and strode into the large living room where the husband, a banker, stood waiting in terror with his wife and two young daughters, all four of them in their nightclothes. One Brownshirt produced a whip and struck the banker on his neck. Blood spurted out and he staggered forwards. His wife screamed and moved to help her husband but a Brownshirt moved to roughly grab her, tearing her night dress and revealing a breast in the process. He eyed her lustfully but, before he could get his hands on her, the boss shouted, "Enough. All you Jewish pigs outside. The rest of you, reduce this place to a heap of shit."

The Jewish family was shoved into the street, still in their nightclothes. The banker's wife was crying and the children screaming. Back in the house, Kaufmann and his friends destroyed the family home piece by piece. Furniture was smashed to pieces. Pipes were ripped out from the kitchen and bathroom, causing water to cascade through the house. The curtains were slashed. The kitchen and bathroom were totally ruined and all that was left of them was a small mountain of white dust and broken porcelain. In their drunken frenzy, the mob managed to forget about the three bedrooms as they returned to the living area where they began urinating, defecating and vomiting over the beautiful carpet.

Outside, a large black car pulled up and the banker was thrown into the back with another petrified soul and driven away. The rest of the family were left weeping outside the villa while the Brownshirts set off in pursuit of further prey.

By dawn they were exhausted. Having wrecked another six innocent families' lives, the boss suggested they went home for some rest and food. They were told to re-assemble at their local bar at mid-morning when they would finish the job.

Kaufmann turned towards Grünewaldstrasse, but the boss called him back.

"Kaufmann, I believe there are a family of Jews living in your apartment building."

"That's right. A particularly nasty lot. A store owner, his wife and their teenage son. They don't look like Jews, don't go to their synagogue and his store is in a non-Jewish area. They don't appear to have any Jewish friends. They're pretending to be good Germans, but they're not. They're just another revolting group of Jews."

"I see," said the boss. "Perhaps we should pay them a visit later today."

"I'd rather you didn't. That lot," he said, pointing to the retreating rabble, "would probably smash the whole building up, including my own apartment and those of loyal Germans."

"What are their names and where is his store?"

The boss pulled out a pocket book and wrote this information down. "Benjamin Gerber," he said to no one in particular, "I'll deal with him later today."

◆　　◆　　◆

Soon after dawn, the Gerbers, who had been slouching half-awake in their living room all night, were disturbed by the sound of the drunken Kaufmann staggering up the street, his boots echoing sharply on the pavement. The door slammed and he went into his ground floor apartment.

"I'd be interested to know what he's been up to," Benjamin said.

The Gerbers were fully aware that something had been happening but they weren't sure exactly what. The skies of Berlin had been red since just after midnight and there had been a non-stop rumble of shouting, screaming and breaking glass. Anxious as they were to know what was going on, they hadn't the slightest intention of leaving their apartment to find out.

"We'll just have to sit it out," said Ruth.

The radio constantly reminded its listeners that righteous vengeance against the Jewish murderers was being dealt out all over Germany. So the family sat tight.

In early afternoon there was a soft, anxious tapping on the door. They froze and held their breath but the tapping continued, more urgently this time. Ruth got up and cautiously opened the door and was shocked to find her neighbour and old friend Julia Friedman standing there with tears pouring down her face. Ruth hastily took her arm, pulled her into their sitting room and closed the door.

"Julia. What is it?" asked an anxious Ruth, gently leading her old friend to the settee.

"Erika and I have just walked up to the Ku'damm."

"Julia. It's dangerous even being seen with us."

"It's fine. Kaufmann's asleep. You can hear his horrible pig-like snoring rising up the stairwell."

"Why are you crying?"

"Because of what we saw on the Ku'damm. There were shops smashed up, synagogues on fire, but the worse thing was the Jewish men being kicked, beaten and then led away by the Brownshirts and the SS. There was a group of local schoolchildren with their teacher standing on the edge of the pavement spitting on the Jews as they were led away. It was like some vile organised school activity."

The Gerbers sat in stunned silence. Now they knew what the commotion was and the extent of the catastrophe that was threatening them. Julia began to cry even more.

"God, I'm so ashamed of being German. I hope this Nazi nightmare soon passes. You must get away," she urged. "It's not safe for you here."

"We're trying to," Ruth replied, "but it's not as easy as all that. Julia you must leave. If you're found here you'll be arrested. Thank you for coming to see us."

"I'm so sorry, Ruth. We used to be such good friends, but it's so frightening. Kaufmann told us not to have anything to do with you or we would be accused of collaborating with enemies of the state and racial inferiors. He said he would have us arrested. Please forgive me."

Ruth embraced her. "Of course we do Julia. Now you really must go before Kaufmann wakes up. Creep quietly down the stairs. Thank you for coming. It's very brave of you."

Julia silently slipped out of the door and Ruth closed it quietly behind her. The family settled down to wait. They turned the radio on and, shortly after four, an announcement told them that the action against the Jews had been completed.

Benjamin got up from his seat. "Right. It seems it might be safe out there. I'm going to see if the store is still standing."

"Please be careful," said Ruth.

"I will. I'll come straight back."

◆　　◆　　◆

Luckily Benjamin's store was not in an area targeted by thugs and it was no real surprise to him that it appeared untouched as he approached the main door. Two men, one wearing a fawn raincoat and the other a leather coat, crossed the road from a waiting car. Benjamin let out a sigh of relief, assuming that all was well with the shop. He reached into his overcoat pocket for his keys, when one of the men grasped his arm and said.

"Herr Gerber?"

"Yes."

One of the men thrust a piece of paper under his nose.

"Gestapo," he snapped. "You will come with us."

CHAPTER FIVE

Panic began to envelop Ruth and Jonathan by early evening. Where was Benjamin? Was he safe? Was he still at liberty?

"I'm going to look for him," said Jonathan.

"No. It's bad enough waiting and wondering what's happened to your father. I couldn't bear it if you disappeared as well."

"But I can look after myself."

"I know, against two or three. But there are dozens of them out there. You wouldn't stand a chance. You'd end up in prison or dead."

The radio continued to spew out anti-Jewish propaganda. The Jews were told they'd have to clean up the mess they'd made and pay for the damage they'd caused. Enemies of the Reich had been arrested. Ruth and Benjamin sat tight. They had no one to turn to and nowhere to go. They just waited.

Two days passed without news. Then, on the third day there was a loud banging on the door. Ruth stood petrified in the middle of the room while Jonathan nervously went to see who was there. Kaufmann stood there, resplendent in his ill-fitting, brown SA uniform. He had a big head which always surprised Jonathan who believed there was obviously little inside the Brownshirt's skull. His face was the shape of a melon and he'd shaved his light brown hair so that there was little left on top. He was short and overweight, but a man of great bravery when helped by a half-dozen of his companions in beating up an old Jewish man. He looked at Jonathan with a smirk on his face.

"You are to report to the front of the Zoo Bahnhof to clear up the dreadful mess you left the other night."

"Where's my husband?" pleaded Ruth.

"No idea. Some members of your sub-human race have killed themselves. Others have been locked up. I neither know nor care what's happened to Gerber. Now get out and clear up the disgusting mess you've left."

Jonathan managed to keep control of his temper and collected their outdoor clothing. He helped his mother into her winter coat and, nervously, they trudged towards the Zoo Bahnhof. Once there, they were told by the brave boys in brown to join a group clearing up glass and other rubbish. Brushes and shovels were provided. Brownshirts, armed with whips, supervised the operation. The group looked over their shoulders as they whispered amongst themselves. From these hushed conversations, Ruth and Jonathan learned that many Jews had committed suicide in Berlin and nearly all of the synagogues had been burned to the ground. Men had been arrested for no apparent reason and, it was thought, taken to Gestapo Headquarters for questioning. Of the fate of many husbands, fathers and sons, a deathly silence pervaded the Jewish community. They had simply disappeared. Families waited in despair.

◆   ◆   ◆

Benjamin was one of those who had been taken to Gestapo HQ. Located in the heart of the Nazi government area on Prinz-Albrecht Strasse, this was one of the most feared buildings in the whole of Berlin. Benjamin wasn't beaten, but roughly handled and frog-marched down to the cells in the cellars. He stayed there all night. He had nothing to eat or drink and the light was kept on, so he couldn't sleep.

After a breakfast of stale bread and water, Benjamin was taken upstairs to a luxurious office, in which a sallow complexioned middle-aged man with thin, immaculately greased, black hair sat behind a desk as large as Benjamin's cell. The guard who had brought Benjamin up from the cellar manhandled him to the desk, told him to stand to attention then took up a position directly behind him.

"Name?" barked the man behind the desk.

"Benjamin Gerber."

"Benjamin Gerber, SIR!" shouted his interrogator.

"Benjamin Gerber, sir."

"Do you know why you've been brought here?"

"No."

The guard struck Benjamin hard across his face with the flat of his hand.

"No sir."

"That's better. You've been brought here because you are an enemy of the Reich."

Benjamin shrugged his shoulders and another hard slap stung his face.

"Are you a Jew, Gerber?"

"Yes sir."

"Then why do you pretend not to be?"

"I don't sir."

"You live in a non-Jewish district, you own a store in another non-Jewish area, you don't attend the synagogue, and your son, until recently, attended a German Gymnasium. You don't even look like a filthy Jew."

"I was born to Jewish parents, as was my wife. We chose not to be religious. Is that a crime?"

"Don't be insolent. I'm asking the questions," he bawled as he nodded to the guard who delivered a hard punch to Benjamin's left ear.

"How you behave and how you look makes no difference. You're still a Jew with syphilitic pus running through your veins."

Benjamin felt close to collapse and his legs buckled but the guard held him up.

"Where are my family, sir?" he asked weakly.

"No idea. Dead for all I care. That would be two less vermin to exterminate. I'll have more questions for you later. Take him away."

Benjamin was taken back to his cell. He sat there all day and night, wondering what would come next. Would he ever see Ruth and Jonathan again? He'd no idea. The light was kept on and proper sleep was impossible. He dozed fitfully, waking up each time to the sharp realisation of his dreadful situation. Even had the light been off, sleep would have been impossible as all around him there were moans, screams and the cracking of whips coming from adjacent cells.

Shortly after dawn, and following another bread and water breakfast, Benjamin was taken back to the palatial office. He felt terrible but was determined to see this through knowing, as he did, that others in the building were being treated far worse than he and still lived. He was again made to stand to attention in front of the greasy policeman's desk, with a different SS guard in close attendance.

"What did you discuss when you met the Englishman Walker?"

"Business, sir. Herr Walker and I have known one another for a number of years and I have purchased many manufactured goods from him to sell in my store."

"Nonsense. Walker is an English spy and, what's more, a Jew lover. Are you aware that his wife is a Jew?"

"Of course, sir. I've known Inge as long as I've known Richard."

"Why did Walker return to Germany? He left here two years ago, so why would he come back if not to spy?"

"He came back to discuss business with me. For no other reason."

"Liar!" screamed the policeman and the guard delivered yet another punch to Benjamin's left ear.

"Will you be joining Walker in England?"

"We've applied for visas for England and America, sir. We're waiting to hear from both countries."

"We don't allow our enemies to leave the Reich. We'll see how you respond when others, less kind than me, question you. Take him away."

◆   ◆   ◆

Ruth and Jonathan lived on the edge of their nerves for two days and then could stand it no longer. They had to find out what had happened to Benjamin. It wasn't a decision they took easily. On their brief excursions outside the apartment, they had heard rumours of more suicides as well as mass imprisonments and even some executions. The Jews had been made to clear up the mess after 10 November, and now rumours were circulating that they would be made to pay for the damage, as well as being subjected to new laws which would further restrict their freedom of movement. The thought crossed Ruth and Jonathan's minds that once they stepped inside the Gestapo building they might never come out alive. But they had to know what had happened to Benjamin, whatever the risks entailed.

They made the journey by U-Bahn to Potsdamer Platz, sitting in nervous silence, and then walked the short way to the Gestapo HQ. Here they joined the inevitable queue, consisting exclusively of Jewish families, desperately anxious for news of their relatives. The line shuffled slowly and quietly forward until, after more than two hours, they found themselves being brusquely ushered towards a desk on the ground floor of the centre of Nazi terror. Several desks were positioned across the main hall. Behind each sat a hard faced woman dressed in a simple grey suit. The official who dealt with the Gerbers was in her thirties with well-groomed blonde hair, neatly tied in a bun. A pair of gold-rimmed spectacles completed her business-like appearance.

"Yes?"

"We're trying to find out what has happened to my husband and Jonathan's father, Benjamin Gerber."

"When did you last see him?"

"Late in the afternoon of November tenth."

"How do you spell the name?"

Ruth's mouth was bone dry and she could barely spell out her husband's name.

"Is he Jewish?"

"Yes."

"He was probably arrested for his part in destroying German property."

Jonathan stood still, his hands clenched together down by his side. He was staring at the floor and sensibly resisted telling the woman what he thought of her suggestion.

The woman opened a ledger and took her time examining what seemed to Ruth to be page after page of small precise writing.

"Benjamin Gerber. Arrested at 18:00 hours on November tenth. Brought to this building then taken to the cells to await questioning."

"Is he still here?"

"I don't have that information."

"Is there another person who might know?"

The woman stared at her without a flicker of emotion on her face.

"Room 30. First floor."

Ruth thanked her and the two of them climbed the steps to the first floor. They quickly found Room 30 and joined yet another queue but this one was mercifully short. After another thirty minute wait, they were admitted to an office where, toward the tall window and seated bolt upright behind a large oak desk, sat a black-uniformed SS officer. Ruth and Jonathan crossed the polished floor and approached the desk.

"Yes?"

The man looked more like a clerk than a bully but, nevertheless, Ruth knew she must approach him with caution.

"I'm looking for my husband, Benjamin Gerber. My son and I were told downstairs that he had been brought to this building and that you may be able to tell us where he is now."

"Spell his name."

Ruth did so and the clerk painstakingly fingered his way through the ledger. Eventually he looked up, stared at Ruth without expression and said, without a hint of emotion in his voice.

"Gerber, Benjamin. Arrested November tenth, 1938. Questioned about involvement in action hostile to the Reich and dealings with a foreign spy. Taken from here to the camp at Sachsenhausen on November thirteenth."

Ruth was devastated to hear such ridiculous allegations against her husband but she composed herself and asked.

"Can we see him?"

"Highly unlikely. That is up to the Commandant at the camp. You'd better go there and ask him."

Ruth thanked him and she and Jonathan made their way out of the building and set off home, reaching the apartment totally exhausted and utterly depressed.

◆   ◆   ◆

Benjamin had been taken to Sachsenhausen, a concentration camp north of Berlin, in a police van with ten others. On arrival they had been marched past the SS barracks and the administration building before assembling on the parade ground outside the Commandant's office. There they'd been told to strip in the freezing weather and put on horribly rough brown uniforms. They bundled up their clothes, took them into an inhospitable hut before being ordered back on to the parade ground.

The Commandant appeared, tall and thin in his black SS uniform which included a cap with a skull on the front.

"You have been brought here because you are suspected of being enemies of the Reich. Behave, work hard and obey orders and you may one day leave here free men. Disobey and you will be punished. Criticise the Reich or engage in any political discussion and you will be executed."

The Commandant strutted back into his office and the guards took the men to the far side of the parade ground where a large allotment was being cultivated. Then they were told to dig. They worked all day and every day. The food was mostly thin soup and hard dried bread. If they stopped work without permission, or talked to their fellow prisoners, they were caned. Benjamin kept his head down and got on with his work.

In the nights, there were whispered conversations in the icy huts. Benjamin listened but took no part in these. One man, a Communist shoemaker named Isaac, spoke with great animation of the days before Hitler. Hitler won't last, he claimed. Soon Stalin's red tide would sweep across Germany and exterminate every single Nazi. The men warned Isaac to keep his ideas to himself. Benjamin said nothing.

The next day Isaac and one other from the hut disappeared. The other man was never seen again but Isaac, in front of the entire prison population, was hanged and his corpse was left dangling from the gallows for three days. Benjamin said nothing.

◆　　◆　　◆

Ten days had passed since "the night of the broken glass" and a week since Benjamin had been taken to Sachsenhausen. Ruth decided that she and Jonathan had to try to see him. On the day that they set out, a letter arrived that dashed many of their hopes. The US Embassy had written to say that their application for a visa had been refused but that they had been placed on a waiting list. Their case would be reviewed when the US Government's new "quota" became operational.

So it was with heavy hearts that they set out to Oranienburg where the camp was located. They didn't expect to be allowed to see Benjamin. On arrival there was the expected queue, shorter than usual, but, after completing the necessary paperwork, they were thrilled and amazed to see Benjamin appear, accompanied by a guard. He looked terrible; sunken cheeks, eyes surrounded by black circles, sores in the corner of his mouth, filthy hair and cracked fingernails. When he saw them his face lit up and he was allowed to embrace them, briefly but warmly. The guard warned them they had five minutes and were lucky to get even that.

Ruth told him about the letter from the US Embassy and Benjamin asked about their British application and whether there had been any communication from Richard. Sadly Ruth shook her head. Jonathan, not knowing how to react, stood in silence and Benjamin wrapped his arms around him.

"Don't worry son. People are being released all the time. They've no reason to hang on to me much longer. I'm sure I'll be home soon."

The journey back to the city was miserable but, when they got home, there was at last some good news; a letter from Richard which included the phrase "thank you for your hospitality." Richard had found a way of having the stamps smuggled out of Germany.

Time dragged on but, one afternoon in mid-December, the key turned in the lock and Benjamin walked in.

"I was taken into the Commandant's office, handed my possessions and told I was free to go. I had just enough money for the S-Bahn. Several of us made the journey to freedom at the same time. One told me that most people taken in on November tenth had been released."

"How are you, Dad?"

"Tired and hungry, but, apart from some loss of hearing in my left ear where they beat me, not too bad. Happy it's all over. Now we must prepare to leave this wretched country. Anyhow, things are looking up. Your mother tells me that we're on waiting lists and Richard's sorted out the stamps."

It was an awful Christmas and an unhappy New Year. In their thoughts for Christmas the Nazi press failed to mention Jesus, whose birthday they were celebrating, on the grounds that he was a Jew. The family were totally isolated. Benjamin wasn't going to work. Ruth had no friends and Jonathan wasn't bothering with his new Jewish school. The reptilian Kaufmanns kept a close watch on them, so the Gerbers made absolutely certain that they did nothing to attract attention. Then, early in January, another letter arrived, this time from the British Embassy. It was about their visa application and instructed Benjamin to "bring the appropriate documentation to me" to a Mr Watts in Room 26 on the second floor of the British Embassy at three in the afternoon in seven days' time.

◆   ◆   ◆

Benjamin and Ruth thought long and hard about how to get the stamps to the embassy without arousing suspicion. If they set off clutching a parcel, the Kauffmans might spot them and contact the Gestapo. Although Benjamin had been released from Sachsenhausen without charge, he still felt like a marked man. They eventually decided that Benjamin would set off to work as usual and then leave in good time to make their appointment in the Wilhelmstrasse. He would tell his employees that he was going to bank some money, which he frequently did, and deal with the sale of the business. In a society where suspicion had become almost endemic, there were always snoopers, even in Benjamin's shop, ready to raise the alarm.

The day before they were due to take the stamps to the British Embassy Ruth got cold feet.

"Benjamin, you really must think of a safer way to get the stamps to the Embassy. You know what the Gestapo are like. If they stop you and ask to see your papers they'll immediately know you're a Jew. Then your briefcase will be searched and that'll be the end of it. The stamps will be spotted, they'll assume you're up to no good, you'll be arrested and the stamps confiscated. You'll end up back in Sachsenhausen and this time you probably won't come out. We have to think of something else."

The three of them sat head in hands, deep in thought.

"I know," piped up Jonathan. "Hide the stamps among your other stuff—a false compartment or something"

"Not enough room," muttered Benjamin.

"Then have two false compartments," his son replied.

"Still not enough room."

"Hand on a minute," said Ruth, "I could sew a false bottom and two false sides."

"Getting closer, but there's still not enough room."

Jonathan re-entered the discussion. "Put as much as you can in the hidden compartments of your briefcase and I'll bring the rest in my sports bag."

Ruth was about to object when she stopped herself. "Jonathan's right. He and I'll travel together. A few well-placed Heil Hitlers and some loose talk about how unpleasant the Jews are will steer any suspicion away from us. It's unlikely that the Gestapo will stop a handsome boy and his mother. More likely they'll be on the lookout for men carrying briefcases."

Benjamin heaved a great sigh of relief. "Great, that should work."

Ruth set to work creating a false bottom and two false sides. When she'd finished, Benjamin carefully put the stamps into place. Jonathan, meanwhile, had been preparing the contents of his sports bag; football jersey and shorts, socks, boots, jockstrap and a towel. Benjamin laid the stamps across the bottom of the bag and the football kit was laid over them. Perfect.

The next day was freezing cold as an icy wind from the North German plain whipped across the city. Benjamin and briefcase set off for work while Jonathan and Ruth sat nervously at home, waiting to play their part in the deception. Just after lunch, Benjamin left his store and was approaching the U-Bahn station when two men, both in the Gestapo uniform of leather coats, stopped him.

"Gestapo. Papers please," said the shorter of the two.

Benjamin reached inside his jacket, pulled out his identity card and handed it to the policeman who flicked it open, studied it briefly and stared at Benjamin.

"You're a Jew I see. What are you carrying in the briefcase?"

"Some money, paying in books for the bank and documents relating to my business which I hope to sell."

"And why is that?"

"My family and I are hoping to emigrate to America."

The taller of the two men then snatched the bag from Benjamin, opened it and began rummaging through the contents. He handed the money to his colleague and told him to count it he began to read through the payment books. After what seemed an eternity to Benjamin, the two agreed that the money tallied with the payment slips. The money and books were returned to the briefcase, which was snapped shut and handed to Jonathan whose hands were shaking, stomach turning somersaults and heart hammering in his chest.

"You seem nervous Herr Gerber," the taller man said.

Benjamin looked at his interrogator. "I was arrested last November, spent some time in your cellars and sent to Sachsenhausen. Later I was released.

The short man laughed.

"Yes. I can see that that would make you nervous. On your way Gerber."

Benjamin was still trembling when he met Jonathan and Ruth outside the Embassy. He had worried himself sick that he would be followed. He paid the money into the bank and then spent the journey looking over his shoulder. He didn't think he'd been followed, but you could never be sure with that lot, he thought to himself. His wife and son were pleased and relieved to see him.

"Everything alright?" asked Ruth.

"Yes," Benjamin replied. "I'll tell you about it later. Let's get inside the Embassy."

The three of them entered the sanctuary of the British Embassy and were politely directed to Room 26 and knocked on the door. A tall fair-haired young man, wearing a blue blazer and grey slacks, answered and invited them in. He closed the door and thrust out his right hand.

"Benjamin and Ruth. I'm Simon Watts. And you must be Jonathan. So good to see you. First things first. Please let me have the documentation."

Benjamin opened his brief case and handed three thin parcels to Watts who immediately placed them in a desk drawer but, before he could lock it, Jonathan handed him a much larger parcel.

"I see you've taken precautions. Good thinking." He locked the stamps in the desk drawer.

"Good. I'm taking the parcels to England myself and handing them to your Mr Walker in London."

"Thank you very much," said Ruth.

"It's a pleasure. It feels good to be getting one over on those revolting Nazis."

A flash of alarm spread over the Gerbers' faces.

"Don't worry. We have this place checked for microphones daily. We're not being overheard, even by our own Ambassador," he said with a wry grin on his face. "I'm sorry I don't have any news of your visa applications, but things are on the move. We're now helping Jewish children to leave Germany and Austria."

"I understand," said Benjamin. "You're already risking a lot for us and we're very grateful."

"Think nothing of it. By the way, you must have friends in high places to pull this off."

"It's Richard who has the friends," said Benjamin.

"So it seems. I'm looking forward to meeting him. He sounds interesting." Simon shook both their hands again.

"Good luck. You can count on me."

"I know we can," said Ruth. "Please give our best wishes to Richard."

"That I will. Goodbye."

◆   ◆   ◆

Piece by piece their escape plan was falling into place and when, three weeks later, a letter arrived from Richard which said nothing in particular but which ended "let's hope there's no war this year". They knew the stamps were safe. Then a letter came from the US Embassy telling them that, while the American immigration quota was full for the time being, many on the waiting list were being encouraged to wait in Cuba where the government were happy to provide temporary landing certificates. Hundreds of hopefuls were already there, and it seemed to Benjamin and Ruth that they'd be better off there than in Germany.

Surprisingly, the landing certificates were easy to obtain and the final arrangements for leaving Germany were now rapidly put into place. Benjamin re-opened the shop with Jonathan assisting, and together they got rid of all the remaining stock at rock-bottom prices. The premises were sold off cheaply, quickly followed by the apartment and furniture. Enough money was raised to emigrate and take ten Reichmarks each out of Germany.

Ruth handed in most of her remaining jewellery, keeping only a few small pieces which weren't worth much but of great sentimental value, in particular a ruby brooch which had once belonged to her mother, and received a receipt. Benjamin and Jonathan went to the Berlin-Amerika line and booked three passages from Hamburg to Cuba. The entire family then reported to the emigration police. All of the necessary paperwork was completed, taxes paid and passports issued. Their passports had either Israel or Sara added to their names and were stamped with a large red letter J.

Each packed a large suitcase and, without an ounce of regret, left their apartment on 12 May 1939. U-Bahn and train took them to Hamburg from where they were due to sail to Cuba on the following day aboard the *MS St Louis*.

CHAPTER SIX

On the following morning, the Gerbers, each carrying an extremely large suitcase, joined a long line of what turned out to be more than nine hundred passengers, almost all of them Jewish, hoping to escape from Germany. They were so far back that it was impossible to see what was happening at the front. The ship was moored at Shed 76. The Gerbers spotted it, a large steamer with two short, fat funnels. There were two masts, adorned with black and white flags. A swastika flew menacingly at the stern. All three were on edge, especially Jonathan whose natural impatience made this kind of waiting intolerable. They edged forward, eventually catching sight of six tables. Seated behind each of these was a customs official, methodically going about his business. Immediately behind him stood a man in civilian clothes, accompanied by a pair of black-uniformed SS guards.

As they moved slowly towards the tables, they saw a family of four being taken away by two of the guards and a plain-clothed man who was obviously a member of the Gestapo. The tension in the queue was growing as the refugees moved forward in silence. Then it was the Gerbers' turn, and the three of them presented their documents to the official who consulted a list before handing Benjamin's passport to the thin-faced Gestapo man. He took an eternity to read it before turning to Benjamin and staring at him with his piercing blue eyes.

"You were imprisoned in Sachsenhausen, Herr Gerber."

It was a statement, not a question.

"You were released despite being suspected of being an enemy of the Reich."

"I was released without charge."

"This time, Herr Gerber. On the next occasion you will not be so lucky. Be warned, if you ever return to the Reich, you will be taken back to Sachsenhausen and you will never leave there alive."

He turned to the guards.

"Search their luggage."

The contents of all three suitcases, which had been carefully packed, were emptied on to the quayside. As the guards completed their fruitless search, they ordered first Jonathan, then Ruth and finally Benjamin to re-pack their cases.

"Be quick," ordered the Gestapo man, "you're keeping the other Jews waiting."

Hastily they re-packed their suitcases as best they could, then stood waiting.

"Search them."

A thorough search of jackets, trousers, other pockets and Ruth's handbag took up another ten minutes. Some kind of dispensation had been granted and each of the Gerbers carried two hundred and thirty Reichmarks, but this was only to be spent at sea. With a look of disappointment on his face, the Gestapo man snapped Benjamin's passport shut and returned it to its owner with a flourish.

"Remember, Jew: never come back."

◆　　◆　　◆

On the bridge of the *St Louis* the Captain, Gustav Schröder, watched the scene on the quayside below and turned to his first officer.

"Those are wholly innocent human beings, Klaus, yet they're being treated like common criminals."

"You're right, sir, but at least most are getting on board. We'll soon be taking them away from all this."

"I really do hope so, but I've heard whispers from Head Office that the Cubans are considering changing their policy about their island being used as a transit camp for the USA."

"I hope that's just a rumour, sir."

"So do I. All we can do is set sail and, if there are problems at the other end, deal with them then. Meanwhile, let's give them a comfortable voyage."

◆   ◆   ◆

Below deck, two tough-looking boiler men were sitting in a large cabin they shared with eight others. One of them, a strongly built man of medium height, a ruddy complexion and with thick black hair, said to his companion, "Remember Günther, we've a job to do on this voyage, apart from our normal duties."

The other man, wiry but thinner and taller with straight blonde hair, replied, "Of course, my dear Otto, we've to keep an eye on the Jews to see if they've sneaked any valuables past our people on the docks."

"That's right. I doubt they'll manage to get anything through but you never know with that slimy lot. Anyway, if there's nothing, we can always amuse ourselves with a Jew or two; remind them why they're leaving the Fatherland."

"We must be careful, Otto. The Captain and the officers will come down on us like a ton of bricks if we're caught."

"Then we mustn't be caught," replied Otto, with a sneer on his face. "Don't forget our second task is to ensure that the crew are loyal. I hope it's a rough voyage. I'd love to see the Jews spending all of their time vomiting over the side."

◆   ◆   ◆

The Gerbers found themselves in a neat, tourist-class cabin with a sea view. The sleeping quarters and bathroom were small but there was a reasonably sized relaxation area. After their ordeal all they wanted to do was to sit quietly. At 20:00 hours, the blowing of the ship's horn announced their departure and the three of them went on deck to watch the ship effortlessly leave the country of their birth behind. They stared in silence as the vessel cruised along the Elbe towards the open sea. Ruth and Benjamin said they felt tired and left for a snooze in the cabin. Jonathan said he would have a look around the ship and join them later.

The *St Louis* left the Elbe and entered the North Sea and, before long, the dark lights of the Dutch coast could be seen to the east. The Netherlands was a free country, thought Jonathan sadly, but he soon cheered up and set off on his trip around the ship. Within an hour he was back in the cabin. His parents were still asleep so he settled down to read *A Tale of Two Cities* in English. He was so excited he couldn't concentrate so he soon gave up and began thinking about life in America. He knew he would never see Germany again. Eventually he drifted off to sleep.

As they sat down to breakfast the following day, Jonathan reported what he had seen; the ballroom, where he'd heard there might be film shows as well as dancing, the first-class quarters which were even more sumptuous than their own and the decks where hundreds of Germans were saying goodbye to their country with a mixture of sadness and relief.

They shared the table with a family of four from Düsseldorf. Introductions were made. Sebastian Hofstadt was a scientist in a munitions factory and felt himself fortunate to be allowed to escape from the frantic preparations for a war which he felt sure would come. His wife Rachel was a proud-looking dark-haired woman and their fourteen year-old son Matthew was rather like a younger version of Jonathan. The young Gerber boy ignored everybody else and gazed in awe at their table companions' seventeen year-old daughter. She was introduced as Hildegard but, she briefly interrupted with a smile, she preferred to be called Hilde. She had her mother's dark, curly hair, high cheekbones and stunning soft brown eyes. She smiled again, this time at Jonathan, and he felt himself blush deeply.

The adults chatted happily for the rest of the meal. They talked about their lives "back home," their destinations and their hopes for the future. Jonathan tried to engage Matthew in conversation, but without much success, and was almost totally tongue-tied when it came to talking to Hilde. Their parents got on so well together that they agreed to share the table for the rest of the voyage. That would leave plenty of time for Jonathan to overcome his shyness. As they stood up to return to their cabins, Hilde examined Jonathan's handsome face and powerful body, almost bursting out of his jacket. His seventeenth birthday was not far away. He was still growing. Soon he would top six feet.

◆   ◆   ◆

Back on the bridge, Captain Schröder and his officers carefully plotted a course which would take them through the Straits of Dover, into the Channel, briefly calling at Cherbourg, and finally the Atlantic Ocean. There was no further word as to whether or not the Cuban authorities would cause difficulty on arrival in Havana Harbour. He chatted with his officers who told him the passengers were a decent lot and they envisaged nothing but good relations with them throughout the voyage. The radio officer reported that he had worked overtime sending wires to friends and relatives of the refugees. Several had received responses, including Benjamin from Richard Walker who wished him good luck and promised to "be in touch." Everybody seemed happy and, if not totally joyful, then at least satisfied. All, that is, except Captain Schröder, who felt a heavy sense of responsibility towards his passengers and prayed he could land them safely in Cuba.

◆   ◆   ◆

The weather was mercifully kind and there was little seasickness. The passengers visibly relaxed as the ship left European waters. As the *St Louis* proceeded across the vast Atlantic, friendships were made and, in some cases, cemented. Even the odd spell of choppy seas failed to upset the growing confidence of most on board. Jonathan, following his morning routine of exercise and breakfast, made his way to the deck on a sunny day. He took his novel with him and had only read a few pages when Hilde appeared and asked if she could sit with him. That was the end of his reading as the two talked about everything; Berlin, Düsseldorf, their schools, persecution, escape, their destinations and their hopes. By dinner they were firm friends. Over the evening meal their parents exchanged glances as they saw evidence of their children's blossoming relationship.

Jonathan and Hilde became almost inseparable. They danced together and went to film shows in the ballroom, although the first of these ended in chaos when the ship's officer rather insensitively screened a Nazi propaganda newsreel. There was a promise not to repeat this type of film.

One morning Jonathan decided to take a look at the engine rooms. He made his way below deck and was strolling along a narrow passage when a door opened and a crewman stepped out.

"What are you doing here? Passengers are forbidden to enter this area."

"I'm sorry, I didn't know."

The sailor pulled Jonathan through the door and thrust him into the room.

"Look what I've found Otto. A rat running about outside."

"What do you think he's after Günther? Food?"

"No. Most likely he's come down here to spy on our superior technology so he can report to his American friends."

"Don't talk rubbish," protested Jonathan. "I know nothing at all about engineering."

"I don't trust Jews. They have funny looking dicks," said Otto.

"Let's have a look then."

"Good idea," said Otto, reaching towards Jonathan's trousers.

At this moment, months of pent-up hatred and frustration boiled over and Jonathan struck out at Otto's chin with his fist. He missed, but landed a mighty blow on the seaman's throat instead. Having seen the power of the punch, Günther would have been well-advised to run for help, but he didn't think quickly enough and made a grab at Jonathan from behind. The young Jew swung his elbow and cracked his second assailant across the jaw. The German dropped to the floor screaming. Meanwhile Otto, his face purple, managed to scramble to his feet and, yelling "you filthy Jew," moved towards Jonathan with his fists clenched. He swung but the boy ducked and responded with a tremendous thump on the Nazi's nose which promptly burst, pouring blood over the sailor's mouth, chin, neck and shirt. A hard kick to the knee finished Otto off and he fell to the floor groaning.

◆   ◆   ◆

Jonathan flung the door open into the passage and rushed back to the cabin where his parents were enjoying a quiet cup of coffee. They could see straight away that something was seriously wrong and asked him what had happened. He blurted out the whole story, half crying and half shouting.

"I knew one day you'd take it out on them. You haven't killed them, have you?" asked Benjamin, his voice on the edge of panic. Jonathan shook his head. Ruth now took command and told them she would find an officer and tell him about the incident. She was gone for ten minutes and, when she returned, she said that they should wait in the cabin. Jonathan was recovering from his hysteria and his mood was now one of anger and worry.

Half an hour later there was a firm rap on the door. Benjamin answered it and found, to his surprise, Captain Schröder waiting in the doorway, asking if he could come in. The Captain was a small man wearing a cap which seemed far too large for him. He had a modest moustache and, when he took off his peaked cap, short grey hair perched above a tanned face. He looked very distinguished in his immaculately pressed uniform. He had an air of authority about him and gave the impression that he would soon be in total command of the situation.

"Shall we all sit down?" he asked.

They did as he suggested. He turned towards Jonathan.

"What is your name young man?"

"Jonathan."

"Well Jonathan, you had no right whatsoever to be below deck and I would expect any member of my crew to stop you and instruct you to return to your own part of the ship immediately. However, I would not expect them to attack you and I do appreciate that you acted in self-defence. But you must never go there again," Schröder said firmly.

Ruth asked what had happened to the men who had attacked their son.

"Both are in the infirmary. One has a broken jaw and the other a bruised throat, badly swollen knee and a broken nose. They will be kept there until the ship reaches Havana. Their lives are not in danger."

"Thank God for that," said Benjamin.

"I shall address the crew in their mess and inform them that anyone who insults or attacks a single passenger will be charged and locked up."

"Thank you very much, Captain."

Schröder stood up and the Gerbers followed suit. Jonathan apologised for his behaviour and the Captain nodded. He grasped the door handle then changed his mind, turned back to look at Jonathan and said to him,

"One final thing, Jonathan. When you get to America, you will find they play a form of football much different to ours. I don't pretend to understand it but it seems to me that you should try it. I'm sure you'll be an excellent performer." With the tiniest of smiles at the corner of his mouth, the Captain left.

◆   ◆   ◆

The rest of the voyage passed more or less without incident, at least as far as the passengers were concerned, although an elderly refugee did die of natural causes. Friendships grew stronger and optimism became greater. As Cuba grew nearer, however, problems mounted for Captain Schröder. Radio messages from Hamburg and the shipping agents in Havana became increasingly pessimistic of the likelihood that the nine hundred refugees would be permitted to land. When the ship docked in Havana harbour on 27 May, a party of Cuban police came aboard and told the Captain that the passengers could not land. The landing certificates had been revoked, he was told.

The passengers had gathered on deck and some were waving happily to friends and relatives on the shore who were amongst the two and a half thousand refugees already in Cuba. Then the police arrived and doubts began to grow. Uncertainty became despair as the Captain outlined the situation. Discussions were taking place, he assured them. He let them know that these negotiations with the Cuban authorities were being conducted by a representative of the Jewish Joint Distribution Committee, based in New York. Meanwhile they sat and waited.

Schröder, fully behind the refugees in their plight, was able to report that the twenty two passengers who already had US visas would be allowed to land. The Cuban government, with a man called Batista leading the way, were asking for thousands of Marks from each passenger to grant them new landing certifications. Nobody on board had that kind of money. Their funds were either safely tucked away in the country of their destination or else gathering dust in Nazi bank vaults.

The situation became worse. An appeal to the United States fell on deaf ears, as did similar requests to other Caribbean countries. Despite his sympathies being strongly behind the refugees, the US President, Roosevelt, was due to face re-election in 1940 and had no desire to upset the voters, many of whom were opposed to a further influx of refugees. The ship attempted to sail to Miami on 2 June, but had been ordered back to Havana harbour by a US Navy destroyer. Eventually, in a mood of abject despair, Schröder told the refugees on 6 June that the ship would have to set sail for the return voyage to Hamburg. One hundred thousand lined the quayside, scores of them weeping as their loved ones sailed back to what many feared would be certain death.

CHAPTER SEVEN

The world's press seized on the story of nine hundred homeless and stateless Jewish refugees with nowhere to go but back to a country which didn't want them. Heaven knows what kind of reception awaited them when they stepped on to the quayside at Hamburg. The Gerber family were amongst those with much to fear. Benjamin was the first to express his concern about what would happen to them on their return to Germany.

"It looks like I'll be back in Sachsenhausen before long."

"And I won't get away with what I did to those two Nazis," said Jonathan.

"You may be right," said Ruth, "but the Captain said that negotiations were continuing and I'm sure neither he nor anyone else trying to find a way out will give up."

"Let's hope so," replied Benjamin, "at least the Captain said we've plenty of food and fuel. There's just under two weeks before we're due in Hamburg. That's plenty of time to find a way out of this mess."

◆　　◆　　◆

The world watched and waited. The joy of the outward journey, with fancy dress balls and tea dances, now evaporated into an atmosphere of gloom and despair. Behind the scenes the Jewish agency people worked day and night to find a home for these desperate people. The Captain knew that the ship was a floating time bomb. There had been two failed suicide attempts while the ship had loitered in Havana. A small group of young Jewish men tried to take over the ship and stop it heading for Europe but the Captain talked sense into them and order was quickly restored. Schröder, closely in touch with the efforts of the Joint Distribution Committee, told his loyal officers when the ship was in mid-Atlantic:

"We must do something for these people if all else fails. I've decided, when we enter the Channel, I'll run the ship aground at the safest spot on the English coast. That'll force the issue. The English will have to take care of them." The officers, totally behind their Captain, then discussed how they would achieve this and a plan was agreed. Meanwhile the refugees, feeling totally humiliated and rejected, waited in growing terror. Some of the crew felt the passengers' pain and frustration. It all became too much for one sailor who took his own life rather than continue to be part of this unfolding tragedy.

◆　　◆　　◆

Jonathan and Hilde were leaning on the deck rail, their arms wrapped strongly around each other, gloomily discussing their future.

"What will happen when we dock in Hamburg?" the girl asked.

"I'll probably be arrested with my father and sent to a camp. What about you?"

"Back to Düsseldorf I guess. My father will be sent back to work in the factory, probably without being paid. Where we'll live, I've no idea. We've no house and no money. All we have is in America and there's no way now to get hold of it."

"Same as us, except what we've got is in England."

"The Captain says that people are still trying to sort something out," she said, grasping Jonathan's hand. "Let's hope they succeed."

They kissed briefly, then Hilde set off for her cabin. A figure stepped out of the shadows, his face heavily bandaged.

"So my Jewish pig, we're on our way back to Germany. I needn't take my revenge on you now. When we reach Hamburg, I'll have you arrested for attempting to murder a party official. You'll end up on the gallows or facing a firing squad, and I'll be there to see it."

Jonathan was past caring about Otto. He didn't regard him as a physical threat so he said to him, "I could easily deprive you of that pleasure by throwing you overboard now. No one would miss a useless thug like you."

Otto backed away, but not without a parting shot.

"And what's more I'll have that Jewish whore arrested as well for consorting with an enemy of the Reich."

Jonathan moved threateningly towards the bully but the Nazi made a run for it. Jonathan decided not to follow. His family already had enough problems.

◆   ◆   ◆

Less than a week before the *St Louis* was due to dock at Hamburg, Captain Schröder at last had some good news from the air waves. He'd repeatedly told the passengers that they would not be returned to Germany and now he was able to deliver on his promise. The world-wide press campaign and the frantic efforts of the Jewish authorities supporting the refugees paid off. Britain, Holland, Belgium and France would welcome a quarter of the refugees each. For Schröder this brought double relief. The passengers appeared to be safe and he wouldn't have to run the ship aground, although he was clear, in his own mind, that he would have done so if he'd thought it necessary. Showing no emotion, the Captain asked his First Officer to arrange for the passengers to assemble in the ballroom in an hour's time.

It was an extremely apprehensive group that gathered to hear Schröder sixty minutes later. They feared the worst but, when the Captain told them of the offer from the four governments, there was a huge, audible sigh of relief. Many had no links at all with these countries, but it didn't matter one jot. They would not be returning to Germany. The Captain raised a hand to signify quiet.

"We have less than a week to organise this. If any of you have existing contacts who might help you in these countries, please let the First Officer know. He will then arrange to get in touch with them. The rest of you must divide yourselves up to be allocated to one of these countries. We shall be docking at Antwerp in Belgium. Some of you will stay in that country while others will travel by train to neighbouring Holland. Those going to England and France will be taken by sea. A steamer is on standby."

There was an outburst of cheering and clapping, but the Captain again raised his hand.

"It has been a very difficult voyage for all of you. I'm delighted it seems that it will have some kind of satisfactory ending. I know these are not the countries of your choice, but perhaps the American government will soon relent and allow you to settle there. Good luck to all of you."

With that he left the room and a babble of conversation broke out. Ruth gave the signal to leave and all three returned to their cabin.

"Sounds like England is the best bet for us," said Ruth. "Do you think Richard will help us?" she asked Benjamin.

"I'm sure he will."

"Right, off you go to give his contact details to the First Officer."

Benjamin rummaged through his suitcase and found a piece of paper with Richard's address and telephone number then left the cabin. Ruth and Jonathan anxiously awaited his return. It was more than two hours before he re-appeared.

"There was a queue a mile long but for once I didn't mind waiting. I've handed over the information. They'll let us know when the wire's been sent."

The officers were working overtime, so it was almost dinner time before a soft knock on the door brought news. The officer confirmed that the message had been sent and he'd let them know as soon as he had a reply.

◆　　◆　　◆

Dinner with their friends from Düsseldorf was an animated affair. In recent days, meals had been quiet and sombre but now they had plenty to talk about.

"We shall be going to Paris," announced Sebastian. "I have a cousin there who runs a small engineering business. There'll be work for me and good education for the children. When the Nazis are gone, we'll return to Düsseldorf."

"We hope to go to England," said Benjamin. "We're waiting for a reply to our wire to some friends there."

Rachel joined the conversation.

"Paris is a beautiful city I believe. I'm sure Matthew and Hilde will be very happy there."

Matthew did look genuinely excited, but Hilde, though pretending to be enthusiastic, was clearly unhappy to be separated from Jonathan.

◆   ◆   ◆

The following morning another officer brought the Gerbers the news that they'd been waiting for. Richard would be more than happy to look after them and would be waiting for them in London when they arrived. The end of the voyage was still almost a week away so they made their minds up to enjoy themselves in the time that remained.

On the final evening, Jonathan and Hilde stood arm in arm and side by side and stared as the coast of England slowly drifted by.

"I wish I was coming with you, Jonathan."

"So do I, Hilde."

"We may never see each other again."

"Why not? England and France aren't far apart and we shall both be free to travel, unlike in Germany."

"Do you really think so?"

"Of course. Look here's the address of the family we're staying with in England. Write to me. You can give me your address in Paris as soon as you have it."

He handed Hilde a scrap of paper then put his arms around her and kissed her for what seemed an eternity. They broke off, said goodnight and then went their separate ways. Hilde took care not to look back at Jonathan, so he couldn't see the tears streaming down her face.

◆   ◆   ◆

The next day the *MS St Louis* tied up at Pier 18 in Antwerp. On the bridge Captain Schröder watched the scene below as the nine hundred refugees went their separate ways. He was glad that he hadn't had to run the ship aground and happy that some solution seemed to have been found. His thoughts were interrupted by his First Officer announcing that he had a visitor. A tall, grey bearded Jewish rabbi stood at the rear of the bridge.

"I'm here to represent all of the passengers, Captain. Thanks to your support, kindness and persistence, we all have a chance of a new life. Should you ever need help, please ask any member of the Jewish community wherever you are. They will all know your name and what you did for us."

Schröder felt embarrassed, but looked his visitor in the eye. "Thank you. I hope all does go well. I'm proud to have done my duty." The rabbi smiled at him then left.

◆　　◆　　◆

The Gerbers, along with the other passengers, disembarked then quickly re-embarked on a small steamer bound for France and England. The rest set off by rail and road to their new lives in the Low Countries. The vessel on which the France- and England-bound Jews found themselves was a converted freighter, the *Rhakotis*. Boarding began at 14:00 hours but the ship remained at anchor while the *St Louis* set off for America to begin a series of cruises. As the *St Louis* passed the *Rhakotis*, many of her crew lined to rails and shouted "good luck" to the Jews.

◆　　◆　　◆

The journey was slow and the small ship was terribly overcrowded and uncomfortable but nobody really cared. They were safe at last. Over two hundred disembarked at Boulogne, including Hilde and her family. Then the *Rhakotis* sailed for Southampton, reaching there at noon on 21 June 1939, midsummer's day. There was a lengthy wait at customs and immigration followed by a train journey to London. It was late afternoon when they reached the English capital. Richard was waiting at the ticket gate at Waterloo Station. As soon as he saw his German friends, he walked towards them and welcomed them with open arms.

PART TWO

Families: June 1939

All happy families are alike; each unhappy
family is unhappy in its own way.
LEO TOLSTOY, *ANNA KARENINA*

CHAPTER EIGHT

About six miles north of Waterloo Station, another family were carrying out an animated conversation in their small sitting room. There were four of them; husband, wife, and their two teenage children, a boy and his older sister. They appeared, at first glance, to be a normal English family of similar ages to the Gerbers. True, they weren't well-off, but neither were they poor, and they seemed typical of the English working class. But they weren't. All but one of them depended for a majority of their income on crime.

Doris was the head of the house. She was a formidable looking middle-aged woman with tightly curled black hair. She had a tough face with thin lips and a determined look in her eyes. An onlooker would see, straightaway, that she was in charge. The father, George, was a skinny looking man with a face like a ferret. His straight, fair hair was thinning on top and his brown eyes darted from his wife to his children in a shifty manner. He looked like a man who couldn't be trusted.

The other two members of the Wallace family sat in silence while their parents talked. The girl, Angela, was seventeen and looked ordinary enough with her pale complexion and curly black hair inherited from her mother. She had a slightly bored look on her face, but overall she was quite good looking and had attracted some interest from the local youths. The boy, Patrick, nicknamed Edgar by his mates after the famous crime writer, was a surly looking fifteen year old with an almost permanent sneer. Although he looked fairly innocuous slouched in his chair, when he stood up he had a muscular physique moulded on to his short, squat body. His straight brown hair lay on his head with only a hint of a parting.

The house in which they lived was small but well-kept. The cosy sitting room was clean, but the carpet and some of the furniture looked a bit threadbare. The grate in the fireplace was empty but for a cheap-looking stand which housed a brush, tongs, poker and shovel. Curtains which had seen better days were at least clean. Upstairs there were a couple of bedrooms: one shared by the adults and the other by the children. The decent-sized kitchen had a large sink, but the toilet was outside in the back yard next to a heavily padlocked shed. The yard, which had a tiny paved area, was protected by a high wooden fence. Washing was hung out to dry each Monday morning. The front door of the house opened to a street of about forty similar adjoining properties.

Fifty yards away was a wide tree-lined avenue of well-built terraced houses which led to the busy High Street. The people who lived there were obviously wealthier than the Wallaces, who themselves aspired to this type of better life, and they had a feeling of general dissatisfaction that had led to this evening's conversation.

"I'm fed up with livin' 'ere," Doris began. "We've got a house the size of a shoe box with no bath or khazi. The furniture and carpets are shabby and the kids are too old to be sharing a room."

"You're right, Doris, but it could be worse," replied her husband. "Imagine living in one of them slums nearer town."

"That's rubbish, George. It's like people in the slums sayin' they're better off than tramps sleepin' rough. The point is we could do better, a bigger 'ouse, nicer clobber, smarter furniture and tastier grub, and more of it. I'd love to own one of them smart new semis up 'Endon way. And 'ow about a new radio? I can 'ardly 'ear a thing outta that tiny box we got. And I fancy a gramophone. I could listen to Al Bowley all day long. And Bing Crosby. And I couldn't go to the Dorchester to listen to Jack Jackson could I? And good ole Joe Crossman."

Doris burst into a tinny contralto.

"Zing went the strings of my heart."

"Leave it out Doris. Ye'll give me an 'eadache. Anyow, 'ow we gonna manage all these extras?" asked George.

"By gettin' more money, dimwit."

"And 'ow we gonna get more money?"

"That's what we're discussin'."

George looked non-plussed. He brought a little bit in through his unemployment benefit. What jobs there were he'd been able to turn down because of his convenient bad chest. His main source of income was pick-pocketing and he lifted enough wallets and purses from the hordes that wandered around the West End to keep their heads well above water. The problem was that there was plenty of competition, especially from Greeks who seemed to be the world champions at picking pockets. George, like his wife, had been brought up in this crowded North London suburb. His father had lived a life of crime and had passed on his dipping skills to his willing son. George's mother had been a prostitute who had died of syphilis when she was forty, although she looked closer to sixty at the time of her death. Angela, their daughter, did her bit as well. She caught the number 643 bus each morning, except Sunday, and worked as a waitress in the A.B.C. Tea Rooms in Wood Green. She gave Doris most of her pay and tips, keeping enough for her bus fares, lunch, ten cigarettes a day and a Saturday night out at the Palais. She seemed happy enough, although her calm exterior concealed a growing loathing for her parents and their way of life.

Patrick, on the other hand, made little or no contribution to the household budget apart from the occasional theft of tools from yard sheds. He'd left the Victorian Elementary School just up the High Street fifteen months earlier and had made no effort to find a job. Most of his time was spent loitering around the neighbourhood with other similarly placed youths. Although Patrick was generally accepted as the head of the "gang," he often had to show the rest who was boss by agreeing to take part in any number of escapades, even though he thought most of them were stupid. Just the previous week they'd daubed paint on the walls outside the synagogue in Stamford Hill. The "gang" left revolting messages like "Jews go ome" and "Jermani nos wot to do with the Jews". Police had been to the Wallace house on more than one occasion to investigate the beating up of a perfectly innocent citizen. In short, he was pretty useless. Both his father and mother assumed he'd go into the family business but Angela knew that he wasn't anywhere near as bad as he seemed and she hoped to be able to lead him away from a life of crime.

The discussion paused for a moment while all four lit Woodbines; Doris and George from their shared packet of twenty, Angela from her ten, and Patrick from his pocket money-sized five packet.

"We'll 'ave to do without these and cut out boozin' unless we can get hold of more dosh," Doris continued. "That bastard Cohen's put up the rent. Bleedin' Jews, they're everywhere. The only money I can earn is doin' washin' for that lot. I don't know why they're 'ere. They should go back to their own country."

"This is their country," said George. "Some of 'em have been 'ere for 'undreds of years."

"Yeah, that's just some of 'em but lots 'ave just come from Germany and other places over there. There's less jobs for us now and more of them bastards pinchin' all the good 'uns. They're a smelly lot, anyway."

"Seen that lot up the 'ill?" Patrick asked, "how they dress? Stupid great fur 'ats, big coats then them crazy big beards."

Doris spoke sharply: "What's that got to do with anythin'? Speak when yer spoken to. You gotta branch out George. Your dippin' ain't bringin' in enough. Why don't you do some of 'em big 'ouses up north? Take the boy with yer. He's small enough to crawl through some of 'em winders."

"It's no good now Doris. Too light. We'll be spotted a mile off. We'll 'ave to wait until it's dark in October. The boy could come down the West End with me and learn the trade. Any'ow Doris," George looked at his wife, "why don't you do a bit of shopliftin'?"

"Piss orf. I'm the organiser. You do the leg work."

"I've got an idea," said Patrick.

"I told you to speak when you're spoken to."

Patrick, who took after his mother, wasn't easily put off.

"But it is a good idea. I could nick bikes."

"That's no good," said George. "We don't wanna be shittin' on our own doorstep. That plain clothes copper Crawford 'as already got 'is eye on us. If 'e 'ears a bike's bin nicked, this is the first place 'e'll come. You'll be pinched and birched before you can say Jack Robinson. And don't forget that mad mick Gibson controls all the dodgy stuff round 'ere: thieving, tarts and the bookies. Step on 'is toes and we'll get a razor across our faces."

"Then I won't do it 'ere. I'll pinch 'em from Walthamstow or Tottenham or somewhere like that. I'll pedal 'em back 'ere."

"An 'ow we gonna get rid of 'em?" asked George.

"'Ang on George. The boy's got a good idea. 'E could bring 'em back 'ere and the two o' yer could strip and paint 'em in the shed."

"What you gonna do when you've painted 'em?" asked George.

"Flog 'em at Romford Market."

"Romford Market! That's bloody miles away."

"Patrick can pedal 'em across. I'll meet 'im there and arrange the sale."

"Ow will you get there?"

"Bus into Stratford then Green Line to Romford."

"Anyway, why Romford?"

"Three reasons. One, arf of stuff flogged there is 'ot; two, the people round there 'ave got money. Ever since that Ford Factory opened up they've been mintin' it in. And three my cousin Bert, yer know Alf's boy, 'as got a stall there. 'E knows 'ow to get rid of bent goods and what's more 'e'll get us a good price for the bikes and whatever else we can get 'old of."

"All right Doris. We'll give it a go. But first the boy comes up west with me. I'll show 'im the tricks of the trade."

Doris nodded. Her father had been a tough railway man and an active trade unionist, not afraid to use violence against colleagues whom he thought were too soft in their attitude to the bosses. Doris had inherited his toughness and might have avoided a life on the dark side but for the aftermath of a drunken night at The Rochester Castle when she'd let that greasy George Wallace get the better of her in the park. Pregnancy, a rushed wedding and Angela followed in quick succession.

◆   ◆   ◆

The next morning father and son were seated side by side on the number 76 bus riding into London. During the journey, George gave Patrick strict instructions. He was to watch, learn and collect. He was to observe his light fingered father at work and then stand at Swan and Edgar's corner and collect the dip's ill-gotten gains and hold on to them. That way, if the police did pinch George, there was a good chance of him not having the evidence on him if he was searched. If anything did go wrong, they'd split up and make their way home independently.

They got off the bus at Waterloo, crossed the bridge and made their way to Piccadilly Circus via The Strand, Trafalgar Square, Leicester Square and Coventry Street. It was a warm summer's day. Patrick was wearing a green short-sleeved shirt and worn, but clean, brown trousers which he was hoping he'd fill with the proceeds of his father's pick-pocketing.

Patrick took up his station outside Swan and Edgar's and watched his father disappear into the crowds. It was as busy as ever, perhaps even busier with hundreds of shoppers jumping off buses and taxis or rushing up the steps from the tube station. Some loitered and chatted in the sunshine while others headed towards the expensive shops in Regent Street and Piccadilly. The crowds were so dense that Patrick felt certain that there would be rich pickings for his father. He was right. Within an hour George re-appeared and skilfully passed two wallets and a purse to his son which Patrick quickly thrust into his pocket. The boy then lit a Woodbine and slowly strolled round the statue of Eros, thinking he could easily do what his father was doing.

Half an hour later he was back at his post but it was more than two hours before George came back and passed over another purse.

"That'll do for today. Meet me back at Waterloo."

The pair of them travelled home, well pleased with the day's work. Back in the house they counted up the contents of the wallets and purses and found that, in notes and coins, their haul totalled just over six pounds. Doris was pleased.

"That'll do nicely. Don't get rid of the wallets and purses. They're good quality. I'll take 'em to Romford with me and get rid of 'em when we shift the first bike. I might as well take those tools that Patrick nicked at the same time."

The surest way to get caught was to work the same patch day after day. So they left it for a few days and the next time targeted the rush hour crowds at Charing Cross Station. The takings weren't as good as Piccadilly, but decent enough. Then the family decided it was time to put Patrick's bike plan into operation.

◆   ◆   ◆

Patrick set off confidently on the 649 trolley bus to Tottenham, arriving in the High Road on another sunny morning. The shoppers were out in force and plenty of them were on bicycles, some with baskets attached to the handlebars. The male shoppers tended to attach their shopping bags to the crossbar. Patrick hadn't done well at school but what he lacked in brain power he made up for with sly cunning. So, instead of grabbing the first bicycle he could see, he watched as people rode up to the shops, parked and went in. He was after a man's model as he wouldn't be seen dead riding a girl's bike. He spotted a very busy greengrocer's and worked out that any customer who walked in would be a while before they were served. This would give him plenty of time to get hold of a bike and make his getaway undetected. An old gentleman on a sparkling new machine that probably cost him most of his spare cash, leant his bike against the greengrocer's and went in. Quick as a flash, Patrick walked up to the bike, wheeled it off the pavement and set off down the High Road. There were no shouts or whistles as he rode steadily south across Lordship Lane, down Stamford Hill and then home. Piece of cake.

His mother and father were waiting for him and the bike was quickly stowed away in the shed.

"Well done son!" his mother said and then his father added his congratulations. "It's a nice piece of work. Should fetch a bob or two at the market."

The next day George and Patrick stripped and re-painted the bike, fixed new mudguards and chain guard, and within eight hours it was unrecognisable from the machine stolen from outside the greengrocer's shop in Tottenham. The fresh paint dried and, a few days later, Patrick set off to Romford. Doris began her trip by bus and Patrick met her at the bus stop in Romford which was in the middle of the Market Place. It was a lovely, sunny day and the shoppers were thronging around the stalls on either side of the street. Doris thought it was too busy to get Bert on his own so that she could conduct her business unobserved, so she decided they should have lunch first. They crossed the street and made their way past Stone's department store and Copsey's furniture shop to Humphrey's bakery and refreshment rooms. After a cup of tea and a sandwich, Doris set off in search of her cousin Bert. Patrick sat on the ground outside the café, watching Copsey's lorries come and go and guarding the bike as if it were the crown jewels.

Doris re-appeared, nodding to Patrick to follow her. Together they approached an ironmonger's stall where a fat, bald-headed man in brown overalls was waiting for them.

"Yer remember Patrick, don't yer Bert?"

"Course. 'Ow are yer lad?

"Fine ta, Uncle Bert. 'Ere's the bike"

The bike was given a thorough once-over by the market trader.

"I'll give you three quid for it."

"Cost nearly six new," said Doris.

"Yeah but that's from a shop. This one's been nicked. Three quid. Take it or leave it"

"What about the wallets, purses and tools?"

"One pound the lot, plus the three for the bike."

"Alright," said a reluctant Doris.

Bert counted out three pound notes, a ten shilling note and four half crowns.

"Nice doin' business with yer. Let me know when yer've got anything else."

The two left to catch the Green Line back to Stratford and made it home in time for tea. Like Doris, George had hoped for more but quickly recognised that it wasn't a bad deal. Angela got back from Wood Green and thought it was good money, better than she earned at the A.B.C. but, she added, she'd rather earn hers honestly.

"Don't worry dear, I've got an idea how you can make some more lolly," said George with a leer.

◆　　◆　　◆

August came and most of the talk in the country was of war. But not in the Wallace household.

"We're doin' alright, but not well enough. It's time Patrick joined you, George. I mean actually liftin' a few wallets and purses, not just collectin' yer pickins."

"Right, he should be ready. We'll give it a go tomorrow."

On the way into London, George reminded his son of the way to go about it.

"Pick the right mark. Old people and women are best. Younger men are more on the look-out and, if you get caught at it, they'll probably frog march you to the nearest copper. Never look 'em in the eye. Go for the easy lift. Wallets in jacket pockets in crowds and purses in 'andbags are the best. The wallets in the pockets can be a bit tricky, but when they keep their stash in their back pockets it's a bit more dodgy coz there's often a button there, sort of lockin' it up. Watch 'em shop and see where they put their wallets and purses. If someone nabs you, scarper. We'll meet up at 'ome."

For a while everything went well for Patrick. He strolled round Piccadilly and Regent Street and even ventured into Oxford Street. He lifted a couple of purses without any difficulty. Then he spotted an old man in a tailor's shop in Regent Street. The shopper bought a jacket, paid in cash, then returned his wallet to his inside jacket pocket. Easy, thought Patrick, as he followed the target towards Piccadilly. As the crowds thickened, he made his move. He walked quickly in front of the man, reached into his inside pocket but, before he could get his hand on the wallet he felt a grip of iron on his wrist.

"Oh no you don't, you little thief. Let's find a policeman."

Patrick reacted quickly. He said nothing but kneed the man between the legs. As the man cried out in pain, his grip on Patrick slackened and he tore his wrist free and set off into the crowd. He heard shouts behind him but didn't look back. In a flash he was down the Piccadilly tube station steps. He walked briskly to the Haymarket exit, marched quickly down the street, headed across Trafalgar Square, then down Villiers Street and along the embankment. Less than forty five minutes after he'd almost been caught, he was climbing, a bit out of breath, up the steps of the number

76 bus at Waterloo on his way home. Patrick sheepishly told his parents about his mishap.

"I don't think 'e's quite ready for wallets in pockets yet," George said to Doris later that evening. "'E'd better steer clear of the West End for a while. Perhaps 'e can lift another couple of bikes."

"Don't worry. We're doin' all right and things are about to get better."

"Ow's that?"

"While you two 'ave been out thievin', 'Itler's attacked Poland. Chamberlain's told 'im to get out or else."

"Or else what?"

"Or else we'll 'ave a go at Germany. 'Itler's a nutter. 'E won't pull out. There's gonna be a war and that means bombs, blackouts, rationin' and men in uniform lookin' for girls. We'll be all right, you'll see."

CHAPTER NINE

Richard assembled the Gerber family on the concourse of Waterloo station and told them his immediate plans.

"I've booked two rooms at a hotel just around the corner. It's too late to travel back to my place tonight. If it's alright, I'll share with Jonathan and you two can have a room to yourselves. It's too late at night to talk about the future. I'm sure you're all worn out, so I suggest we all go straight to bed and meet for breakfast in the morning. Sorry, I'm not thinking straight, have you eaten?"

Benjamin assured him that they had enjoyed plenty to eat on the steamer and at Southampton, and that they could easily last until morning.

"Just one thing, Richard," continued Benjamin, "who's paying for all this?"

"Don't worry, I'll sort it out. I know you're struggling at the moment, but you'll soon be a rich man and we can settle up then."

"Thank you, Richard. That's very kind of you."

"My pleasure. I'm afraid you'll have to lug your suitcases for little longer, but the hotel's only a short walk away. I was lucky to get a room. This station's been incredibly busy for the past six months with refugees arriving from Germany, Austria and now Czechoslovakia. Lots of children as well with the Kinder transport, although most of them came in via Liverpool Street. The hotels are nearly always full."

They checked in. Richard explained that his car was parked near the hotel. He'd fetch it in the morning and drive them to his home in south-west London. Once they were in the room, Richard asked Jonathan how he was.

"Very tired, incredibly relieved and very excited."

"Do you think you'll miss Germany?"

"The Germany I knew as a boy, but not the Germany I've lived in for the past six years."

"I know. My own boys felt the same when we left. Good night."

Jonathan thanked Richard, turned on to his pillow and, within minutes, was fast asleep.

Breakfast was a treat in the morning. There was corn flakes and orange juice followed by a large plateful of scrambled eggs with tea, toast and marmalade to finish. Over breakfast, Richard explained that they would soon be driving to his house in south-west London. His youngest son Michael would leave his room to Benjamin and Ruth, and share with his brother Paul. Jonathan would have to stay with the family of Richard's boss, Reg Martin and his wife Mary, and share a room with their youngest son John, who was nineteen. The eldest Martin boy Roger, who was twenty four, still lived at home, which was just a few hundred yards from Richard's house.

The Gerbers were not in the least bit nervous. They'd been persecuted, Benjamin had been imprisoned, Jonathan attacked, much of their property stolen by the Nazis and they'd floated around the Atlantic on the *MS St Louis* waiting for the world to help them. Now they were in a new country and they knew they were amongst friends and that Richard would see that they were all right.

They checked out from the hotel and the Gerbers waited with their suitcases for Richard to bring the car around. Benjamin was worried that the three of them, each with a large suitcase, wouldn't fit into the car but, when the sleek black Ford with a large boot appeared, he could see that there was room for all.

It was an overcast day but dry as they edged their way through the heavy morning traffic along the south bank of the Thames. There wasn't much of a view, although they did get a glimpse of Big Ben and the Houses of Parliament in the distance as they crawled along York Road. South London seemed far less attractive than the renowned sights north of the river. Streets of small-soot covered houses were thrust tightly against one another, but things improved as they picked up speed heading south on the Guildford Road. Soon they were cruising through streets of brightly-painted, new-looking, semi-detached houses, each with a small pretty garden at the front.

Thirty minutes later, the car drew up outside one of these homes. It was semi-detached but looked quite large. Made of red brick and with a grey slate roof, the house had a large bow window at the front, painted light blue with a matching front door which opened to reveal a tall, brown-haired, handsome woman with a large smile on her face. Introductions were made and they all moved indoors with their luggage, except for Jonathan's case which stayed in the boot for later transportation to Reg and Mary's. Richard's wife Inge offered them tea or coffee and biscuits. The Gerbers chose coffee. Inge pointed out that the English were addicted to tea and that she had grown to like it. Richard told them that this mid-morning ritual was called "elevenses." When it was over, they got down to business.

"We need to get things sorted out pretty quickly," Richard began. "Firstly, you have to register as aliens. You'll have to go up to London and do this in Piccadilly. I think it's fairly painless. Inge and our boys are British citizens. Though they were born in Germany, I'm British which has made things a lot easier for us. It won't be as simple for you but, now you're in, they won't send you back."

Ruth spoke, "It's what we expected but, I'm sure you'll understand, we're better off here than we would be in Germany."

"Of course," said Inge. "We'll do all we can to make you comfortable and happy here."

"Thank you," said Benjamin. "We'll go into London to register tomorrow or the day after."

"Next," continued Richard, "we need to sort out your money. I'll retrieve your stamp collection from the bank. I've looked into this and the best place to take them is Stanley Gibbons in The Strand in London. They're the biggest stamp shop in England, if not the world. They won't necessarily buy the stamps, but they'll put a price on them and point you in the direction of reliable dealers."

"Excellent. Thank you, Richard."

"Once you've sold the stamps, we'll need to find you somewhere to live. You're welcome to stay here as long as you like, but I'm sure you'll want to find your own place as soon as possible. Inge's got some ideas on this."

"I think you should rent a property rather than buy one. The times are very uncertain and who knows what'll happen when war comes. I hope that we'll all be safe but, during the last war, many aliens were locked up, including some who had lived here for many years and were British citizens. We've no idea what will happen this time. I don't think that the time is yet ripe to put down roots, which is why it's better to rent a furnished property rather than buy one. If you are interned, you won't need to worry about your valuable property and its contents."

"I know it sounds harsh," said Richard, "but we've all got to be prepared for this war. When it comes there'll be bombing and thousands of buildings will be destroyed. It's better for a landlord to sort out compensation than you."

"Wherever you end up living in London, or most other big cities, the German bombers will come," continued Inge. "They'll bomb the East End of London because of the docks and we'll be attacked here because of the aircraft factories. Nowhere will be safe. There's a strong Jewish community living in North London and I think you should look there for somewhere to rent for the time being. I know you're not practising Jews, but many of them are recent German refugees and, to start with, I think it'll help you to settle in. The problem with the part of London where we are now is that most of the houses are new and there's very little decent property on the rental market."

"And," said Richard, "it's a short trip into the City of London where there are several excellent schools. Are you hoping to go to school, Jonathan?"

"Yes, I am."

"He hasn't been to school for a year," Ruth said. "Will they have him?"

"I've no idea," said Richard, "but I do have some contacts who might help."

"You seem to have a lot of contacts Richard," said Benjamin.

All of them chuckled and Inge continued, "I've some German friends in North London. We'll go up there together. I'm sure they'll know the right landlords to approach. Now it's time for lunch. Afterwards Richard will give you a quick look round the neighbourhood and then our boys will be back from school. After tea Richard will take Jonathan to our friends' house."

"I think Benjamin and I would like to come too," said Ruth, "to thank them."

"Of course."

◆　　◆　　◆

The sun had crept into the sky and, by the time Richard and the Gerbers set off on their walk, it was warm. Most of the houses looked similar to the one they'd just left. The gardens were lovingly kept. There were a few sparkling new shops: bakers, greengrocers, butchers and a Post Office/ newsagent.

Behind one avenue there was a beautifully mown large field where a dozen or so men dressed in white were engaged in some game where one of the men tried to knock down some bits of wood with a ball. The bits of wood seemed to be protected by another man armed with a club. When the man with the club hit the ball, the other men either stopped it, ran after it or caught it.

"What game is that?" asked a bemused Ruth.

"Cricket," replied Richard. "It's a kind of national obsession with us, like drinking tea."

"How long does a game last?" asked Jonathan.

"This one will go on until nightfall, but it's only a local club game. Big games, played by famous sportsmen, last for three, four or even five days."

"Good heavens!" said Benjamin. "They must get awfully tired."

"Not really. See that building over there?" The other three nodded. "There are nine other team members in there, probably drinking tea and playing cards. They're waiting for their turn with the bat. The people who hardly ever get a break are the umpires, that's like the referee in football, but cricket has two. The two gentlemen in white coats with brown hats are the umpires. They sometimes have to stand on their feet for a whole match, with only a short break for lunch and tea."

"I'd like to try it," said Jonathan. "I'm sure I could hit that ball out of the field."

Richard laughed, not unkindly. "It's not as easy as it looks. But you should try it. Cricket's a wonderful game."

Back at the house, Paul and Michael Walker had returned from their grammar school. Paul was the same age as Jonathan and Michael a year younger. Conversation was switched from German to English. The Walker boys spoke excellent English with only a slight German accent. Jonathan volunteered to act as interpreter for his parents if required. The two families got on well together, but soon it was time for Jonathan to make his way to his temporary home. Richard took all three Gerbers in his car on the short trip to the Martin's house. More warm smiles greeted them when they arrived at a residence remarkably similar to Richard's.

Three cheerful people, all with fair curly hair, were waiting in the hallway to welcome them. Reg and Mary Martin were the adults and the young man was their son John. They introduced themselves and John and the visitors were then ushered into the sitting room. Ruth tried out her improving English by asking John about himself and was told he was on vacation from Cambridge University where he was studying physics. Mary gave apologies for her elder son Roger whom, she said, was still at work. Reg explained that Roger was a journalist on the *London Evening Globe*, a paper which had opposed the government's policy of appeasement.

"I'm pleased to hear that your papers are allowed to say what they think. If you criticised government policy in Germany, the paper would be closed down and the staff marched off to a concentration camp, or worse," said Benjamin.

"Richard and Inge have told us how bad it is in Germany. You must feel terrible having to leave your homeland," said Mary.

"No, we're relieved," said Ruth, "and we're so lucky to have friends like your family and Richard's to look after us. Thank you very much."

◆　　◆　　◆

By the time the two youngsters had come down to breakfast the next morning, Reg had set off to his work as a department store manager and Roger had returned. He was also curly haired and tall, looking like the sportsman that he was. He shook Jonathan's hand firmly before continuing to recount in frustration to his mother the details of his latest story of yet another missed opportunity by Neville Chamberlain. The PM was dragging his feet over courting the Soviet Union as an ally against the Nazis. Mary gave her son a funny look.

"Sorry Jonathan," said Roger, "can't get all this foreign affairs stuff out of my head. Anyway, tell me a bit about yourself. Would you like to speak English or German?"

"English please."

A lively discussion followed, mostly about sport. Roger's 100m time was faster, just (he'd had to convert it from his 100 yards time), and Jonathan's best sport was football. Roger was keener on rugby.

"Do they play rugby in Germany?"

"I'm not sure. I've never played it. What is it?"

Roger gave a brief description of a game of rugby.

"Is it like American football?"

"Sort of. Why?"

"The captain of our ship said I would make a good American footballer."

"If that's the case, you'll probably make a good rugby player. Anyhow, must dash. Nice talking to you Jonathan. I'll be late tonight Mum. I'm taking Jane to the cinema after work."

"What are you going to see?"

"*Destry Rides Again*. It's a western with James Stewart and Marlene Dietrich. Bye all!"

Reg had given Richard time off from his work to help settle the Gerbers in. Richard accompanied his German friends to the Alien Registration Office in Piccadilly. With war rapidly approaching, supervision of aliens was being tightened up. A bureaucrat in a grey suit with matching hair told them they would have to appear before a tribunal to be classified if war did come. They were told that they had to register any change of address immediately if they moved from their present one and that they may be interned in the event of war.

On that gloomy note, and with registration completed, they set off for the Strand and the Stanley Gibbons stamp shop. Richard did the talking and introduced Benjamin to one of the sales consultants who asked for a description of the collection. This caused several sharp intakes of breath, a puffing of cheeks and raising of eyebrows from the Stanley Gibbons man who pronounced that, assuming the stamps were in good condition, the whole lot would probably be worth more than twenty thousand pounds. He gave Benjamin a list of dealers whom he said would be interested in some, if not all, of his collection.

The four of them had lunch in the Lyons Corner House at the bottom of the Strand, opposite Charing Cross Station, and then caught the train home. When they arrived at the Walkers, Richard suggested that Benjamin telephone the stamp dealers to find out whether or not they were interested in the collection. Benjamin's English was a bit dodgy and he was on the phone for more than an hour but it was time well spent as he found three dealers, all north of the Thames, who were very interested in his collection and he arranged to see them the following afternoon. Richard then rang his bank to organise the collection of the stamps the next morning. With the stamps well on the way to being sold, Benjamin and Ruth could now make serious plans about spending the money. Firstly, they had to repay the Walkers, then find somewhere to live and finally sort out Jonathan's schooling.

The stamps were sold and the money, which happily was a bit more than predicted, banked. Inge, Benjamin and Ruth spent a whole day in North London where they met some friends of Inge's who put them in touch with a landlord who owned a small two-storey house just off the High Street. They made an appointment to meet the landlord at the house the following day.

The three of them returned twenty-four hours later. It was a decent day and the house looked delightful in the sunshine. It was terraced and a neat wall enclosed a small front garden. A tree-lined grass verge separated the pavement from the wide road. The landlord said that the building dated from 1910. Outside it was in beautiful condition. It was the same story inside with a large sitting room and decent-sized dining room leading to a spacious kitchen. In the hall a set of steps led to a cellar which was served by electric lighting and several wall sockets. Upstairs there were two good-sized bedrooms and a clean modern bathroom, as well as plenty of storage space. The smart rear yard had a shed and was surrounded by a wooden fence. It was exactly what the Gerbers needed. The rent was a bit steep, but they could afford it. It was temporary, but the uncertainty of their position made it ideal for the time being. They agreed to move in at the beginning of September, in ten days' time.

While his parents were house-hunting, Jonathan spent the day learning to play cricket with John and the Walker boys at the local cricket club. Buzz the groundsman had turned a blind eye to their use of the outfield. Jonathan found bowling difficult and he kept throwing the ball rather than keeping his arm straight. He was swift and agile in the field but his batting was a bit hit and miss. He often missed it with a huge swipe but when he connected the ball travelled a long way. There were several stoppages while the ball was retrieved from the adjoining gardens.

All that remained was to find a school for Jonathan. Reg knew of an excellent boys' school in the city, close to St Paul's Cathedral and easily accessible from north London. Richard wrote to the Headmaster on Benjamin's behalf. A prompt reply invited the boy and his parents to visit the school toward the end of August. Since Jonathan hadn't been to school for a year and all his previous education had been in Germany, the Head said he would have to sit a brief entrance test before the interview.

The family travelled by train and walked to the Embankment where the school was located. Signs of impending war could be seen everywhere: sandbagged buildings, signs identifying air raid shelters, people in uniform and pedestrians carrying gas masks. The Headmaster made them welcome when they reached the school. Jonathan was taken off to sit his test by another member of staff and the Head suggested that Benjamin and Ruth spend the next hour walking around St Paul's. Time was soon up and the family were sitting in the Head's study with coffees. The Head, whose name was Lawton, was a tall, dark-haired man in his fifties. He was wearing a smart blue suit, polished black shoes and his straight brown hair was immaculately groomed, probably with the aid of a liberal dose of pomade. He wore a moustache, bigger than Hitler's, on his thin face. Mr Lawton excused himself for a minute and went out to have a word with the teacher who had supervised Jonathan's test. Then he returned and sat down.

"Mr Shields is checking the test now and he won't take long. He did say that you've a remarkable grasp of English, Jonathan. Tell me about your schooling in Berlin."

Jonathan spoke about his gymnasium in Berlin for ten minutes. A knock interrupted him and Mr Shields entered and handed the test paper over to the Head.

"You've done remarkably well. I'm sure I can find a place for you here."

"Thank you sir."

"I need to make one thing absolutely clear. You're German and Jewish but this school will have no truck whatsoever with any racial or anti-Semitic behaviour. My staff and I don't care what religion a boy has, or even if he has no religion at all. There is no colour prejudice whatsoever. Any boy found guilty of abusing another on grounds of race, religion or the colour of his skin will be immediately expelled. I'm pleased to say that, in my fifteen years as Headmaster, I've never yet had to throw a boy out. You'll be happy here Jonathan."

"Thank you sir."

A brief discussion followed about the fees, which weren't cheap, but that didn't matter. The Gerbers were wealthy. Mr Lawton then agreed that Jonathan would study English, History and Geography for his Higher School Certificate and then asked about sport. Jonathan told him that football and athletics were his best sports and he was learning to play cricket. Football was played at the school, Mr Lawton told him, and athletics and cricket in the summer as well as rugby, the sport that Jonathan had discussed briefly with Roger and was keen to try. The Head assured Jonathan that he would cope well with rugby. Handshakes were exchanged and the Gerbers made their way back to their temporary home for one final weekend.

◆   ◆   ◆

It turned out to be the last weekend of peace for almost six years. At dawn on Friday 1 September, Germany invaded Poland. The British and

French governments had already promised to come to Poland's aid if they were attacked, so the two Prime Ministers sent Hitler a "back-off or else" warning. Britain prepared for war. The evacuation of children to the safety of the countryside from cities and other vulnerable spots began. The German armies continued to march eastwards, ignoring Anglo-French threats. A final note from Prime Minister Chamberlain was sent on Sunday 3 September. Hitler ignored it, and Britain and France were at war with Germany.

It was a beautiful summer's day. The Gerbers and the Martins were gathered in Richard's front room to hear Chamberlain's radio broadcast, during which he declared war, at 11:15.

"Britain and France are declaring war on Hitler and the Nazis, not Germany," Richard declared.

Not long after the end of the broadcast, the three families heard the wail of an air raid siren. Some squeezed into the Anderson shelter in the garden, others made themselves comfortable under the stairs, while Roger and his girlfriend Jane stayed in the lounge. Not long afterwards the all-clear sounded. It had been a false alarm.

On the next day, the Monday, the Gerbers made the move to north London. As they were unpacking and setting up home, the Wallaces were less than three hundred yards away planning how to make the most of the new criminal opportunities the war would bring.

CHAPTER TEN

"Right, we're at war. Let's make the most of it," said Doris.

"Some of me mates 'ave bin evacuated to the country. Will I 'ave to go?" asked Patrick.

"Nobody would 'ave yer. No chance," said his mother.

"I 'ope it don't last too long, otherwise Patrick might get called up to fight," George said.

"I'm sure you'll find a way of makin' sure that don't 'appen. Anyway, they might call you up before 'im."

"What, wiv my chest? Leave it out."

"There be bombs," said Angela. "I don't much fancy that."

"When they come," replied her mother, "we'll make use of that an' all."

"'Ow we gonna do that?" asked Patrick.

"You'll see when they come," said his mother.

They were studying the blackout regulations, not out of some sense of civic duty, but to see how they could turn these to their advantage. Street lighting was a thing of the past. Cars had to mask their headlights and torches had to be hooded, reducing their beams to a pinprick. All windows had to be totally blacked out.

"It's gonna be pitch black out there. Just think of all the fings you could get up to in the dark," Doris continued.

There was a sharp knock on the door. It surprised the four of them. They didn't get many visitors. George got up and opened the front door. Their least favourite policeman was standing on the pavement outside.

"'Allo Mr Crawford. 'Ow can I 'elp you?" he said nervously.

"Just a little chat, George. Can I come in?"

"Course you can."

Detective Constable Crawford was a tall man in his early twenties. He had short black hair, without a parting, and was wearing the uniform of a plain-clothes policeman; a light brown belted raincoat and dark brown trilby which he politely took off as he came in.

Crawford followed George into the sitting room where he found the rest of the family looking at him expectantly.

"'Allo Mr Crawford," said Doris. "Cuppa tea?"

"No thanks, Doris. I'm not staying long. Just wanted to ask you about the spate of bike thefts we're getting not far from here."

Patrick's little business was booming. He'd pinched bikes from Tottenham, Walthamstow, Highbury, Clapton and Hackney, but had been careful to steer clear of his own neighbourhood. As a reward, he'd been allowed to keep one for himself. This one was almost brand new but they'd repainted it then scuffed it up so that it looked well used.

"You see," continued Crawford, "I've spotted Patrick riding a bike round here and I wondered where it came from. Wasn't nicked, was it Patrick?"

"No it weren't, Mr Crawford. Dad got it for me."

"Where from, George?"

"Some bloke down The Rochester Castle. Paid 'im a couple of quid for it."

"And where did he get it from?"

"No idea. I didn't ask."

Crawford looked round the room. The previously shabby furniture now had fresh covers and the carpet was new. Expensive looking blackout curtains hung in front of the window.

"A bike, curtains, carpet and furniture covers. You're doing all right. Where's the money coming from?"

An indignant looking Doris started. "I work my fingers to the bone, Mr Crawford. With all those new refugees round 'ere, there's plenty of washin' to be done and they're too bleedin' lazy to do it for themselves."

"Now there's a war on, I expect you'll be joining up, George."

George patted his chest. "Not wiv me asthma, Mr Crawford. I'd be no use."

The policeman gave him a look of utter disdain.

"I'm off now but I've got my eye on you lot. Sooner or later I'm going to nab you."

He got up, put his hat on and walked out the front door. The Wallaces sat in silence for a minute and then George said.

"Bastard. I 'ope 'e gets knocked down in the blackout."

"Don't worry," his wife said, "'es got nuthin' on us."

◆   ◆   ◆

For a while, the Wallaces carried on more or less as usual, apart from cutting down on bike thefts. They were fed up with getting told to put that light out by the air raid wardens. Little 'Itlers people were calling them. Rationing had started, but whatever the Wallaces needed they either stole or bought on the black market. George reported from the West End that, once nightfall came, it was full of folk drifting about in the darkness. All were looking for something: the men for sex and the girls for business. Everywhere there were uniforms of all colours, many of them loitering outside the Regent Palace Hotel, just off Piccadilly Circus. Some went into the hotel with the girls while the others took their escorts to the dark streets behind the hotel or even as far afield as Hyde Park, where they had to share the darkness with homosexuals. Posters were everywhere urging Londoners to "Take Your Gas Mask Everywhere" and inviting women to do their bit for National Service.

"Time to earn your keep, Angela. We've 'ad lots of expenses what wiv blackout curtains and furnishins and you gotta admit the grub's bin good."

"I pay my way. I give mum lots of me A.B.C. money each week."

"It's not enough, ducky. There's plenty down the 'dilly would fancy a nice young girl like you."

The penny dropped and Angela stared at her father in horror.

"There's no way I'm workin' as a tart. It's an 'orrible thought. Besides I might catch somethin'. And somebody might attack me."

George stood up and walked towards his daughter.

"Yer'll do as yer bleedin' well told, my girl."

"I ain't doin' it and that's that," shouted Angela.

George slapped her across the cheek. Angela was speechless and buried her head in her hands and started to cry.

"If yer don't like it yer can piss orf and live rough on the streets. No daughter of mine is goin' to live in this 'ouse without payin' 'er way.

George's voice softened slightly. "And don't worry 'bout bein' attacked. Patrick and I will be close by lookin' after you."

This was the first that Patrick had heard of it, but he shrugged his shoulders and sat in silence.

Doris joined the discussion. "You don't 'ave to go the 'ole 'og. I'm sure there's plenty that'll pay for a nice quick 'and job."

"I wouldn't know what to do."

"You can practice on Patrick."

Doris stood up and walked towards her husband.

"You filthy beast, George Wallace. Don't worry, Angela. I'll tell you all about it. Give it a try. If you don't like it, you can pack it in."

Angela very reluctantly agreed and the next night the three of them went up to town. Angela was young and pretty, not like some of the seasoned pros who had been patrolling the streets for years, most of whom looked as if they'd seen better days. The darkness, however, hid some of their worst features. She soon attracted the attention of a soldier and was back on patrol five minutes later with two half-crowns in her purse. She repeated the trick three times and well before midnight they were on their way home two pounds to the good. There'd be a problem if they stayed out after twelve as the only all-night buses going their way would have dropped them at Stratford. Still, they reasoned, they'd soon be earning enough to afford a cab.

"Ow was it, ducky?" asked Doris when the three got back home.

"Easy, but I 'ated it," replied Angela. "Some of the regulars gave me a dirty look."

"'Fraid of the competition I expect. Never mind, there's plenty for all."

Everything went smoothly for a while. Patrick cautiously resumed his bike thieving, taking great care to steer clear of Crawford. Doris carried on with her regular trips to Romford Market and Angela brought in some useful extra money two or three evenings a week, though with ever-growing reluctance. George was still lifting wallets and purses with great success. The darker nights, making burglary so much easier, couldn't come soon enough for them. Then a new visitor, far more frightening than Crawford, arrived.

It was a Saturday night. Angela was at the Palais and Patrick was out roaming the streets with his mates. Doris and George were having a quiet cigarette before setting off for an evening at the White Hart when their visitor arrived.

"Mr Gibson," said George, his stomach turning somersaults, "'ow nice to see you."

"Likewise George, and you too Doris," he replied, glancing at George's nervous-looking wife. Gibson was one of the very few people who put the wind up her.

"I see things are going alright for you," said Gibson in his soft Irish burr, "what with bike thieving, picking pockets, the odd burglary and your pretty daughter tossing soldiers off down the 'dilly, you must be bringing in a pretty packet."

Gibson was a large bald-headed man, overweight with a fat face, ruddy cheeks and ginger moustache. He was wearing a dark suit. He looked quite jolly, but there was no doubting the menace in his voice when he spoke.

"I see you've had the good sense to stay off my patch. Very wise. You're showing promise. Maybe I can put some jobs your way."

"That's very kind of you, Mr Gibson," said Doris. "We'll be 'appy to 'elp."

"I've got something just now. Where's the boy?"

"Out wiv 'is mates."

"I see he's got a bicycle. Very handy. I need a lookout for my bookies. All he has to do is ride up and down the street and, as soon as he spots a copper, sprint like mad to tip the bookie off. My man could be in a pub, street corner, house or wherever. It'll be a nice little earner for him."

"That's very good of yer, Mr Gibson. When do you want 'im to start?" asked Doris.

Gibson tore out a sheet of paper from a notebook and jotted something down.

"Tell him to come to this address on Monday at ten. We'll see how he goes. If he does well, I might be able to find something else for him. I run a string of ladies in my guest houses. Your boy can keep an eye on those as well. He might even get to sample the goods. When it gets darker, you'll be stepping up your housebreaking no doubt. We could go into partnership. I'll help you get a better price for your goods."

Neither of the Wallaces was stupid enough to tell Gibson that they already had an outlet. If he was offering to help, then that was that.

"By the way," Gibson said as he left, "it's a dangerous world out there in the darkness. You make sure you're carrying some protection."

◆   ◆   ◆

The war was going nowhere. Men (and some women) were enlisting. Ration books and ID cards had been issued. The odd ship was sunk by German submarines, U-boats, and Winston Churchill had joined the war cabinet. The Germans were too busy overwhelming the Poles to bother about Britain and France. It was all so quiet that many took the opportunity to take a late holiday in the autumn sunshine. War? What war?

◆   ◆   ◆

The Gerbers moved into their new house on Monday 4 September. The unpacking was left to Benjamin, while Jonathan and Ruth caught the number 76 bus to Victoria. Their destination was the Army/Navy Stores. They came out with Jonathan fully equipped with uniform, gym shoes and football boots, shorts and shirts for his new school. They did some more shopping, and then, weighed down with bags and parcels, caught the bus home.

Benjamin took Jonathan to the school on the following day. Both were surprised on arrival to find so few boys. The Headmaster told them that the younger pupils had been evacuated to a boarding school in the country. How long they'd be there, he couldn't say and he couldn't predict whether or not the sixth form would remain in London.

Benjamin left his son in the care of the school and walked to Piccadilly to register their new address. There he was told that, as the country was now at war, aliens would be treated on a case by case basis. Some enemies of the state had been immediately locked up. The official told Benjamin that he would soon receive a letter instructing his family to appear before a tribunal. He would receive two weeks' notice of this, so that he would have time to prepare his case. In the meantime, he was to report to the local police station.

Staff and pupils treated Jonathan well, as the Headmaster had promised. As he wasn't the only German Jewish refugee in the school, he escaped being treated as an oddity. He coped well with both the lessons and the language and, by the end of the day, felt very comfortable. At home he reported enthusiastically on his day and his father passed on the information from the Alien Registration office. Ruth had taken charge of the house, the garden and the shopping. Benjamin went to south-west London to see the Walkers one evening and told them how well they were all settling in. He updated Richard on his position at the Alien Registration Office and his friend quickly volunteered to provide a reference if necessary.

"Oh!" said Richard, "I nearly forgot. A letter arrived here addressed to Jonathan. It's in the kitchen. I'll go and fetch it."

Richard returned with the letter and handed it to Benjamin who examined it closely.

"It's from France, I see. Must be from that girl Jonathan met on the *St Louis*. Thanks. I'll pass it on."

"By the way," said Richard, "You must visit us one weekend. I'll have a word with Reg and let you know."

At home, an excited Jonathan read the letter from Hilde. It was disappointingly newsy. Her parents were well and her father was working. Both she and Matthew went to good schools and she liked Paris. She was looking forward to hearing from Jonathan now that he had her address. Encouragingly, she finished the letter with an X.

On the second Wednesday of the term, Jonathan and his classmates walked to Charing Cross Station and caught the train to south-east London where the school's playing fields were situated. They played football and Jonathan excelled. His size and physique made him a natural centre half. He tackled strongly, showed great pace in defence and, when called upon to head the ball, sent it many yards up field. He created quite an impression, but remained quiet and modest. On an adjoining pitch, there were H-shaped posts at either end. Jonathan asked the teacher what they were.

"That's a rugby pitch. Ever played it?"

"No sir, but I think I'd like to."

"We'll be playing rugby later in the term. I think you'll do well when you learn the game. It's a bit tricky at first."

The weekend reunion in south-west London took place in mid-October. All three Gerbers stayed in Reg's house. Both his sons had gone away, Roger to join the army and John to do some hush-hush work for the war effort. After a lovely meal on the Saturday night, all three families gathered in the Martins' sitting room. Inge asked about Jonathan's school and Mary asked about the new house. Benjamin told them about the tribunal.

"You should be alright," said Richard, "but you can understand the government taking these precautions. There's a huge number of refugees in the country and there are bound to be a few rotten apples. What worries me is that the government will overreact and intern everybody. Still, we'll cross that bridge when we come to it."

Reg asked Benjamin how he was spending his time.

"I'm at a bit of a loose end," he admitted. "I'm used to working and being idle doesn't really suit me."

"I wondered about that. How would you like to come and work for me on the purchasing side of things for two or three days a week? Richard's often disappearing up to London," he said with a wry grin, "and I could do with a bit of help."

"That's very kind of you Reg. I'd love to do it but I insist you don't pay me. We refugees aren't supposed to take British citizens' jobs and, besides, I don't need the money."

"Right, that's settled then. Shall we say Tuesday at ten?"

"That's fine. Thank you Reg."

An obviously very pleased Benjamin looked at his son and asked what news he had about the family they'd met aboard the *St Louis*.

Jonathan passed on the best wishes of the Hofstadts to his parents and told them that they seemed to be doing well in Paris. He had replied to

Hilde, even daring to begin to make his feelings for her clear, and was keenly looking forward to her next letter.

◆   ◆   ◆

Back home, the Gerbers decided to make themselves known amongst the other Jews in the district. It wasn't as if a wave of religious enthusiasm had swept over them but it seemed that, as newcomers, a lot could be learned about North London from people who had been there a while, especially the refugees. One evening the three of them attended a social gathering in a hall adjacent to the Stamford Hill synagogue. They were slightly upset to see horrible things about the Jews painted on the wall outside. They mentioned it to a woman they were siting with in the hall.

"Don't worry about that. It's nothing like Germany here. Probably one of the local thugs who've got nothing better to do did it. The Wallace boy, I'd guess. It'll be a good thing when he's called up to fight."

The evening went well and they promised to return to similar events in the future but didn't commit themselves to attending services in the synagogue, not that anyone seemed to care.

◆   ◆   ◆

It was late October and still there was no war. Many evacuees returned home from the country. Cinemas and theatres, which had been closed on the outbreak of war, began to re-open and some football matches were played, although many of the better players were in the forces. The only action was at sea where a German battleship, the *Admiral Graf Spee*, was sailing around the South Atlantic sinking British merchant ships. Churchill, in charge at the Admiralty, promised that the Nazi raider would be sent to the bottom of the sea. Everywhere there were signs of London at war. More posters, "War Savings", "Lend a Hand" and "England Expects National Service".

◆   ◆   ◆

The dark nights enabled the Wallaces to step up their criminal activities. Angela, very reluctantly and with a growing sense of fear and dislike of her family, continued to accompany her brother and father to Piccadilly. As her parents had predicted, there were a growing number of men from the forces willing to pay the five bob for a hand-job, and she never returned without a couple of quid and a sense of disgust. While she was plying her trade, father and son watched in the shadows. George was armed with a razor and Patrick carried a sheath knife. Money wasn't exactly rolling in, but they were doing alright. The blackout curtains had cost a small fortune, but at least that meant that they hadn't been threatened with prosecution by the ARP warden for showing a light.

The best news was that the hated copper Crawford had joined the Navy. In late autumn Gibson put in another appearance. He was well pleased with Patrick's work as a bookies' lookout. Now he wanted the boy to do a similar job with his brothels, keeping an eye open for the law, as he put it.

The darkness allowed George and Patrick to spread their wings and head north to help themselves in some of the wealthier houses. They targeted Hendon, Finchley and Edgware where nicely spread out new private estates provided rich pickings. It was easy if the houses were unoccupied, but most families were staying in as the days shortened. Weekends were better. Families liked a night out after their dull, ration restricted, weeks. Patrick's size and dexterity was useful and it was usually he who squeezed into deserted houses before letting his father in through either the front or back door. Jewellery made up the major part of their hauls, although they did pick up some cash from time to time. The ever-resourceful Doris disposed of the goods, making sure that Gibson didn't spot her.

The family worked seven days a week with daytime lookout work for Patrick, dipping for George and two or three nights up west for Angela, watched over by George and Patrick. One night, when Patrick was lurking in a doorway off Glasshouse Street, a soldier approached and asked if he was interested in business. Patrick swore at him and the soldier ran away when the boy threatened him with a knife.

"Some dirty queer approached me," he told his father on the way home.

"What 'appened?"

"I told 'im I'd cut 'im and he ran off."

"Good lad... 'Ang on, this could be another little earner."

"Leave it out, dad"

"No, you won't 'ave to do anything. Just lead 'em to a nice quiet spot where I'll be waitin'. We'll pull the blades on 'em and empty their pockets."

"What 'appens if they fight back?"

"Good question. We need somethin' to 'it 'em with first."

"I know just the thing, them 'andles on the tube which people 'ang on. Make nice coshes. I'll pick up a couple tomorrow."

They were talking as if compiling a shopping list and Angela listened to this in ever growing horror. She liked being a waitress in the A. B. C. Tea Rooms and couldn't get out of the house quickly enough in the morning. Each evening she sat on the bus home in sheer dread about what the night would bring. She had to get away.

By late December they were exceeding even their own expectations and they almost lived like kings and queens, although this made not a scrap of difference to Angela who had no wish to live like this unless she won the football pools or married a rich man. Then they had a bit of bad news. Crawford may have gone but his replacement, a plain-clothes detective called Scott, was even worse. He'd been a beat bobby for years, but the shortage of keen young men, many of whom had been called up, had led to older officers being promoted to jobs for which many were totally unsuitable. Scott was one of these. He wasn't much of a physical threat, he was barely five foot nine and flabby, but he had a nasty conniving mind and that was dangerous. One Saturday night he was waiting outside The White Hart when George and Doris left at closing time. He had black eyes, a red nose and thin lips which barely opened when he told Doris and George that he'd got his eye on them and would be paying them a visit soon.

◆   ◆   ◆

Jonathan and Patrick's paths crossed one Saturday afternoon towards the end of November. Strolling through the local park, he spotted a group of boys of about his age playing football. Coats had been put down at both ends for goals. Jonathan began to watch from the edge of the pitch.

"What you starin' at?" one of the boys shouted.

Jonathan shrugged his shoulders.

"Fancy a game. We're one short and losin'," the same boy said.

"Alright."

He took his place in defence, made a couple of decent headers and intercepted a few passes. Then one of the opposition boys ran straight at him.

"Go on, Edgar," shouted his team mates.

Patrick tried to slip the ball past Jonathan who stuck out his powerful left leg and got hold of the ball. Patrick continued his run and tripped over Jonathan's outstretched leg, falling flat on his face on to the muddy ground. He pulled himself to his feet and snarled at Jonathan.

"Yer foulin' bastard. That's a penalty."

One of the other boys joined in.

"No it wasn't, Edgar. It's a fair tackle."

Patrick limped back to the middle of the pitch, still muttering to himself. Jonathan began to have a bigger impact on the game and, when they decided to call it a day, his team were a goal ahead. As he walked away, a sullen Patrick approached him, called him a cheat and told him not to play in any more of their games.

"Anyway, oo are yer?"

"We've just moved into the district. We've come from Germany."

"A bleedin' kraut. Yer'd better steer clear of me. I'm the cock round 'ere."

Although he hadn't a clue what that meant, Jonathan replied, unperturbed by the threats, "Don't worry, I will"

"Don't mess with Edgar Wallace or I'll cut yer."

The name rang a bell with Jonathan but he thought no more about it and headed home.

◆   ◆   ◆

It was a desperately cold winter. The so-called "phoney war" continued and was still being fought exclusively at sea. The British people's vitally important supplies from America were being continuously disrupted as merchant ships were sunk crossing the Atlantic. Sometimes the enemy used submarines and at other times surface raiders. The one piece of good news came in December when the captain of the German pocket battleship *Graf Spee* was forced by British warships to scuttle his vessel outside Montevideo harbour in South America.

◆　　◆　　◆

The Gerbers had been called before a tribunal in late October. They answered the questions truthfully and left Richard's name and address as a supporting referee. Several weeks later they received notification that they had been placed in Category C, which meant that they were not a threat to anyone and could continue as they were.

Jonathan maintained his good progress at school. His sporting prowess and modest, open personality made him popular and soon he had several new friends. With the cinemas open again, a small group of them made regular trips to such treats as *The Four Feathers*, *Gunga Din*, *Beau Geste* and, best of all, *Stagecoach*. Before the cinema visits, they regularly played football for the school. Jonathan had established himself as a commanding centre half in the team.

The promised rugby game took place during November. The teacher recognised that Jonathan was fast and positioned him on the wing. It was cold and he stood outside a line of four others waiting for the ball to come to him but, for twenty minutes, it never did and he became increasingly frustrated and bored. Then a boy on the other team came dashing towards Jonathan.

"Stop him, Gerber," cried the teacher.

Jonathan ran towards his opponent and crashed his solid shoulder into his chest. The boy went down like a sack of potatoes and lay gasping on the ground. The teacher blew his whistle to bring the game to a halt and looked at the injured player.

"He'll be alright. He's just winded. Normally, Gerber, you should wrap your arms round the legs, or sometimes the waist, and take them to the ground. That's the best way to stop them."

"Yes sir," said Jonathan who then watched the other players for tips on how to do this. Following a sort of turtle shaped activity, which the teacher called a scrum, an extremely large boy from the other team came charging at Jonathan with his right arm held stiffly in front of him and the ball safely tucked under the other arm. Jonathan moved quickly forwards to challenge the threat. He ducked beneath the hand and hit the boy with a crunching tackle in his midriff. He wrapped his arms tightly round his opponent, drove him backwards, then dumped him on the ground.

"That's the way, Gerber," the teacher called out while stopping the game to revive the victim of Jonathan's tackle. There wasn't much more for him to do. Most members of the other team chose to pass the ball before Jonathan got near them. Towards the end of the game, he received the ball.

"Run, Gerber," shouted the teacher.

Jonathan skipped round his opposite number and set off towards the white line that passed between, and on either side of, the H-shaped posts. Others pursued him but without any chance of making up the ground and soon he was placing the ball on the grass beyond the white line.

"Try," said the teacher who then blew a long blast on his whistle.

After the game, the teacher congratulated Jonathan.

"Well done Gerber, you'll make a decent player."

"Thank you, sir," said Jonathan modestly.

On the way home that night Jonathan had another run-in with Patrick. He was wearing a raincoat over his school uniform which included white shirt and a smart school tie. He turned in from the High Street and was confronted by three youths.

"'Ere's that kid from the posh school," said one. "What school you at?" Jonathan told them.

"Never 'eard of it," one of them said.

"'E speaks funny," another said. "Which country you from?" Jonathan told them.

"I told yer 'es a bleedin' kraut and I bet 'e's a Jew boy an all. Let's do 'im over," said Patrick.

Jonathan would have preferred to turn his back and walk away, but he quickly recognised that he wasn't going to have this option.

Two of the youths approached Jonathan, their fists raised. He dropped his satchel and hit the first a steamroller blow on the side of the face. The boy dropped to the ground screaming. The next boy, who hadn't got a clue how to fight, came at Jonathan arms flailing. A swift uppercut to the jaw dumped him on his backside. He scrambled to his feet and backed off, joining his mate in retreating a safe distance.

"Cut the bastard, Edgar."

Out came Patrick's knife and he thrust at Jonathan who kicked the wrist with such force that the knife dropped to the ground. Patrick howled and then reached down to pick up the knife, but Jonathan was too quick and a swift kick saw it skate across the pavement and fall harmlessly down the drain. Jonathan advanced on the three of them but they knew when they were beaten and started running. The satchel was retrieved as the three louts disappeared into the distance. When they felt safe, they stopped and started hurling abuse at him. Patrick delivered the final insult, desperately trying to make up for another loss of face he'd suffered in front of his mates who'd always thought he was some kind of tough guy.

"I bet you are a bleedin' Jewish bastard as well. You've 'ad it now. I'm gonna get yer you Nazi Jewish twat."

The die was cast. War had been declared on Jonathan Gerber.

CHAPTER ELEVEN

Both households enjoyed a happy Christmas under the circumstances. The extra money the Wallaces were making from their various enterprises meant more cigarettes and an increase in the number of visits to the White Hart. George enjoyed extra beer at 6d a pint and Doris was able to step up her consumption of port at 7d a tot. The only drawback for the family was Angela's attitude, both to the way her parents and brother carried on and to the revolting things they made her do. Somehow, she had to get away from them.

The Gerbers spent Christmas with Reg and Mary in south-west London. The Martin boys were still away and neither parent knew where they were. Like parents throughout the land, they were worried, but tried not to show it. The Walker family and Roger's girlfriend, Jane, joined them for Boxing Day. The war seemed far away as they ate, drank, chatted and played Monopoly.

Jonathan returned to school in the New Year. His rugby improved and he soon found himself playing centre three-quarter in the school team. Whether or not he liked it more than football, his enjoyment of the game was growing. Although he hadn't yet excelled at his studies, due initially to some language difficulties, some signs of potential were beginning to show and he worked hard. He hadn't told his parents about the run-in with the three youths and that soon became a distant memory. And still there was no war.

◆　　◆　　◆

The Wallaces received an unwelcome New Year's visitor. Detective Constable Scott knocked on their door one mid-January afternoon.

"I thought I'd find you 'ere this time of day. It's too early for thievin'. Thank you, Doris. I will 'ave a cuppa tea," he said as he took off his hat and sat down.

"I'm a bit like Mr Crawford in that I know everythin' you're up to. And also like Mr Crawford, I'll nab you if I can and you'll both be sent down. Unless, that is, we can come to some sort of arrangement."

"What sort of arrangement, Mr Scott?" asked Doris, as she returned with the tea.

"Well I thought, seein' as 'ow your various businesses are flourishin', a fiver a week should suffice."

"That's blackmail," exclaimed Doris.

"No, it's not. It's a generous contribution to yours truly's retirement fund and it'll make certain that you stay out of the scrubs, George and you 'olloway, Doris me dear."

Scott drank his tea, commentated on the state of the war and then got up to leave.

"I'll work out 'ow yer gonna pay me and I'll let you know soon."

The Wallaces were flabbergasted. As winter moved into spring, their cash flow slowed down. The lighter nights meant fewer opportunities to use the darkness and they were paying off Scott. They weren't poor by any means, but they'd become accustomed to an improved lifestyle and they couldn't think of a better way of upping their income. George tried to persuade Angela to increase what she offered to the punters but she was adamant that she'd gone as far as she was prepared to and, in any case, she wouldn't be doing hand jobs much longer. Becoming increasingly fed up, they struggled on throughout the summer. Little did they realise it but new opportunities were just around the corner.

◆   ◆   ◆

Although there was still no war, rationing was tightened and the country lived on in gloomy austerity. Ruth followed the government's advice and cultivated vegetables and the arrival of spring after the cold winter brought welcome relief for miserable Britain. That relief extended to the Gerbers but, little did they know it, much worse was to come for them.

Jonathan continued to excel at school. He was becoming a respected sportsman as a leading member of both football and rugby teams and scored a spectacular try in one game to earn the school a late victory. Studies were progressing well and soon he was studying meteorology and climatology, reading Shakespeare's sonnets and learning about the Thirty Years' War in seventeenth-century Germany. His teachers were confident he would pass his Higher School Certificate when he took the examination in June 1941.

In the late spring Jonathan took part in athletics. He ran fast and jumped far but, as the days went by, he became less self-assured, since he had a lot on his mind. Regular letters were continuing letters with Hilde and looked forward to seeing her, perhaps in the late summer. But, like millions of others, his plans began to unravel on 9 April 1940.

The war exploded into action on that early spring day. The Germans attacked, and soon overwhelmed, Norway and Denmark. An Anglo-French force had sailed across the North Sea to make a nuisance of itself, but it was ill-prepared and badly equipped and they were soon back with their tails between their legs. The British newspapers began talking of a fifth column of Nazi sympathisers in Norway, working behind the scenes to prepare the way for the Nazi hordes. They even suggested that there might be fifth columnists closer to home as well.

Things stayed quiet for a month, and then the real action began. The German army, the Wehrmacht, poured troops into Holland, Belgium and Luxemburg, supported by dive-bombers in a repeat of the tactics employed in subjugating Poland in less than a month during the previous autumn. But, for Hitler, defeat of the Low Countries was a mere appetiser. The main course was now open to him: France.

Back in Britain, the call for internment reached fever pitch. Fuelled by the popular newspapers, like The Sunday Pictorial and The Daily Mail, the police began to round up Category B aliens, those that they'd been keeping an eye on. Even some Category C people, those living on the south-east and east coasts in possible invasion areas, were taken away and locked up.

Jonathan's concerns for Hilde and her family grew day by day. The two were now exchanging letters on a regular basis but he hadn't heard from her since the German army began its push towards France.

The Germans attacked France through the densely wooded Ardennes while the French sat smugly behind their heavily fortified Maginot Line. Soon the Anglo-French army found themselves hopelessly outflanked and the Germans began to drive them towards the Channel.

The police continued to round-up Category B aliens and the Gerbers began to become increasingly concerned about their own position. Richard spoke to Benjamin at work. "It's looking pretty grim and, if France falls, which seems likely, they could grab every refugee in the country, including your family."

"But why? We're refugees from Nazi persecution. Surely they don't suspect us of disloyalty?"

"I'm sure the authorities don't, but the press are, as usual, exaggerating the situation. They're talking about fifth columnists attacking from the rear while the Germans attack us from France, parachutists dressed as nuns and all sorts of unlikely scenarios. You need to prepare for the worst, Benjamin. I'll drive round to your place over the weekend and pack my car boot with your valuables, in fact everything that isn't absolutely essential. If you do get arrested, you house will be empty and an open invitation for the thieves to move in."

"Thank you Richard."

◆　　◆　　◆

The British and French armies were driven on to the beaches of Dunkirk in northern France by the Germans. Then a quite remarkable rescue mission was launched, with ships ranging from Royal Navy destroyers to small fishing craft and paddle steamers lifting more than three hundred thousand defeated troops to safety in Britain. The press portrayed this as a triumph but, in reality, it was a defeat of huge proportions and Britain stood alone against the might of Germany. Prime Minister Churchill called on the citizens to stand together against the Nazi threat. The enemy was just over twenty miles away from the shores of southern England. Invasion seemed a strong possibility and the intensity of the round-ups increased.

◆   ◆   ◆

The Gerbers knew it was just a matter of time before their number came up. They did their best to carry on their usual lives, but it was not easy living in perpetual fear of the almost inevitable knock on the door.

Just around the corner, the Wallaces were in their sitting room as it grew dark when they had an unexpected visitor in the shape of Detective Constable Scott.

"Come on you two," he said looking at George and Patrick, "I've got a job for you. George go and make yourself presentable. Put a jacket and tie on. Patrick, go and find a nice big bag."

"Where we goin' Mr Scott?" asked George.

"I'll tell you when we get there. I've got a car outside. Get a move on."

The car was a black Wolsey and looked like a police vehicle even if it wasn't. Scott drove due east towards Romford. Nobody spoke for a while. George was next to Scott in the front seat while Patrick was in the back, nursing a large canvas bag. Eventually the policeman broke the silence.

"Right, listen you two, we're gonna do an 'ouse near Romford. I've sneaked a look at the list of the foreigners to be interned. The people who live at this 'ouse are on it, but they ain't due to be picked up just yet. So me and you, 'Detective' Wallace, are gonna' arrest 'em. We'll 'urry 'em along, bung 'em in the car and drop 'em outside Barkin' nick, then piss orf. Meanwhile Patrick 'ere will be 'elping 'imself to some tasty pickins in the empty building. As soon as we've dropped the mugs off, we'll come back and get 'im."

"Ow many of 'em are there, Mr Scott?"

"Just the two, 'usband and wife. Should be a piece o' cake. 'Ere we are. Out yer get Patrick. I'll see if I can open a back wind'er. You can slip in through there. As soon as we're off, yer in. Wait 'ere for us to pick you up."

Patrick nodded, got out and disappeared into the shadows. Scott pulled the car up outside a nice-looking terraced house on the other side of the street. He got out and knocked on the front door. A nervous looking elderly man answered.

"Mr Abrahams?"

"Yes."

Scott flashed his warrant card, but it was back in his pocket before Abrahams could get a proper look at it.

"We're police officers. You and your wife are to come with us immediately. You're being detained under Regulation 18b."

This sounded convincing to George, even though he knew it to be a pack of lies.

"Do we have time to put our house in order?"

"You've got five minutes to pack a suitcase each. We'll come in to make sure you get a move on."

The three men walked into the neat sitting room where a bemused Mrs Abrahams was waiting. Her husband explained the situation to her.

"Will our house be safe while we're away?"

"Of course madam. The police have been instructed to keep a special watch on the empty properties of those who have been detained. Now please hurry up. We've other calls to make."

"Where are we going?" asked Mrs Abrahams.

"You'll be told that when we get to the station. Jenkins," he said, nodding to George, "go upstairs and help Mr and Mrs Abrahams to pack their suitcases."

The three went upstairs. Scott waited until he could hear the sounds of clothes being taken from drawers and wardrobes before slipping into the kitchen and opening the back window. The flustered Abrahams couple re-appeared in hats and coats, clutching their luggage.

"I'll secure the premises," said Scott, returning to the kitchen. He locked the back door and gave the key to Abrahams. The owner of the house closed and secured the front door behind him and all four climbed into the Wolsey, after loading the Abrahams' luggage in the boot. As they drove off, Patrick emerged from his hiding place. It didn't take him long to spot the open window and he climbed in, pulling the empty bag in behind him and switching on his torch. He then ransacked the house, filling the bag with all that it would take; clocks, pieces of jewellery that Mrs Abrahams had forgotten in her panic, small paintings, pottery, cutlery, pots, pans and plates. There was just about enough space to carefully lower the bag out of the kitchen window. He followed it out and returned to his place of concealment to wait for his father and the policeman to return.

Scott and George drove into Barking and dropped the Abrahams and their luggage outside the police station. Scott told them to wait on the pavement while the two villains parked the car. Instead, they drove off back to Romford to collect Patrick and the loot, leaving two elderly Jewish refugees standing helplessly outside the police station.

They picked Patrick up, shoved his bag in the boot and set off home.

"That was easy, wasn't it?" said Scott.

"Piece o' cake, Mr Scott."

"The big joke is that they really will be arrested and interned in the new few days."

All three laughed loudly.

"Never mind," said Scott. "they're only Jews. Right, we'll take this lot back to your place. Your missus can get rid of it in the usual way. I want 'arf."

◆ ◆ ◆

Italy declared war on Britain and France on 10 June. Four days later the Germans entered Paris. France surrendered and Britain stood alone against Hitler's growing empire. The fear of the British people, who now believed that the next stage of the war would be an invasion of their shores, manifested itself in attacks on shops and businesses owned by Germans, Austrians and Italians. The popular press insisted they were all locked up where they couldn't do any damage to the war effort. Prime Minister Churchill agreed and mass arrests of the remaining enemy aliens began. Benjamin and Ruth sat in their house waiting for the inevitable. At least their valuables were safe, thanks to Richard. The dreaded knock on the door came at the beginning of July. They were driven to the police station with those same three suitcases that had left Germany and crossed the Atlantic just a year ago. The police asked where Jonathan was. The Gerbers were left at the police station while the arresting officers drove to the City to collect their son.

Jonathan was enjoying a geography lesson when the Headmaster came into the classroom, with a pained expression on his face, and, apologising for the interruption, asked the boy to collect his things and follow him to his study. The police were waiting for him and they took him back to north London to be re-united with his parents. Nobody knew where they would be sent. The following morning they joined a large group climbing into a black police van. As they meandered out of London, Jonathan thought of Hilde. He hadn't heard from her since the beginning of May. Would he ever see her again? Was she still alive? Would the Germans go looking for the passengers from the *St Louis* who had made new lives for themselves in France, Belgium and Holland? While he was asking himself these questions, the bus pulled in through the gates of Butlin's Holiday Camp at Clacton in Essex.

PART THREE

Internment: July 1940

So I departed and was free from imprisonment.
WILLIAM ADAMS

CHAPTER TWELVE

The Butlin's Holiday Camp at Clacton was a pleasant place but it wasn't exactly as it had been before the war, barbed wire having been hastily erected around its perimeter. Benjamin shuddered as he climbed down from the coach that had brought them from London. The last barbed wire compound that he had seen had been at Sachsenhausen. "Surely it wouldn't be as bad as that?" he thought quietly to himself.

A consignment of troops was waiting to greet them and they were hastily shuffled, clutching their suitcases, to an area which had been tennis courts in happier times. An officer appeared with a corporal and, after a brief nod from the former, the latter called the roll. The Gerbers answered their names. Family groups were then taken away, two or three at a time, by small patrols, presumably to be shown to their accommodation. The Gerbers waited patiently for their turn. Eventually two soldiers brusquely told them to follow them and they soon found themselves in a rather pleasant avenue of small single-storey buildings. Young trees were gently swaying in the breeze at the edge of the pathway.

"Here's your chalet," barked one soldier. "You have an hour to unpack your suitcases. Then report to the Kent dining room, where you'll be given further instructions."

Ruth thought of asking some questions but then, realising that the soldiers couldn't or wouldn't supply the answers, she kept quiet. They entered the chalet and found a small neat room with two pairs of bunk beds, a washbasin and a set of drawers. Jonathan volunteered to sleep on the top of one pair with his father down below. Ruth took the lower bed on the other.

They unpacked their bags in silence, put their possessions in the drawers and then sat down on the lower beds. All three were clearly traumatised.

Less than twenty-four hours earlier they'd been settling in to their new lives and now their freedom was gone. The impact of the arrest had been softened by Richard's warning that they were likely to be rounded up but, nevertheless, all three were fairly depressed by the sudden turn of events.

"Come on. Snap out of it," said Ruth. "We're here and we're alive. They're not likely to kill us. If we were still in Germany, things would be a lot worse."

This cheered the other two up a little, but the pervading atmosphere of uncertainty remained. Soon it was time to set off to the Kent Dining Room. Fortunately the camp was well signposted and they found first the toilet and shower block and then the Kent Dining Room. A vast group of people were sitting at the tables, talking quietly amongst themselves and nervously looking around. Everyone looked utterly confused. The low murmur of voices gradually petered out when the same officer who had been present at the roll-call strode noisily in. His corporal followed him, clutching a sheaf of papers.

"Pay attention," snapped the officer. "You are all enemy aliens and will be held here until such time as I'm told otherwise. While you're here, you'll follow the rules of the camp to the letter."

At least half of those present looked totally bemused. They understood little of what was being said. Their English was either poor or non-existent. Jonathan put his hand up.

"Yes?" said the officer.

"Are most people in here Germans?"

"German or Austrian."

"A lot of them don't seem to understand English. I'll be happy to act as interpreter if you wish."

"Very well. Come and stand at the front next to Corporal Miles."

It was symptomatic of the chaos that surrounded the round-up of aliens that thought hadn't been given to language difficulties. There would be plenty of others in the room who could have done this job, but Jonathan was determined to give himself plenty to do to keep his mind off his sadness.

Jonathan joined the two soldiers at the front. The officer read out a whole list of instructions which Jonathan quickly and efficiently translated into German. Meals were to be taken in this room at 08:00, 13:00 and

18:00 hours. Anybody who was late would miss the meal. Smoking was restricted to two forty-five minute breaks a day. Letter writing and receipt of all communication with the outside world was expressly forbidden. There would be neither newspapers nor access to radios. Exercise could be taken within the camp grounds, but there would be a curfew following the evening meal after which all internees will remain in their chalets unless they had to visit the latrine block. Anybody attempting to escape would be taken to a prison where they would be locked up in conditions far worse that the holiday camp.

"And," continued the officer, "as I said at the beginning, you are all enemy aliens. My country is under threat of invasion from yours and, as far as I'm concerned, some of you may well be willing to help the enemy should he land on our shores. My job is to ensure that not one of you is in a position to help the Nazis should they arrive. I intend to fully carry out my orders. With your suspect status in mind, the authorities may wish to question some of you and those will be taken to London by train and interrogated by the security services."

Jonathan looked at the assembled mass and doubted that there was a single one amongst them who wanted anything other than for Germany to be defeated in the war. He kept his thoughts to himself, but did risk a question.

"Could you tell us how long we'll be here?"

"As long as the Home Office decides to keep you under lock and key and that could be for the rest of the war. Report back here at 18:00 hours for your evening meal. Dismissed."

◆   ◆   ◆

The Gerbers and the other internees settled into a routine. Jonathan began to rise early and carry out his exercise programme before breakfast each day. Soon others joined him and, within three days, fifty or so men and older youngsters were working out vigorously under his instruction. After breakfast Jonathan read and studied. He'd had the presence of mind to bring several books with him. His parents and most of the other internees strolled around the camp grounds. Nobody made close friends, but chatting quietly amongst themselves helped to alleviate the boredom. One family had been in England for seven years and had had a holiday at this particular camp during the previous summer.

"It cost us £3.10s for the week and we had a wonderful time," the father of the young family told Benjamin.

The grounds of the camp were very attractive and spacious. There was a delightful sunken garden, a boating lake and a playing field as well as the tennis courts where they assembled for roll-call each morning and evening. Most of the facilities weren't in use; the ballroom, bars, coffee bars and billiard room were closed for the duration, but one area that became very busy was the children's playground.

The conversations that Ruth and Benjamin had with the other internees indicated that almost everybody was either German or Austrian and Jewish. Each morning after breakfast a short list of names, mostly young or middle-aged men, was read out. They were told to report to the camp office immediately after breakfast. Then they disappeared but, to everyone's intense relief, were back in time for the evening meal.

A week into their stay, Benjamin's name was called out and he vanished for the day, arriving back at the camp, like the others, in time for dinner. Back in the chalet after they'd eaten, Ruth asked her husband what had happened.

"Nothing really," he said. "At first they were a bit aggressive and asked me where I'd lived in Germany, what my job was and how I'd got here. When I told them I'd been imprisoned in Sachsenhausen and sailed here on the *St Louis*, they eased up on me."

"How did you get there?" asked Jonathan.

"By train to Liverpool Street with two police officers guarding us, then across London in a black police van to a large park. We couldn't see much out of the van, but I had a vague feeling that I recognised the park. Perhaps we'd been there with Richard. Anyway, we were taken into a large and beautiful old house, questioned, given a sandwich and a cup of tea, then driven back to Liverpool Street. It was all rather painless. I doubt if I'll be taken there again."

Ruth and Jonathan were relieved. Then Benjamin added, "There was one thing: I'm certain I saw Reg and Mary's boy Roger while I was there. When we were waiting outside the room in which we were to be questioned, a tall officer walked quickly by. I'm sure it was Roger Martin. He didn't see me and I don't feel it would have been right to attract his attention."

◆   ◆   ◆

The daily grind continued and lethargy set in amongst the internees, except for the Gerbers who occupied themselves as best they could. But, despite appearances, they were overwhelmed with worry. How was the war going? Had the Germans invaded? What would happen to them all? On top of this was Jonathan's concern for Hilde and her family in occupied France.

Quite suddenly and without warning, they were told one morning at roll-call to pack their things and assemble by the camp office, now called the Guard Room, at 09:30. There were about fifty in all on the list. Someone asked the Corporal where they were going, but he walked off without replying.

This time there were five army lorries waiting for them. The atmosphere was very tense and the guards treated them with contempt. The Gerbers climbed into the lorry with their luggage and took the seats immediately behind the driver, whom they couldn't see because the entire interior of the truck was protected with canvas to deny the passengers a view of the outside world. Two guards, armed with rifles, sat at the rear.

The journey began in silence, but soon a series of quiet conversations broke out. A man sitting next to Jonathan explained in perfect English, without the hint of an accent, that he had lived in England since 1914. His German mother had died just before the start of the first war and he had come to this country with his English father. He had been a travelling salesman and knew these roads like the back of his hand. Periodically he put his eye to a hole in the canvas and reported on the progress of their journey. The first big city they passed was Birmingham. Shortly after this they pulled into a large yard where sandwiches were handed out followed by some disgusting tasting tea from vacuum flasks. Then they set off again and another big city came into view, Manchester their unofficial guide told them, adding that Liverpool appeared to be their destination. He speculated that their final port of call might be the docks for transportation to Canada or Australia or the Liverpool jail.

He was wrong on all counts because, as dusk began to fall, the lorries drew to a halt and they were all told to get out and bring their luggage with them. It seemed that they were at a very large building site, with dozens and dozens of half-built houses nestling on either side of unmade roads. The internees were marched to a large incomplete building which contained a spacious hall, presumably to be used as social centre for the residents when the buildings were finished. Here they were served some thin tasteless soup with stale bread. On the walk from the lorries, more barbed wire was spotted. They seemed to be far worse off that they had been back in Clacton.

◆   ◆   ◆

The Gerber family were escorted with about nine others to a street which, as they peered through the gloom, they guessed consisted of about half a dozen blocks of terraced houses, with eight houses to each block. The roads were wide, but in a bit of a mess and the struggling group had to pick their way carefully round the numerous potholes.

All twelve members of the group were assigned to one block and Benjamin led the way up two flights of stairs to a small room in the roof. There were three mattresses lying on the floor and no other furniture at all. There was a small window which appeared to look out to the houses on the other side of the street. Jonathan set off to explore the rest of the house and reported back soon afterwards that there was a bathroom and toilet on the first floor, a kitchen on the ground floor, with nothing more than a sink and a stove, and a room next to the front door where three men were trying to sleep. Jonathan decided that was probably the sitting room.

"The English have an expression out of the frying pan into the fire," began Ruth, "which seems to describe our situation very well, but we'll just have to put up with it and hope for better times. Meanwhile, let's try to get some sleep."

Jonathan prodded the mattress and announced that it was full of straw. A moment's silence followed and then all three burst out laughing, giving way to the kind of gallows humour so essential for their survival.

"Are the British trying to emulate the SS?" asked Benjamin.

"Not really," replied Ruth. "They just panicked when some of their rubbish newspapers started campaigning to lock us all up. This won't last long."

After a more or less sleepless night, the Gerbers looked out of their window to find that it was raining heavily. They'd lain on their mattresses in most of their clothes and felt pretty rough so they made their way downstairs, hoping for a decent wash. There was a short queue outside the bathroom and they patiently waited their turn. When it came, each was horrified to find that there was no hot water, but they did the best they could. Feeling only a tiny bit better, they made their way outside and found the road in a shocking state. The potholes were full of water and the rest of the surface had become a bog. They could now see more clearly the extent of their confinement as they saw the three metre high barbed wire fence attached to thick wooden posts. Men, women and children were milling about in the rain waiting, someone told them, for the morning roll-call. Fifteen minutes later, when they were all soaking wet, a sergeant appeared and shouted out their names in turn. When he'd completed the task, he ordered them to report to the dining hall for breakfast.

Dining was inside a large tent, next to another smaller temporary structure which housed the kitchen. The rain lashed down on the tent with the thudding almost drowning out what little conversation there was. The meal was cold, undercooked and tasteless. When it was over, they were ordered to return to their billets. Mercifully, the rain had stopped but it was still wet and unpleasant underfoot. There seemed nothing to do but stand around outside their houses and chat with the other internees. Every street appeared to be packed with people just milling around and it soon became obvious that not everyone was German or Austrian. Jonathan's acquaintance from the lorry journey joined the Gerbers.

"Hello. I'm Klaus," he said.

The three of them introduced themselves.

"I know this place from my travels before the war," Klaus began. "It's called Huyton. It used to be a small village with a fine church. Then they decided to demolish some of the slum houses in Liverpool and move the people here."

"Well, where are they?" asked Ruth.

"As far as I can make out, some of the estates here are occupied but this one, it's called the Woolfall Heath Estate by the way, has been set aside to detain people. That's why they didn't bother to finish building it perhaps."

"How do you know all this?" asked Benjamin.

"Got it from one of the guards. I expect most of them are pretty tight lipped, but this one seemed happy to talk."

"By the way," he continued, "you may have noticed that it's not just Germans and Austrians here, but Italians as well. And not all the Germans and Austrians are Jewish. So, watch it."

Klaus moved off, presumably to collect some more snippets of information, and the Gerbers continued to stand aimlessly outside their house. Soon they were joined by a young man who introduced himself as Joachim. He explained that he was a member of the crew of a German merchant ship that had been captured by a British cruiser in the Atlantic. The Gerbers were immediately wary of him and became even more so when he asked if they were Jewish. Nervously, they admitted they were. This prompted an outburst of apologies from Joachim who said that he was appalled by the way that the Nazis had treated the Jews and that this had made him ashamed to be German. He was not a member of the Nazi party, he told them, and he looked forward to the day when Hitler and his cronies were dead and buried. Then Germany could return to being the fine country it was before they contaminated it. He smiled sympathetically and then warned them that a small number of the crew of his ship were rabid Nazis and could be dangerous.

◆   ◆   ◆

The roads got worse, the houses became damp and the food got no better. Morale amongst the internees sank lower with each passing day. Each of them had their own private worries. The Gerbers wondered whether Richard knew where they were and Jonathan continued to fret about Hilde and her family. How long would they be in Huyton and where would they send them next. Canada? Australia? There was absolutely nothing to do but wait. Klaus appeared from time to time with information. The Germans hadn't invaded but the Luftwaffe were trying to knock the RAF out of the sky. A ship full of refugees had been sunk in the Atlantic by a U-boat after leaving Liverpool en route for Canada. There had been great loss of life. Two of the Jewish internees at Huyton had hanged themselves. It was all horribly depressing. The Gerbers had met more than one internee who had fought with distinction for Great Britain in the previous war and there were several others who had already been interned between 1914 and 1918. The whole thing was a total shambles. People fell ill in the damp and unhealthy conditions, but there was only one doctor to treat them. The authorities had to ask the doctors amongst the internees for assistance and over a dozen stepped forward, more than happy to help.

Things could hardly get worse but they almost did. One morning, about a week into their stay, Jonathan was standing outside of his house, having just had a pleasant chat with Joachim, when he was approached by two men; one tall and blond haired and the other shorter with black hair. Both were tanned by the sun and appeared to be in their thirties.

"Why were you talking to that traitor, Jew?" the black haired one asked.

Jonathan stood his ground then stared deep into the eyes of the two men, each in turn. Then he took a step towards them. The two men saw something in Jonathan that they feared and they began to walk away.

"When Germany has won the war, Jew, your race, together with people like our shipmates, will be wiped from the face of the earth."

Jonathan didn't reply and the two Nazis continued their retreat.

◆   ◆   ◆

Suddenly it was all over. After two weeks of misery in Huyton, the Gerbers were amongst two hundred names called out at morning roll-call. They were told to pack their bags and be ready to leave after breakfast. Later, as they stood waiting for their transport to arrive, Klaus popped up with his latest gossip.

"It's the Nazis who are being blown out of the sky by the RAF. I bet we're not going to Liverpool jail. Could be Canada or Australia."

As they rumbled along the road towards Liverpool, Ruth turned to Benjamin and asked, "What was worse, Huyton or Sachsenhausen?"

"Sachsenhausen of course. Conditions were pretty dreadful at Huyton, but I never felt I might be beaten up or killed."

It was mid-morning before the lorry pulled up and they climbed down to find themselves on what they presumed was the quayside at Liverpool. They looked at each other with expressions that needed no words. Where on earth would they be going next?

CHAPTER THIRTEEN

The dockside was littered with vehicles of all shapes and sizes; lorries, charabancs and black Marias. Groups of bemused-looking men, women and children were spilling out of them on to the quayside clutching their luggage. Everyone was told to wait for further orders. So they did, standing and chatting in the warm sunshine with their suitcases at their feet. Amid the hubbub, there were the occasional screams from confused babies. An army officer appeared accompanied, as usual, by an NCO. He nodded to his subordinate who then shouted to get the large group's attention. The NCO instructed the internees to pick up their suitcases and follow him. A number of soldiers fell in alongside them. The Gerbers, and the others, realised that they'd reached the point of no return. Their destination would soon become clear. If they were shipped to Australia or Canada, there was little chance that they'd return before the end of the war. Assuming, of course, that they reached their destination in one piece after running the gauntlet of the German U-boats.

Eventually they were brought to a halt and ordered to board a small steamer which was certainly nowhere near large enough to transport them to the other side of the world. As if by magic, Klaus appeared at their side.

"That's the Isle of Man ferry," he informed them. "I went there on holiday a few years ago. It's a lovely place. We should be alright there."

"How far's the Isle of Man?" asked Jonathan.

"Only about eighty miles. We'll be there in time for tea."

They clambered on board. There were too many passengers for the number of seats available so Benjamin and Jonathan had to stand while Ruth sat. The ship gave a blast from the horn and set off from the vast docks on a calm sea, which hopefully meant that there wouldn't be much seasickness. It soon became obvious that those on board had been fetched from holding camps all over Britain. An Italian man with a broad Scots accent told them that he ran a catering business in Glasgow and had lived there since before the previous war. He'd been briefly locked up in Edinburgh Castle before being transported to Liverpool.

The voyage passed without incident, although Jonathan did spot the two Nazis who'd threatened him at Huyton. They were allowed on deck as the ferry approached Douglas and they could see the island ahead with its rolling hills easing their way down toward the sea. Approaching the quay side, the vast sweep of Douglas Promenade was before them, with an almost unbroken chain of tall buildings stretching towards the promontory at the far end of the bay. It had been just over three hours since the ferry had left Liverpool and the sea had stayed calm throughout. Despite the circumstances, Douglas looked fine in the sparkling sunshine and this lifted their spirits a bit. As they got closer they saw barbed wire surrounding many of the streets. They heaved a collective sigh of relief. It could have been a lot worse, although the wired compounds told them that this would not be a holiday.

Internees disembarked at the pier where a group of about fifty soldiers was waiting for them. Here the Gerbers received a nasty shock which threw them into fresh worry and confusion. A sergeant called for silence.

"You will now be allocated to your billets. The men will stay here in Douglas. Women and children will be taken to another part of the island. You may now have a few minutes to say goodbye to one another."

Jonathan, it seemed, qualified as a man and would stay in Douglas with his father. The three of them were devastated but, as usual, Ruth made light of their misery.

"I've been told it's a small island and we won't be far apart. I'm sure that once the authorities have sorted themselves out, we'll be able to visit each other. Remember, it could be worse. We could still be in Huyton or, worse still, Berlin."

Benjamin and Jonathan put on brave faces.

"You're right Ruth, as usual," said Benjamin. "I'm sure we'll all be together very soon."

The three then wrapped their arms around each other in a strong embrace before Ruth broke away and joined the other women, many with children, who left for heaven knows where.

A list of names was read out and those on it set off walking along the promenade, glancing at the buildings, most of which seemed to be hotels or guest houses, generally in terraces, three or four storeys high, with a basement. Benjamin and Jonathan were amongst this group which turned left off the promenade and headed uphill. It was a hot day and their suitcases were heavy. Trudging up the slope, they passed a small church on their right shortly before a right turn followed by an immediate left, which brought them into a heavily fortified square. Despite the barbed wire, it was quite impressive with tall terraced buildings, similar to those on the promenade, covering three sides of the square. Jonathan noted with satisfaction that the grassed area in the middle was level and seemed suitable for football.

"I'm Captain Daniels and I'm the Commandant of this camp which is called Hutchinson Camp," announced an officer who was standing in the square waiting for them. "This is your home for the foreseeable future. You will be allocated rooms in one of the boarding houses or hotels. You will find conditions here far better than those places you have been brought from whether it be Walton Jail, Lingfield Park Racecourse, Huyton or wherever. But, I must remind you, you are all enemy aliens. Any minor misdemeanours will be punished. We have detention facilities in the camp. Serious matters will be dealt with by the Manx Police; that's the local force. Any attempt to escape will result in a lengthy period of imprisonment."

He paused to let this sink in and then continued.

"Corporal Briggs will now allocate you to your billets. After you've found your rooms and unpacked your suitcases, you will re-assemble in this square where you will be given further instructions."

The Corporal bellowed out instructions and Benjamin and Jonathan found themselves on the top floor of a four storey building which looked pretty substantial and seemed to be about forty years old, like many of the early twentieth century houses in North London. When they reached their room, which was on the top floor, they were surprised to find a double bed which brought on some light hearted banter about snoring and pulling on the sheets and blankets during the night. The room was quite large and was furnished with a wardrobe and two chests of drawers, both of dark oak. They were high enough above ground to have a splendid view of Douglas Bay with the sea sparkling in the late afternoon sunshine. Benjamin started unpacking the suitcases while Jonathan nipped off for his usual look around, returning to report that the house was now full. He guessed there were about two dozen men in it. There was a bathroom and separate toilet on each floor. A kitchen, dining room and large sitting room took up the ground floor.

"I'd say it's pretty comfortable," said Benjamin.

"It's not ours and we're not free to come and go as we please," replied a sullen Jonathan.

"That may be, but we'll keep our heads down and our noses clean. Remember what your mother said."

"Sure, dad. You're right," Jonathan paused, "as usual."

The camp members reassembled in the square. Captain Daniels informed them that they should report for roll-call in the square at 08:00 and 17:00 hours each day and that they were responsible for cleaning their own rooms. After dinner had been served in their houses, the officer asked that each house elect a House Captain who would be responsible for organising rotas for the cleaning of public rooms, laundry, the collection of supplies for the kitchen at ten o'clock each morning, the delivery and collection of mail and liaising with the recently appointed Street Leader, who in turn would report to the Camp Leader. The Camp Leader would be the link between the internees and the authorities.

"Typical army," murmured someone, "to have such a long chain of command."

"Just like school," said another.

"Ooh, I hope not," said a third with a snigger.

The camp members seemed happy with these arrangements and were especially cheered by the mention of mail and set off to dinner in a good mood.

◆　　◆　　◆

Dinner was excellent. It was a seaside landlady's meal; Lancashire hot pot followed by rice pudding and a surprisingly drinkable cup of coffee. The Germans and Austrians were not entirely familiar with English cuisine, but it wasn't a great deal different from their own. The cook, having been told that the majority of diners were Jewish, made certain that the meals were strictly kosher, although Benjamin and Jonathan weren't bothered by this at all.

The house members then withdrew to the sitting room to elect their Captain. It didn't take long. Jonathan, eighteen going on thirty, proposed his father, after pointing out that Benjamin had run a successful business in Berlin and was well-used to organising people. With two exceptions, from the Nazi merchant seamen who now found themselves in a houseful of Jews, he was elected. The Nazis then left and the rest spent an hour or so chatting amongst themselves before setting off to bed. It was a beautiful evening but, because of an evening curfew, there was no chance of a post-dinner stroll.

Benjamin and Jonathan sat in their room, which was pretty miserable. The windows had been painted blue and there was a single orange bulb: air raid precautions should the Germans decide to bomb the Isle of Man.

"You heard mention of mail?" said Benjamin.

"I did. We should write to Richard and let him know we're alright."

"No. You should write to Richard. I'm not sure my English is good enough yet."

"What should I say?"

"I doubt if you'll be able to write what you please. The letters are bound to be censored. For the time being, just say we've been interned and that everything is alright. Tell him we've been separated from your mother, but she isn't far away. Ask after his family and the Martins and say we hope that they are all well."

"Fine. You'll need to check with the Street Leader and find out where I can get writing paper, envelopes and stamps."

"I'll do that in the morning. I have to see him anyway to report that I've been elected House Captain," Benjamin said with a grin.

They went to bed and slept well. Jonathan was up early to take exercise before roll-call and, after an excellent breakfast, Benjamin set off to meet the Street Leader. His father re-appeared about an hour later clutching a pile of newspapers and a radio which he set up in the sitting room, where he also left the papers. Germany was in complete control in France, which heightened Jonathan's anxiety about Hilde and her family. The British mainland was still under threat, but the Germans were losing the war in the air. The newspaper reckoned the enemy wouldn't invade whilst the RAF ruled the skies.

On their second full day on the island, a soldier provided a football and soon impromptu games were being played each morning with Jonathan, of course, the star turn. Days still seemed long but nowhere near as bad as at Clacton or Huyton. Benjamin kept busy organising the house. One of his first duties had been to pass on Jonathan's letter to Richard to the authorities, the Street Leader having acquired paper, envelopes and stamps from the local Post Office. Football became a major attraction for the younger internees and soon familiar faces appeared. Joachim was in another house in the street with Klaus. The seaman was a very good player, but poor old Klaus had two left feet and spent most of the time laughing at his own incompetence. There was even talk of organising matches against the other camps and Benjamin was asked to approach the Street Leader to see if this was possible.

◆   ◆   ◆

Each evening after dinner, the house members sat and talked in the sitting room, all except the surly Nazis who slunk off to their own room. The rest were a cross-section of all that was good in the world. There was a teacher, two university professors, a scientist, three musicians, an artist, a doctor, a surgeon and various skilled craftsmen like shoemakers, cooks and bookbinders. Benjamin knew that this pattern was repeated in the other houses and, collectively, this represented an enormous reservoir of talent languishing in internment, when they could have been making a substantial contribution to the war effort. At nine o'clock each evening, the radio was turned on and everyone listened in silence to the BBC News, with Jonathan translating English words and phrases where necessary. The news wasn't all that great, but what Prime Minister Churchill called "The Battle of Britain" was going well.

In their room before bed, father and son talked about Ruth, worrying and wondering if she was doing well. Benjamin said he would get her address the next day so that they could write to her. Jonathan turned to his father and said.

"Don't you think it's time we actually saw mother? These English soldiers don't seem too bad. I'm sure they might organise some family reunions if we asked them, even if it's only for an afternoon."

"Good idea. I'll speak to the Street Leader in the morning and see what he thinks."

The Street Leader also thought it was a good idea and promised to do what he could. Father and son were in the sitting room discussing this when Joachim came in.

"Time for football, Jonathan."

Jonathan had been entrusted with looking after the football and the pump. He dashed up to his room to collect it. As he put his hand on the door, he heard movement inside. He walked in and found the two Nazis ransacking the drawers and wardrobes.

"What do you think you're doing?" shouted Jonathan.

The two started at him open mouthed, then the blonde one started towards him.

"I'll take care of him. You grab what you can. Jews shouldn't have possessions so we're confiscating them."

His blood was immediately up, as it had been during the confrontation with the seamen below decks on the *St Louis*.

Jonathan was a thoroughly decent young man of great strength and courage but he preferred to use these attributes on the sports field. He was neither bad tempered nor violent, but one thing he loathed above all others were the Nazis. These two were as arrogant as the rest he'd met and his property was under threat so, when the blonde man approached him, he didn't wait for an invitation to act. He rushed forward, grabbed hold of his assailant who crashed against the wardrobe and fell to the floor.

"You filthy pig," he shouted as he pulled himself onto his feet, approaching Jonathan with his face scarlet and his fists clenched. Jonathan ducked below his assailant's wild swing and cracked him a fierce blow on the side of the head. The German screamed and fell backwards, cracking his head on the chest of drawers. The black-haired Nazi looked terrified but, before he could decide whether to retaliate or find a safe way out of the room, the door flew open and Benjamin rushed in closely followed by Joachim. Jonathan was grabbed before he could do more damage and then a soldier arrived and arrested all five of them. He pointed his rifle threateningly at them and marched them to the camp HQ.

Benjamin and Joachim gave brief statements and were quickly released. The two Nazis were given a thorough grilling by Captain Daniels and left under armed guard. Then it was Jonathan's turn.

"The war's not being fought here Gerber," the Captain began. "This is just the type of situation we're keen to avoid. What have you got to say for yourself?"

"I'm sorry sir, but they were stealing stuff from our room. When I came in, the blonde one went for me so I hit him."

"Do you always use violence against people who upset you?"

"No sir. Only Nazis."

The Captain chuckled. "Well you certainly pack a powerful punch. The man's still groggy and his ear looks like a red cauliflower. You may have damaged his hearing."

"Good."

Daniels laughed again. "Well, they won't trouble you anymore. They've been transferred to another camp on the far side of the island."

"Thank you, sir. Please don't think that all Germans are like those two. There are a lot of good Germans, like my friend Joachim for example."

"Thank you, Gerber. I know that. You can go now. Just one thing though."

"Yes sir?"

"I've no idea when you'll be released but, when you are, fight for England. A couple of thousand like you and we'll have the Nazis licked in no time."

Jonathan smiled, thanked the Captain and left.

An anxious Benjamin was waiting for Jonathan on his return.

"Everything alright?"

"Yes thanks. The Captain's got rid of those Nazis."

"I know. Four soldiers have just taken them away with their bags. The blonde one didn't look too well. He was staggering all over the place. By the way, there's a letter for you."

It was from Richard. He was pleased and relieved to hear from them. Everyone was well and sent their best wishes. Strings had been pulled and he would be visiting them on the last Wednesday in August. It was a perfect end to what had been a difficult day.

The three of them met at the camp HQ. Richard had stayed the night in Liverpool, caught the morning ferry and was due to sail back in the early evening. They were not alone. An officer from Army Intelligence sat in the corner in silence throughout their re-union. Presumably he was there to make certain that no state secrets were exchanged. There were warm handshakes and expressions of joy and friendship all round. Richard asked after Ruth and was saddened to hear that, apart from a couple of letters, they had had no news of her since their arrival a month previously.

Benjamin told Richard about life in the camp and Jonathan spoke enthusiastically about football and daily exercise. Richard said his family were fine, as were Reg and Mary Martin, but he hadn't a clue about their boys. John was still engaged in secret work and Roger was in the Army and hadn't been home on leave for some months. The threat of invasion was still very real. Food rationing was beginning to bite, Richard said, but they were coping well. Then he became a bit more serious.

"There's been a bit of a backlash against internment; questions in parliament, articles in the press and general public dissatisfaction. Funny thing mind you, the papers now calling for a review of internment are the same ones asking for aliens to be locked up in the first place.

"Nearly everyone who could have been locked up has been locked up. That's ridiculous. There's plenty in England who should be under lock and key, but not every single non-British citizen and even some citizens.

Think of all that talent that could be put to good use for the war effort languishing behind barbed wire," continued Richard.

"Yes, we've read that in the papers and it's certainly true that there are plenty here who could make a big contribution to the war effort," said Benjamin.

"Anyhow," said Richard. "A small number have been released."

"We've heard rumours," said Benjamin "and there's been quite a bit about that as well in the newspapers."

"I don't want to get your hopes up but I'm going to chat to one or two of my contacts to see what can be done. They seemed to have stopped interning Category C women. At one time I thought my wife Inge and the boys might be caught up in all this lunacy, but that threat appears to have passed. I can't promise anything but, as far as I can judge, Ruth is likely to be released before you."

"Thank you Richard. That would be wonderful. A start at least," said Benjamin

Their friend continued. "If that happens I've arranged for her to stay with Reg and Mary until such time as you're home."

"Thank you again, Richard. Our family never had a better friend than you."

The soldier in the corner stood up.

"Time's up sir."

"Right," said Richard. "I'll do all that I can and I'll be in touch. Please give all our love to Ruth when you get to see her."

The three embraced and Richard left. He was searched thoroughly, as he had been on arrival. He asked the soldier searching him as he left what he hoped to find.

"Food sir. There's more of it here than on the mainland and some visitors have left with a fortnight's shopping."

Benjamin and Jonathan were overjoyed to see their friend and their happiness grew further at evening roll-call when it was announced that wives interned on the island were to be brought to Douglas to visit their husbands at the end of the week. Those with children were slightly saddened that their boys and girls were not included, but at least it was something, perhaps even the beginning of the end of internment.

CHAPTER FOURTEEN

As Ruth watched her menfolk march away, there was a tear in her eye, but she had been determined not to let them see how sad she was. She herself was already en route in the opposite direction with the rest of the women and children. Several times she looked back towards the retreating Benjamin and Jonathan but, eventually, they disappeared from sight. The women and children passed a little harbour, crammed with small boats of all colours and shapes and, before long, reached a red-bricked railway station where they passed through the ticket hall and then were guided onto the platform by a group of sympathetic soldiers.

Waiting for them was the smallest train she had ever seen. Ruth was used to the grand German trains. This seemed to have much narrower carriages with the rails much closer together than usual. The squat steam locomotive was bright green and the miniature carriages brick red. Ruth wondered how all of the passengers would get on board, but she was lucky to be one of the first to climb on. She found herself a window seat and sat down with her suitcase on her lap. It was cramped and they was barely enough room for the eight passengers and their luggage, but everybody seemed to find themselves a space. When the compartment was full, a soldier slammed the door and locked it.

The train set off. It was a beautiful warm day and the view of the fields, farms and rolling hills was somehow re-assuring. Cows, sheep and even goats grazed lazily in the sunshine. Naturally, Ruth didn't know any of her fellow passengers, but some did know each other and chatted quietly as the train passed through several stations. After about forty-five minutes, the train eased to a halt and Ruth caught a glimpse of a platform with soldiers.

"This is Port St Mary," a voice shouted. "Women with children please collect your luggage and leave the train."

Nobody moved in Ruth's compartment, but they could see some women with children assembling on other parts of the platform. Then the train set off and, fifteen minutes later, stopped again with more soldiers waiting to receive them.

"Port Erin. All remaining passengers please leave the train with your luggage."

The women did as they were told and Ruth joined the others. Before she had a chance to examine her companions, they were off again, following the soldiers outside the station, which looked like a smaller version of the one in Douglas, before being shown into a church hall. They stood patiently, wondering what would happen next. Ruth looked around. There were about fifty women with a wide range of ages. Some were well-dressed whilst others were in worn working clothes. A few looked well fed but the majority were thin and looked in need of a decent meal. Many were Jewish in appearance, but a few were obviously not Jews. Amongst the elderly ladies, a handful appeared not to be well. "What possible threat could these be to the British war effort?" thought Ruth.

Her daydreaming was interrupted by another soldier who began to read out names, in twos and threes, and listed the billets where those small groups should go. Ruth and two very well-dressed young women set off to their guest house, following directions given by the soldier. "How odd," she thought. It would be quite easy to escape. There was no barbed wire, but then she caught sight of patrols of soldiers who stood, armed and with threatening postures, obviously intent on keeping the prisoners where they should be. It was a considerable walk on a warm day but the internees enjoyed it. They spotted that the town centre seemed to have some attractive little shops as they walked downhill towards the sea. They saw the beautiful beach as they walked along the front before heading uphill to their billets

Ruth found her room in a large guest house. She unpacked her case and she glanced around the room. It had a single bed which was a relief. She had spotted a couple of women of her age giving her lascivious looks while they were waiting in the church hall. There was a small chest of drawers, a wardrobe and a wash basin. She poked her nose onto the landing outside and found a bathroom with a toilet next to it. Back in her room, she sat on the bed. She was already missing her husband and son terribly, but she cheered up a little when she remembered her own last words to them. If they could survive Huyton and Berlin, this would be easy by comparison.

The owner of the guest house was Mrs Murphy. She'd been asked to run the house and was being reasonably well-paid by the Home Office to do this. Ruth knew this from a brief conversation she had with the landlady on the first night after dinner, or high tea as Mrs Murphy called it. Later in the evening, the Camp Commandant came to talk to the forty strong group of internees in the sitting room. She introduced herself as Dame Joanna Cruikshank. She was grey, thin and appeared to be in her sixties. Dame Cruikshank gave a brief resume of her career which included service in the previous war. More recently she had held very senior positions in various organisations, including the Red Cross. She would make their stay in Port Erin as comfortable as possible, but she would stand no nonsense. She sounded as though she meant it.

The residents of the guest house were a mixed bunch. One woman was heavily pregnant. Ruth wasn't at all sure about the well-dressed pair who'd walked with her from the church hall. Ruth was to find out later how they managed to afford such fine clothes. The two lesbians had decided to forget about Ruth and concentrate on one another. One of their first actions had been to arrange a room swap, so that they could share. The young woman originally down to be with one of them was only too happy to change. Many of the "guests," as Mrs Murphy now called them, had come to England from Austria in the spring of 1938, having fled in terror when Hitler had marched in. They had little money and threadbare clothes and one or two pitied them, but they were quick to point out that they would probably be in a camp or dead by now had they stayed in Austria.

The "guests" settled into a routine. The beautiful weather encouraged some to swim in the sea. They were allowed to visit the small town where those with money emptied the shops of clothes, materials and cosmetics. Ruth didn't bother and spent her days helping Mrs Murphy with the housework or strolling down to the beach in the late summer sunshine. Keeping busy helped to take her mind off her loneliness and, besides, she liked Mrs Murphy who was a small, squat, grey-haired woman. She had a straightforward northern accent which Ruth, who was improving her English day-by-day, found easy to understand.

Mrs Murphy was enjoying her post-breakfast cigarette and a cup of tea.

"You refugees have been a godsend to me," she said to Ruth. "Before the war I was full all the time. Then the declaration came and we were told there wouldn't be any more 'olidays. The island was to be used for other things. No more 'olidaymakers. First we were told to make ourselves ready for 'undreds of evacuated children from the mainland, but they never came. Then we were told we'd 'ave to look after enemy aliens. Sorry, that's what you were called by the government people. I'm sure you mean us no 'arm. Until you lot came, I wasn't sure 'ow I was going to make ends meet, but now things are looking up nicely."

Ruth told her something of herself and her family and then asked Mrs Murphy what things had been like before the war.

"I was fully booked from May to the end of August. People came over for the Whitsun 'oliday and then we were chock-a-block for the TT motor cycle races."

Ruth asked what "chock-a-block" meant.

"Sorry dear. I forgot you weren't totally up to scratch in English. It means packed out."

Ruth smiled and thanked her.

"After the TT races, that's for motor bikes. It was summer 'olidays. Families came from Ireland and Lancashire mostly. Never a dull moment."

"What else happens on the island?" asked Ruth.

"Apart from shopkeepers, theatre, cinema and ballroom owners, everyone's involved in either the 'oliday trade, fishing or farming."

"Do you have any family?"

"My 'usband was a fisherman across in St. Mary's. 'E was lost in a storm five years ago".

"I'm so sorry."

"My boys 'ave grown up. They're both in the army. God knows where," she said as a look of sadness passed over her face.

◆   ◆   ◆

Ruth kept busy, but thoughts of her family were never far away. Under Dame Cruikshank's leadership, the camp became very well organised. Some of the women began to use the public library, even though they struggled with the language. English classes were started in an adjacent guest house under the guidance of an elderly lady who'd been a teacher in Hamburg. They were very popular. Other classes began with "guests" sharing their skills in spinning, weaving and dressmaking. These too were well-attended, despite the fact that materials were sometimes in short supply and some of the machines had seen better days. One "guest" opened up a beauty salon and another started a hairdressing business. Both were soon doing a good trade. Some who had been cooks leant a hand in the kitchen and others helped with the laundry. A camp bank was set up. When they'd arrived at Port Erin, many of the women, Ruth included, had deposited their money in the local branch of the Isle of Man Bank, but soon the camp bank became operational. "Guests" went to shops, bought goods, collected an invoice, then took this to the camp bank where they were given money to cover the cost of the purchases. Then they returned to the shop and paid for, then claimed, the goods

Ruth didn't need money. She was happy to use the camp bank for the few things she required. She was busy and a bit happier since she was now corresponding with her husband and son. Most of her time was taken up with helping Mrs Murphy. Apart from the housework, she organised rotas for cleaning and for taking baths. She soon had a reputation as a totally reliable guest and this soon came to the attention of the camp authorities. The Commandant knew that some "guests" were in need of clothing, so she arranged for the delivery of clothing parcels from relief agencies on the mainland. Ruth got the job of sorting these out on arrival and distributing the clothing to those who needed it most.

Despite the fine weather and the excellent camp organisation, many of the women became bored and petty bickering was commonplace. The worst offenders were the pro-Nazi Germans, but these were such a tiny minority they caused few problems. Even well-adjusted people like Ruth found it a bit of a strain at times. Then came the news that family reunions had been organised for the end of the month in Douglas. Those who had husbands and grown-up sons elsewhere on the island were overjoyed. The women in the Port St Mary camp were included in this arrangement, but not their children.

Suddenly there were queues at the beauty parlour and the hairdressers. Everyone wanted to look their best when they saw their husbands for the first time, in some cases, for several months. By the time the train had left Port Erin and stopped to collect the rest at Port St Mary, about a hundred excited women were on board. There was a happy chatter throughout the journey, in contrast to the nervous murmurings there'd been on their first ride on the island. The usual troop of soldiers met them on the platform at Douglas and they were shown to waiting charabancs to take them to Derby Castle to meet their husbands.

The menfolk had no such luxury and had to walk from their camps. They arrived sometime before the women, who were late. Derby Castle wasn't really a castle but two large houses built very close together to give the impression of something grander. And the meeting wasn't actually to take place in the castle but in a huge ballroom built right next to it. To Benjamin and Jonathan, waiting nervously for Ruth and the others to arrive, the room seemed almost as big as a football pitch and they tried to picture hundreds of happy holidaymakers dancing round the floor during what seemed to be those far off days before the war.

Inside the ballroom and on the gallery above it, tables and chairs had been set out for the reunion. Jonathan reserved a table for his family while Benjamin waited at the entrance for Ruth. The charabancs arrived and the women climbed off and headed for the ballroom. Husbands rushed to meet them and then more than a hundred couples flung themselves at each other and there were several minutes of noisy hugging and kissing. Tears flowed freely as they made their way to the tables. Jonathan stood up, with a huge smile on his face, as his mother and father approached hand-in-hand and there were more embraces.

"You look well," said Benjamin.

"So do both of you. You look as if you've been lying on the beach sunbathing."

"Well we haven't," said Jonathan defiantly. "I've been playing football and exercising and dad's been dashing all over the place doing his job as House Captain."

"That sounds grand," said Ruth. "Tell me about it."

Benjamin explained what his duties were and asked Ruth what she'd been up to. Ruth told him about clothing parcels, Mrs Murphy, the lesbians and the odd nasty Nazi.

"We had a couple of those," said Benjamin "but Jonathan got rid of them."

Jonathan told the tale of the two merchant seamen, then added that he'd become friends with another German sailor called Joachim.

A gigantic army urn had been set up in one corner and the couples queued for tea. As they drank their tea, Benjamin picked up the conversation.

"We've had a visit from Richard. Jonathan wrote to him saying we're alright and asking after the families, and a reply came saying he was on his way to see us."

"How is he?" asked Ruth.

"They're all well, although the two Martin boys have vanished into thin air, doing important war work. The war's not going too well for us. There I've said it now. Us. We no longer feel German. I can't wait for the day when we're all out of here and get on with helping to defeat the Nazis."

"I feel the same," said Ruth "but, from what I've read in the papers and heard on the radio, it's going to be a long war. It could be quite a while before we're out of here."

"Richard did say that some Category C aliens were being set free. He's going to see what he can do to speed things up for us. He thinks you've got the best chance of getting away soon. Women are getting priority."

"And," interrupted Jonathan, "if Richard says he'll do something, he will."

All too soon it was time to return to their camps. Dame Cruikshank, who had travelled with the women, told everyone that the reunion appeared to have been a great success. She hoped this would be repeated soon with, perhaps, children included.

There were no tears as the three said goodbye. They knew that Richard would do his best for them. Ruth climbed back on to the charabanc and Benjamin and Jonathan walked back to their camp. It had been a memorable day and left all three in high spirits.

◆   ◆   ◆

Ruth carried on playing a leading role in the organisation of the guest house. Mrs Murphy found her assistance invaluable and the two became close friends. Even the Nazis were quiet. One or two Aryan German women detested Hitler's mob, but were fiercely patriotic and Ruth helped the others to understand that these people didn't hate the Jews and were disgusted by the way that they had been treated by the Führer and his gang, but they still fiercely loved their country.

The war seemed far away, especially after the Germans started bombing London in early September. In the middle of the month, Dame Cruikshank announced that some paid jobs were available in guest houses and hotels, in the shops in the town, on the quayside and on neighbouring farms. Ruth volunteered to organise the applications. The criteria she chose were that the women should be reasonably healthy, reliable and in need of money. The two well-dressed women didn't put themselves forward for these jobs. They hadn't caused any trouble in the guest house and seemed decent sorts, so Ruth asked them one morning why they hadn't put themselves forward.

"Well, for one thing Ruth, we don't need the money," said the mousy blonde one who was called Heike. "Well, perhaps that's not strictly true. We did spend a lot when we first came here, but there's not much in the shops now. The food's good, our bed is comfortable and the weather's wonderful. What more could we want?"

"Besides," said the other, whose name was Marlise, "the jobs on offer aren't exactly what we're used to."

"What did you do before you came here?" asked Ruth.

"We were in a big house in Mayfair in London," said Heike. "I worked in the kitchens and Marlise was a chambermaid. We cleared out of Vienna when the Nazis came in. We're not Jewish, but we couldn't bear to be within a thousand miles of Hitler's scum."

"What did you do in Vienna?" asked Ruth.

"Oh a bit of this and a bit of that," replied Marlise.

"How were you treated in London?"

"Pretty well," said Heike. "The money wasn't bad but the best thing was we were in London, not stuck in some country house miles from anywhere. We could nip out most nights and earn a bit of extra money down the West End."

"How?" asked Ruth.

The two Austrian girls looked at each other and then burst out laughing. Ruth was tongue-tied for a moment and then the penny dropped.

"Oh," she said "you're, how shall I put it, ladies of the night."

"You could call it that," giggled Marlise.

Ruth felt embarrassed at her naivety and sat in silence for a few seconds, starting at her hands. Then she burst out laughing and the other two started again.

"Well," said Ruth, "you won't get much business here."

"We were wondering about the soldiers. They must be dying for it. Course we wouldn't bring them back here but, when the dark nights close in, maybe a quick knee trembler or hand job might be possible. We need to keep our hands in." All three burst out laughing again.

◆   ◆   ◆

"What an extraordinary lot we are," thought Ruth to herself later. On this small island just about every kind of person had been thrown together by the needs of war; upright mothers, nervous spinsters, lesbians, Nazis, anti-Nazis, patriots, prostitutes, Jews and gentiles. Ruth felt a certain sense of satisfaction that this disparate band had managed to live together without any real problems. But she also knew it wouldn't last. Winter was on its way. Sunbathing would be over. The days would get shorter and more boring and the tensions would mount. "Will I still be here then?" she thought. She had no idea.

CHAPTER FIFTEEN

Richard and Inge Walker were sitting in their garden in suburban south-west London. It was a beautiful September day, the first Saturday of the month. They'd had an early lunch to enable their boys to watch the cricket match at the local Wanderers ground and the weather was perfect for the last match of the season. The youngsters, Paul and Michael, who were in their late teens, were becoming very keen on the very peculiarly English game. They played at school and had joined the junior section of this cricket club. Paul was a promising spin bowler whose hero was Hedley Verity of Yorkshire. His brother was a hard-hitting batsman who one day hoped to emulate Denis Compton. Sadly the war had put paid to organised cricket at test and county level, so they'd yet to have had the opportunity to see their heroes in the flesh.

Under other circumstances it would have been a perfect day, but the war had shed a gloomy cloud all over the country. True, the RAF had shot hundreds of German planes out of the sky over the past months, and were still doing so, but the threat of invasion grew daily and was expected later in the month. Richard had joined Benjamin's department store's Territorial Army Anti-Aircraft (Searchlight) Company and was part of a huge band of volunteers ready to face the Nazis when the time came. He had recently returned from visiting Jonathan and Benjamin on the Isle of Man. That journey, and its possible aftermath, was the main topic of conversation on that warm, late summer day.

"I had another letter from Jonathan this morning," began Richard.

"How are they?" asked Inge.

"Considering they're locked up on the Isle of Man, pretty well. Jonathan thanked me for coming to visit them and sent his best wishes to all of us. Ruth visited them last week. Jonathan said she seemed in good health."

"What a waste," said Inge, "decent folks like them kicking their heels on the Isle of Man when they could be doing something to help the war effort. Is there anything you can do about it?"

Inge was fully aware of Richard's cloak and dagger activities in the pre-war years and that he'd used what influence he had to visit the Gerbers.

"I've been thinking about that. You remember Harry, don't you?"

"Yes."

"He's still running that art gallery in Bloomsbury. I thought I'd ask Reg if I could pop up to London to see him on Monday morning."

Just before five o'clock, their conversation was brought to an abrupt halt when the air raid siren sounded. There had been occasional warnings throughout the summer but, as on the day that war had been declared twelve months previously, these had turned out to be false alarms. The newspapers and radio had reported a few small-scale raids, but nothing that had amounted to very much. Although there was no reason to suspect that this would be any different, Inge went into the house to prepare flasks of coffee and water bottles. Within five minutes, they were ready to make their way to the Anderson shelter, a corrugated tin structure at the bottom of their garden. Paul and Michael came dashing back from the cricket ground, cursing the fact that play had been suspended with the match in the balance.

They lay down on their camp beds in the shelter, expecting the all-clear to sound very soon. It didn't. While they were lying there, staring at the roof, all four could hear what seemed to be a violent thunder storm in the distance. Inge said that the day was warm and close so wasn't surprised at the storm. Richard wasn't so sure.

The all-clear sounded at 06:15 and, when they emerged from the shelter, they were astonished to see huge areas of dense black clouds in the east over London.

"Looks like this is it," said Richard. "The first full-scale air raid on London. How much damage, I wonder? How many dead?"

Inge took the flasks and water bottles back into the house and made the evening meal. Richard gathered together torches, oil lamps and matches and took them to the shelter. He then made a second trip with blankets and pillows.

"If they come again today, we could be there all night. Best be prepared," he said.

The meal proceeded in almost complete silence. A second raid started before they had a chance to get an update from the radio's nine-o-clock news. The flasks, bottles and sandwiches were already prepared. Ruth carried them with her while Richard locked the doors and windows.

The rumbling noises they'd heard earlier continued for far longer this time and made sleep difficult. All four dozed fitfully so that, when the all-clear sounded just before five in the morning, they felt washed out. It was still dark but, when they looked east, the sky over London seemed to be on fire. Great streaks of orange, red and yellow streamed upwards. The capital seemed to be ablaze.

"How could anybody live through that?" said Inge.

◆   ◆   ◆

Richard Walker was an optimist, but also a realist and he knew full well that two nights of air raids, the capital had taken another bashing on Sunday, would have played havoc with London's transportation system. With this in mind, he set off very early on the Monday morning to see Harry, whom he expected to find in his gallery. He was right about the trains and a journey that usually took a little over half an hour took about four times longer. Things went smoothly until Clapham Junction then it was all stop-go until the train crawled into Waterloo almost ninety minutes late. The tube seemed to be running OK, so he took a train to Leicester Square then changed to the Piccadilly Line for the short trip to Holborn.

It was a short walk to Harry's art gallery in Bloomsbury which he was pleased to note was open for business.

"Richard. How good to see you. What brings you up to London in these troubled times?"

Harry was a German with a Russian name, a Russian wife and a Jewish father although he himself was a practising Christian. He was a small man, not much over five feet tall with thin and receding grey hair, slicked back as usual with pomade. Harry wasn't his real name, but Richard never called him anything else, so accustomed had he become to calling him Harry. He was also one of the most remarkable men Richard had ever met. He'd fought for Germany in the First World War, eventually ending up in the Air Force where his brother had been shot down and killed. After the war, he became a journalist and was appointed London representative of the German Press Agency. From there it was a short step to becoming Press Attaché at the German Embassy in Carlton House Terrace. Here he made many valuable contacts who would later be so important to the Foreign Office, including Richard Walker and Roger Martin. However, he hated the Nazis and this, together with his Jewish ancestry, got him the sack. Not long afterwards he was given British citizenship. He first became an art dealer and later opened up his modest gallery. It came as no surprise to Richard that Harry had escaped internment, given his service to His Majesty's Government.

Richard shook his friend's hand.

"How are you Harry? Actually, I've come up to London to ask a favour of you."

"Sounds intriguing. Wait a minute, I'll just shut up shop and we can go and have a cup of coffee. I know just the place where we can have some privacy."

The coffee shop was opposite the British Museum and they found a seat in the corner where they wouldn't be overheard.

"How's your family?" asked Harry.

"Fine. And yours?"

"Alright, I suppose. My boy Peter wants to be an actor would you believe? He'll be called up soon. I hope the Army will knock that idea out of his head. He'll never make much of a living in the theatre."

"Are you still involved in the, er, clandestine world?"

After he'd lost his job at the German Embassy, Harry had kept in touch with a couple of anti-Nazi staff there. Harry called these his "sources" and he passed on the information he obtained to the British Foreign Office and the press via Richard's relationship with Roger Martin, who was a journalist on a London evening paper. Harry's first source had been posted to the Netherlands, but he soon found another, and information continued to flow out of 9 Carlton House Terrace.

Harry replied to Richard's question. "Not really. Not since the round-ups of all the nasty Nazis was completed last Christmas. Thanks to our friends in the German Embassy, I had a comprehensive list of every dangerous German resident in Britain; spies, Gestapo, men and women from the Abwehr, Nazi party recruiters and other untrustworthy characters masquerading as domestic servants and journalists. You and Roger must have enjoyed your part in all that. How is he, by the way?"

"We did and he's fine. He's something in the Army, I believe. Any of those nasty Nazis still at large?"

"I very much doubt it. Those spies we caught before the war were jailed. When war broke out, their sentences were extended indefinitely. Anybody caught spying now gets the hangman's noose. Dodgy characters we identified before the war were deported and, after September last year, all the rest were interned for the duration. I wouldn't be surprised if a few hadn't changed sides to escape the gallows."

"It's about internment that I wanted to talk to you. I've got three friends, German Jewish refugees, detained on the Isle of Man. The father, Benjamin, has actually been a guest of the SS in a concentration camp. They're no threat to anyone and would be useful to the war effort if they were released. I wondered if you had any contacts who might help to get them out?"

"Yes. That collar-the-lot business of Churchill's was stupid. I bet there are thousands in the same boat. I'm not sure what I can do, but there is one person who might help."

"Who's that?"

"Van."

"Vansittart! What's he up to now?"

"He's a very senior civil servant and has the ear of important people. I'm still in touch with him socially. I'll invite him to dinner and see what he says."

Robert Vansittart had been the senior civil servant in the Foreign Office before the war. He hated the Germans and detested the British government's appeasement of Hitler and Mussolini. He'd set up his own network of agents, Harry amongst them, and fed secret information about Nazi Germany to anti-appeasement politicians, notably Winston Churchill.

Richard thanked Harry who noted down the Gerbers' details, but told him not to expect too much and suggested he try other avenues in case his approach failed. The two shook hands and Richard made his way back to Waterloo.

◆   ◆   ◆

The journey home was quicker than in the morning. Although the citizens were being constantly warned that careless talk costs lives, he learnt from the chatter in the train that the East End, where London's docks were, had borne the brunt of the air raids. The odd bomb had fallen elsewhere; near Victoria Station and further west along the banks of the Thames. The general opinion was that the Germans had dropped off their unused load as they flew back to northern France.

Richard went straight to the store, thanked Reg for the time off and worked for the rest of the day. When he got home he told Inge of his morning with Harry. After dinner, they made their preparations for the night ahead. The siren went as darkness fell and they made their way to the shelter. They crept into bed and soon heard what appeared to be several planes overhead.

"Perhaps they're taking a different route into London tonight." suggested Inge.

Soon she discovered she was wrong as a series of loud explosions screamed at them through the tin walls. Several times the shelter shook as the bombs fell close by.

"It's the aircraft factories," said Michael. "That's what they're after."

Luckily, they lived nowhere near the aircraft factories even though the impact of the bombs made them feel that they were dropping in their back garden. The rest of the night was relatively undisturbed, although they could hear bombs dropping in the near distance. The all-clear sounded just after midnight and they made their way wearily, but thankfully, back to their beds.

At work the next day, Richard learned that nearby Richmond, Surbiton, Malden and Purley had also been bombed but the damage there had been relatively light. Nevertheless, the air raids weren't being confined to London. The war was getting closer.

A couple of evenings later, Reg telephoned Richard to tell him that Roger had arrived for a flying visit and invited him across for a drink. The two former anti-appeasement plotters had hardly seen one another since the war started and their greeting was full of warmth and enthusiasm.

Roger was wearing the uniform of a Captain in the Army Intelligence Corps and told Richard that he was stationed at nearby Richmond where, he added, a small number of bombs had fallen earlier in the week. He kept details of his work close to his chest, but did say that it suited his skills.

Richard told him about his visit to Harry, and Roger wasn't surprised to hear that the former source had been involved in the round-up of those enemy aliens who posed a real threat. He then skilfully steered the conversation towards internment and then told Roger about the Gerbers.

"Harry's going to have a word with Vansittart," said Richard. "Perhaps he can bend the ear of someone in the Home Office."

"It's a bad business. A small part of my job, please keep this to yourself, is questioning the so-called enemy aliens. Ninety nine point nine per cent of them don't pose even the slightest threat to us. But they're starting to release them in dribs and drabs, especially women. I'll see what I can do."

The rest of the time was spent talking about the war, bombings, the infrequency of football and rugby matches and Paul and Michael's growing love of cricket. Richard asked after Roger's girlfriend Jane and was told she joined the Army. Since she was a trained accountant, Roger said, she'd probably end up in the Pay Corps. Richard thanked him and set off home for another night in the shelter.

◆   ◆   ◆

Ruth was looking forward to seeing Benjamin and Jonathan again soon. It was almost a month since the last get-together at the Derby Castle and she, and the other women, were anxiously awaiting news of the next one. She settled into her routine of housework, organisation and dealing with charity clothing parcels. One day, toward the end of September, Dame Cruikshank approached her at the Camp HQ while she was sorting through recently arrived clothing.

"Ruth. A few women internees have been released and next week a police officer from the mainland called Cuthbert is going to start to set up tribunals in Douglas to look into speeding up these releases. Women, I understand, get first priority. The tribunals treat each individual case on its merits. I think it would be a good idea for you to apply to be released."

"But what about my husband and son? They're in Hutchinson Camp."

"I know that, but it's not so easy for them. Women are perceived to be less of a threat than men but I'm sure that, when the time comes for them to seek release, the authorities will take into account that they have a wife and mother who has already been screened and released."

"How do I go about it?"

"Leave that to me. I'll get the necessary documentation together. You just sign it."

Ruth thanked Dame Cruikshank and carried on with her chores. The next day at roll-call, a family reunion for late October was announced. When the cheering died down, Ruth wondered whether or not she'd be attending. The Commandant was as good as her word and the documentation was soon signed, completed and dispatched. Shortly afterwards she was told to travel to Douglas to appear before a tribunal. Four others would be attending with her.

The five travelled together by train under armed guard. On arrival they were shown to a waiting room next to where they would be interviewed one at a time. As soon as these were over they would return to the camp where the outcome would be known within a month.

When Ruth appeared before the tribunal, she found three people waiting to question her; a police officer, who appeared to be in charge, an Army officer and a sinister looking woman in civilian clothes who was introduced as Mrs Stevens. Ruth wasn't told what the woman's function was. She was asked to sketch in her background; life in Germany and England and what she'd being doing at her camp. It didn't take much longer than thirty minutes and, when it was over, she was told to wait for the others and they would all return to the camp together.

"By the way Mrs Gerber," said the policeman as she walked towards the door, "Dame Cruikshank thinks very highly of you and, er, you seem to have friends in high places."

Ruth mouthed a silent "thank you" to the dame, but hadn't a clue as to what the rest of his comment referred to. She travelled back to the camp and waited. Three days before the planned family reunion, she was told she would be released on the following day. She was torn between delight at being released and disappointment at missing out on seeing Benjamin and Jonathan. Perhaps she could stay for a few more days? She thought not and decided that this was just another inconvenience which they would all have to deal with.

She wrote a long letter to Benjamin and Jonathan and asked Dame Cruikshank to see it reached them at Hutchinson Camp before the reunion, so that her unexpected absence would be explained. She thanked the Commandant then sought out Mrs Murphy and thanked her for her help and friendship. There was a tear in Ruth's eye as they embraced. Then she quickly composed herself and promised her landlady that she would bring her family for a holiday as soon as the war was over.

The weather had become autumnal and she felt a chill in the air as she reported to the authorities at Douglas Pier. She was given tickets for the steamer and a travel warrant to London. She was told that the police in Liverpool would give her further instructions. It was a choppy crossing but Ruth didn't notice. Her head was full of confusing thoughts. What would happen to Benjamin and Jonathan? Where would she go when she reached the mainland? What was London like after the bombing she'd heard about? Was her house still standing?

The steamer docked at Liverpool. Ruth and the others being released were told to report to their local police station when they reached their destinations. Even if they were no longer enemy aliens, they were still aliens, a police officer reminded them. The internees stood outside and waited for a police van to take them to Lime Street Station. A police vehicle appeared and the driver warned that the railway timetables were a shambles and it was impossible to say when they would get to where they wanted to be. As they left a police officer asked which of them was Mrs Gerber. Ruth stepped forward and the officer told her that a Mr Richard Walker would be waiting for her when the train reached Euston.

CHAPTER SIXTEEN

The day before the second planned reunion at the Derby Castle ballroom, Benjamin returned from his daily mail collection clutching the letter from Ruth. Jonathan was out playing football so he decided to wait until he returned before opening it. It was, after all, addressed to both of them.

A sweaty Jonathan appeared just before lunch and the letter was opened. It was in English, a sign that Ruth was making a conscious effort never to speak or write in German again. Jonathan read it out loud. She told them that she was being released and was so sad to be missing their meeting. In all probability, she would be in London by the time they read her letter.

Both father and son panicked at the thought of her living alone in war-torn London. Then they remembered Richard's promise to look after her and assumed she was safe south-west of the capital.

"Well that's good news," said Benjamin. "Let's hope we can get away soon."

Both knew that releases from internment had already begun. The first to leave were mostly scientists, especially those who could make a significant contribution to the war effort. All those released up to that point had one thing in common; they were Category C aliens just like Benjamin and Jonathan. This raised their hopes that they too might soon be free.

Jonathan immediately wrote to his mother at Richard's address and the two then settled down again to camp life. Things were looking up. Some of the men were being paid to work for the local traders and farmers. An acute shortage of coal in mid-October led to the need to revive the ancient Manx tradition of cutting peat for fuel. Jonathan volunteered for this and got paid some modest sums for his work and, of course, it made him even stronger. He had an enthusiastic band of followers for his early morning keep-fit sessions. One watching soldier advised him to join the army when he was released so that he could become a PT Instructor.

By the time he'd done his exercises, played football and carried out his peat-cutting duties, Jonathan was very tired and had taken to spending part of every afternoon in his room, reading and dozing. Even that period of relaxation vanished as an afternoon education programme began. All the camps on the island had plenty of school teachers and university professors in their ranks and Hutchinson was no exception. Jonathan enrolled for English Literature and History classes and was able to make up some of the ground lost in his studies since he'd been taken away from school.

Meanwhile Benjamin had taken up sport himself. Some bright spark had removed the brass knobs from the bedsteads in the hotels and guest houses and organised daily games of kugeln, a kind of bowls played without a green. Benjamin had never played the game before, but soon got the hang of it and became a competent player. The Douglas camps set up an inter-camp football league and Jonathan and Joachim spearheaded a strong Hutchinson team that swept almost all before them, a draw with a tough Central Camp team being their only setback. All the matches were played at Onchan Camp, just outside Douglas, which had its own properly marked football pitch with real goals, instead of the usual ad hoc arrangements like coats. It was agreed beforehand that one team would play in white and the other in anything but white. It took a while to get used to this, but eventually the players did and there were a number of hard fought games. One rather odd addition to the Hutchinson team was an Italian who wore a Great Britain tracksuit. He'd been born in Britain of Italian parents and had swum for the country of his birth in the Berlin Olympic Games of 1936. He wasn't much of a footballer, but his enthusiasm and obvious patriotic pride made him a welcome member of the team. "What on earth was he doing here?" thought Jonathan.

◆　　◆　　◆

The news that tribunals to consider release were sitting in Douglas soon reached the internees. Benjamin spoke to his son after supper one evening in late October.

"I think it's time we applied to be released."

"Right. How do we go about it?"

"You put together a letter requesting that we be allowed to put our case to the tribunal. Point out that we're in Category C and that your mother has already been sent home."

Jonathan did as he was asked and Benjamin gave the letter to the Street Leader. They had a fairly quick reply, acknowledging their application which would be dealt with in due course.

"I think that means that we're fairly well down the list," said Benjamin.

"Yes," replied Jonathan. "But we're on it. That's the main thing."

Letters from Ruth arrived regularly. She was staying with the Martins until Benjamin and Jonathan were released. Although well, she missed them terribly. Jonathan was getting really worried about Hilde, from whom he had heard nothing before the fall of France. Even though she would have no idea about his being on the Isle of Man, any letter would have been forwarded from the mainland. Jonathan knew that had she been able to write, she would have. Assuming she was in hiding, in prison or, worse still, dead, hardly a day passed when he didn't think of her.

The camps in Douglas, and elsewhere, housed an extraordinary collection of talents. Apart from teachers and scientists, there were musicians and artists. Top class concerts were held and a room in one of the larger hotels became an art gallery where superb paintings, drawings and sketches were exhibited. The quality of teaching was such that Captain Daniels doubted that a better education could be found in many British Universities.

One day, after football, Joachim and Jonathan were sitting on the side of the road catching their breath.

"Why do you think these professors, artists and so on work so hard?" asked the sailor.

"They're making up for lost time," replied Jonathan. "Back in Germany and Austria, the Nazis wouldn't let them work and Jewish music and paintings were forbidden by law. You surely remember the bonfires of Jewish books and works of art?"

"Not really. I come from a small coastal town near Lübeck. There wasn't much cultural activity there. We did have plenty of Nazis though, especially Brownshirts. They made the lives of the Jews hell. But then, of course, I was at sea most of the time, so I didn't witness a lot of the brutality. What I did see made me hate the Nazis forever."

One old journalist in the camp, whose Jewish paper in Hamburg had been closed long before the war, started a camp newspaper. It was typed on to a stencil and then copies were produced on a hand operated duplicating machine. There were articles about camp life, advertisements for classes, goods for sale or swap and reports on football matches. Much space was also devoted to pleas for release so that the internees could get on with the business of helping their new countrymen to defeat the Nazis.

The newspapers and the BBC kept those on the island abreast of what was happening in the war. It seemed to be a simple battle of survival. Britain and the Empire were standing alone against the might of Nazi Germany and Italy without a single ally. Extensive bombing raids continued night after night, except when poor visibility made accurate attacks impossible. Without being told so by the newspapers, Benjamin, Jonathan and the others knew that German target areas were now spreading well beyond London. During several late evenings they heard the drone of German planes as they headed to drop their deadly loads on Liverpool or Glasgow. From time to time, standing on the hill at the top of Douglas, they could see the tell-tale orange glow and white flashes as the German Air Force pounded the great port city of Liverpool.

"I wonder what it's like in London," said Jonathan.

"They're still getting it every night as well as other cities," replied Benjamin.

"I hope mother's alright."

"So do I. I hate being stuck here all safe and sound while she's facing this horror on her own."

"She's not alone," insisted Jonathan. "Reg and Mary are with her, as well as Richard and Inge. They'll look after her."

"You're right, of course."

◆　　◆　　◆

Day after day, the Gerbers and their fellow internees followed the same ritual; work, sport, study, sleep and worry. Captain Daniels appeared at five o'clock roll-call from time to time to announce the names of those being released on the following day. Benjamin and Jonathan knew they wouldn't be amongst the lucky ones. They hadn't yet been invited to attend a tribunal.

Toward the end of November, the Street Leader informed Benjamin that he and Jonathan were to appear before a tribunal the following day. The next morning they were taken, under guard, to the Douglas Court House. For more than an hour they were closely questioned by Scotland Yard's Detective Inspector Cuthbert who was accompanied by an Army Intelligence officer and a woman civilian. Neither of these said a word. Jonathan offered to act as interpreter as usual, but his father insisted he didn't need help, so improved was his English.

"Tell me about your final years in Germany," he began, turning to Benjamin.

"I had my own retail business. Gradually, I lost both customers and staff as anti-Jewish measures began to take effect. After Kristallnacht, I was arrested by the Gestapo and imprisoned in Sachsenhausen Concentration Camp. I was released after a few weeks."

"Why were you released so quickly?"

"I was imprisoned without charge or trial. I behaved when I was in the camp. Many others were released quickly. Only those who were politically active were kept locked up."

"Were you treated well while you were in detention?"

"I was beaten when I was being questioned by the Gestapo, but they left me alone in the camp."

"How did you escape from Germany?"

"In the usual way. We applied for exit visas, handed over a lot of our wealth to the Nazis and set sail for Cuba on the *St Louis*. We had landing certificates and were to await permission to join my wife's brother in Detroit."

"I'm aware of what happened on the *St Louis*. How do you live in London? Do you have any money?"

"Enough to live comfortably without relying on the government."

"How did you get your money out of Germany? I thought you said that the Nazis seized most of your possessions."

"Much but by no means all. A very close English friend of ours, with the help of a fine young man in the British Embassy in Berlin, enabled me to smuggle my valuable stamp collection out of Germany."

"I see. Your friend's name?"

"Richard Walker"

"And his address?"

Benjamin gave this and the policeman took down the details.

"Will this man vouch for you?"

"I'm sure he will. My wife, who was released last month, is living with Richard's boss until we're all together again."

"And what will you do to aid the war effort?"

"Anything I can. I fought in the last war. I'm probably too old now for the Army but I'd willingly join the Pioneer Corps or the Auxiliary Fire Service."

Cuthbert turned to Jonathan.

"What will you do, young man, if you're released?"

"I'd like to go back to school in London and complete my Higher School Certificate sir. After that, it rather depends on the war. I'll enlist and fight for Britain if it's still on. Otherwise I'd like to go to University."

"Captain Daniels speaks very highly of you both. My colleagues and I will discuss your cases and let you know of our decision in a week or so through the Captain."

Jonathan wrote to his mother telling her of the tribunal. Ten days later, at the evening roll-call, Captain Daniels confirmed that they would be released on the following day. Suitcases were packed and goodbyes said. Jonathan conducted one last PT class and then promised Joachim that he would meet up with him after the war, knowing that his friend wouldn't be released until it was over.

After breakfast, they reported to the guardroom. Travel warrants from Liverpool to London and steamer tickets were issued from the police at the quayside before the ferry set sail for Liverpool on a cold December morning.

◆   ◆   ◆

It was an uneventful crossing. On arrival at Liverpool, they were astonished at the devastation of the docks. Large mangled cranes lay on their side and the piers were so severely damaged they looked unusable. It was surprising that there was anywhere for the small steamer to off-load its passengers. They struggled with their luggage down the gangplank and walked to the police building, having avoided several large craters on the way. The police registered them and repeated the warning that they should report to their local police when they reached their destination.

They joined the other released aliens, amongst them the Anglo-Italian swimmer, in climbing aboard a coach which took them to Lime Street Station. The journey took some time, requiring several detours to avoid streets where many houses had been destroyed. In one road, every house seemed to have been hit and more than half reduced to a pile of rubble.

"We'd have been better off staying on the Isle of Man," Benjamin said, with a hint of a smile in the corner of his mouth.

"But we wouldn't have been free," replied Jonathan.

Lime Street Station was a total mess. It didn't appear to have been bombed, but it seemed that thousands of travellers were milling around the concourse with their suitcases and kit bags. There were sailors, possibly going home on leave, soldiers and airmen, perhaps on their way to re-join their units, as well as hordes of civilians. All were waiting for trains that were either running late or had been cancelled. It was a gloomy day and the dull chatter of the waiting passengers made Benjamin and Jonathan a bit fed up. What had promised to be an exciting day was turning out to be anything but. The public address system poured out a stream of announcements and apologies about the progress, or lack of it, of trains for London, Birmingham, Leeds and Manchester.

Two hours after their arrival, the Gerbers heard an announcement about the imminent departure of a train to London. This seemed to catch the attention of more than half of the people on the concourse and they surged forward towards their platform. Every seat was quickly taken and they joined the crush in the corridors sitting on their suitcases.

The locomotive struggled its way out of the station. It seemed barely credible that it could pull the carriages, so great was the number of people crammed into them. It soon picked up speed but, when they reached Crewe, a voice from the platform shouted that the train departure would be delayed for an hour. Last on to the train meant first out, so Benjamin and Jonathan were at the front of the queue in the station buffet. They ordered a spam sandwich and a cup of tea each. The food wasn't up to much but, as it was the first they'd eaten since breakfast, it was very welcome.

They were soon back on the train and found that quite a few had got off at Crewe, possibly to change trains. They squeezed into a compartment and sat opposite each other in the window seats. A couple of soldiers were puffing on their cigarettes but there was little or no conversation. Thankfully, the remainder of the journey was completed without further hold-ups or delay.

◆　　◆　　◆

It was dark when they reached Euston and they were thrilled to find both Ruth and Richard waiting for them.

Richard interrupted the hugs, kisses and tears. "Let's get out of here before Adolf pays his nightly visit. Ruth and I have already unpacked everything at the house."

If Liverpool looked badly damaged, London looked like the world was about to end. Houses destroyed, fires still burning, smoke everywhere and an army of uniformed men and women scurrying about in the gloom trying to restore some sense of normality to the city. Everyone could see that this was an impossible task, but Richard and the Gerbers expressed admiration for the efforts the workers were making.

"Your area suffered a big raid a few weeks ago, but your street escaped. Ruth and I found there'd been a break-in. Someone broke the back windows and let themselves in. They probably thought you'd think it was caused by a raid but they forgot to break the rest of the windows as well. As far as we can see there's nothing missing and no damage. I've patched them up with some timber but you should get a glazier round in the morning. Let's hope no one gets in while we're picking you up from Euston."

Thankfully the house was as Richard and Ruth had left it three hours before. It was cold so Benjamin put on a couple of electric fires while Ruth prepared a meal. It was agreed that Richard would stay the night. There was no point in running the bombing gauntlet tonight.

Just before nine the siren sounded which signalled a hasty exit to the cellar where everything had been set up for the night. Twenty minutes later bombs started raining down. Richard guessed they were about three miles away but the raid felt a lot closer. Benjamin and Jonathan were terrified at first, but one glance at the calm faces of Ruth and Richard reassured them and they settled down to spend the first of who knew how many nights under attack.

PART FOUR

Blitz: September 1940

These things all went together to
make the most hateful, most beautiful
single scene I have ever known.
ERNIE PYLE, *ERNIE PYLE IN ENGLAND*, 1941

While the Gerbers were making the most of their enforced holiday on the Isle of Man and Richard and Inge Walker were chatting in their garden on that sunny September afternoon, George, Doris and Patrick Wallace were slumped in chairs in their sitting room. It was a lovely warm day in North London. The sky was a pale blue, undisturbed by even the lightest of clouds and the sun blazed down. Any normal family would be enjoying an afternoon in the park but this, of course, was not a normal family. The gloom inside the house was in direct contrast to the brightness outside. All three looked depressed.

"Where the 'ell's Angela?" George asked.

"Gone to Brighton with that new friend of 'ers, Pam," replied his wife.

"She should be 'ere. She should be worried like the rest of us."

Patrick took a drag on his Woodbine.

"What we worried about dad?"

"Not enough bleedin' money, that's what," his father shouted in response, "or 'adn't you noticed? You got yer fags and you spend yer time 'angin around with yer mates. What you doin' to bring some cash in?"

"S'not my fault the bike business ain't goin' well. Every time I nicked one, there's bin somethin' in the paper. Word's got round. People are lockin' their bikes up now. What do you expect me to do? Carry 'em back 'ere?"

"Leave the boy alone George. Ain't 'is fault. Besides 'e's doin' 'is bit for Gibson with the bookies and the tarts."

"Gibson. Don't mention 'is name. Every penny we earn, 'e gets 'is cut. What's a man supposed to support 'is family on?"

"You'll just 'ave to think of somethin'. What about that copper Scott? 'Asn't 'e come up with anythin'?"

"Nothin'. All the bleedin' foreign Jews are locked up, so that dodge we carried out near Romford is out. Breakin' and enterin' is hopeless on these light nights. Besides, people 'ave stopped goin' away. They're stuck in their 'ouses guardin' 'em in case the Germans come. I'm doin' all right liftin' wallets and purses down west, but it just ain't enough. The dog tracks used to be a good spot for that, but it's no good now. 'Ardly anybody goes anymore and most of the places have closed. They're all savin' their money to buy stuff on the black market. Thought I might give the 'orses a go, but I bet it'll be the same there as at the dogs."

"What about nickin' cars?" Doris asked.

"No good that either. Bloody rationin'. No petrol. Many people 'ave locked their vehicles away till the war's over. Most of the cars about are official, coppers and the like, and I ain't risking' pinchin' one of them."

Doris looked pretty fed up. She'd been thinking about a new home and furniture, perhaps even a car, but those dreams seemed as far away as ever. Of course, they were doing OK and certainly as well as the time before they'd expanded their criminal activities more than a year ago. Suddenly her face lit up.

"Tell you what. 'Ave you seen that the government's after as much metal as it can lay its 'ands on. It's for buildin' planes, tanks and stuff. Can't you get 'old of some?"

George looked at his wife. She was usually the one with all the good ideas, but it was a sign of their desperation that even she was clutching at straws.

"Leave it out, Doris. The government wants people to give the stuff to 'em not sell it. You'll be askin' me and the boy to grab the railins' in the park and offer 'em to Winnie next."

"Yer right. Sorry."

"There is one thing mind you. Me medical certificate."

George had persuaded a doctor to give him a medical certificate so that he was exempt from being called up by the forces. It was still early days and his age group wasn't yet being targeted for conscription. But the longer the war went on, the more likely it was that George would find himself in a muddy field somewhere with a rifle in his hand. It wouldn't suit him at all. George was a shirker, a skiver and a coward to boot.

"So what. It'll keep you out of the war, but 'owzat goin' to 'elp us?"

"There's plenty of lads 'oo don't wanna join the army. I could make meself up a bit, turn up at the tribunals in disguise, pretend I'm them and they're scot free. They'd pay a bit for that."

"Don't be bleedin' daft," said Doris. "What about yer name on the certificate?"

"Can't read it. You know what doctors are like with their scrawl."

"Sounds dodgy to me."

Patrick stubbed his cigarette out and told his parents that he'd got a good plan.

"What's that?" asked his mother.

"'Arf inchin' stuff from shops. Me mates are always 'elpin 'emselves to sweets."

"We can't live on bloody sweets," replied his mother angrily. "Anyway, I'm gonna put the kettle on."

Their unproductive planning was interrupted by the sound of the air raid siren from the top of the police station in the High Street.

"There goes Moaning Minnie," said George. "Probably another false alarm."

Patrick got up out of his seat and went into the street. Thirty seconds later he was back, a look of panic on his face.

Doris and George followed him outside. They were shaken by what they saw. To the east all they could see was a mass of sliver shapes gliding together in beautiful formation and sparkling in the fresh blue sky.

"Look at that lot."

"'Oo's are they? Ours or theirs?"

"Theirs, yer dumb idiot. Why else do you think the siren's sounded? They're 'eadin' this way. Quick George, lock the 'ouse up. Let's get down to the shelter."

The nearest public shelter was about a three minute walk away on the High Street. Fortunately a lot of other people had thought it was a false alarm so, when the Wallaces reached the shelter, there was room inside. Many of the larger houses in the area had basements and one of the big blocks of flats had a huge underground cellar where it was assumed that people would be safe. The building they headed for was a rectangular box made of reinforced concrete and totally protected by sandbags. It had a thick steel door.

Patrick, looking up to the sky, announced that there was some smoke over Dagenham way but that the planes had turned and seemed to be heading for the docks. He looked at the shelter.

"This don't look much good. What 'appens if a bomb 'its it?"

"Then we'll all be dead," replied his mother. "Now get in."

The three of them entered the shelter and squeezed onto one of the benches that ran the length of each side wall. The door was still open and they could hear bombs exploding not too far away. The ARP Warden arrived, clutching an oil lamp, and slammed the door shut. The shelterers sat in silence as they listened to the muffled crump, crump of bombs outside. Nobody in the shelter had even the tiniest experience of what they were facing and, not surprisingly, they looked petrified in the lamp-lit gloom. They could hear every bomb as it dropped, but they knew that the explosions were some way away and that, for the time being at least, they were safe.

After more than two hours they heard the welcome sound of the all-clear. They slowly made their way into the street, wondering what on earth they would find outside. Even though it was only six o'clock, it seemed like the darkest of nights. To the south of them, the whole sky was filled with menacing thick, black clouds of smoke. It looked as if a thousand buildings were on fire. There was no sign of the silver planes. They must have returned to wherever they'd come from.

"Looks like the docks 'as bought it," said George.

"I bet everyone's dead down there," observed his son.

"Don't matter that much," replied his father as they set off home. "Most of 'em'll be Jews."

Doris glared at her husband.

"Don't talk rubbish, George. There's lots of proper English living in the East End."

"Well let's just 'ope that most of them that got blown up were Jews."

They expected to find Angela waiting for them when they reached their house, but there was no sign of her. Doris thought she was probably still in Brighton and Patrick asked his parents if they thought the south coast had been bombed.

"'Aven't a clue," his father said. "If they did, she could 'ide under the pier."

The three of them ate their tea. Patrick, unusually for him, chatted away saying that, once the RAF got at the Germans, there'd be no bombs. Nobody seemed to be listening. His parents sat deep in thought, but the silence was shattered by the wailing of the siren at half past eight. This time they didn't even consider a false alarm. They jumped up, George locked up the house and they quickly made their way to the shelter. They took nothing with them. They expected to be back by bedtime but the raid was even more severe than the one in the afternoon and lasted until almost five in the morning. Nobody in the shelter got a wink of sleep, so intense was the never-ending noise as bomb after bomb dropped on the defenceless docks. When it was over, they staggered out, tired and hungry. It was almost dawn. The whole sky to the south of them was a lurid painting of vivid orange flames and coal black dense smoke. The noise must have been deafening as bombs continued to blast off long after the German planes had departed. In the distance, they could hear the clanging of bells as fire engines, ambulances and other emergency vehicles rushed to the rescue of the stricken population.

The Wallaces reached home and collapsed into their chairs. Doris put the kettle on. Again, they sat in silence, sipping their tea. Doris remembered her daughter and went upstairs to see if she was in bed. She wasn't.

"Must still be in Brighton," she told the others.

"I think we'll be safe 'ere," said George. "Nothin' much to bomb in these parts."

"Except us," his wife replied.

George ignored her.

"Any'ow, I got to thinking while we was in the shelter, this bombing ain't too bad. I've got a few ideas as to 'ow we might make a tidy little sum out of it."

CHAPTER EIGHTEEN

Doris and Patrick were too exhausted to listen to another one of George's hare-brained schemes. The night in the shelter had taken its toll on them and they struggled upstairs to the bedrooms where Doris collapsed on to the bed fully clothed. Patrick managed to climb under the covers. With no one left to talk to, George followed moments later. All three remained comatose until about eleven when, still feeling some effect from their traumatic night, husband and wife fell out of their bed. Doris banged on their children's door and asked if Angela was there. There was silence so she walked in. Patrick was still fast asleep and Angela's bed hadn't been slept in. She pulled the covers off her son, grabbed him by the shoulders, shook him and told him it was time to get up.

The adults were downstairs eating their breakfast when Patrick stumbled in, cursed his mother for waking him up and sat down for something to eat.

"You ain't washed, yer dirty beast. No food till yer clean," his mother said in a sharp voice to which both husband and son were well accustomed.

Reluctantly Patrick got up and slowly walked out of the room. He was back five minutes later, still sulking, and began to eat his cornflakes. The room was in complete silence, apart from the slurping noise that Patrick made as he spooned the cereals into his mouth.

"Now what's this bright idea you got, George?"

"I'll tell you later. First, I've got a job for the boy."

"I was goin' to the park to play football with the others," Patrick complained.

"Bugger that. There's a war on. You got a job to do."

"What is it?"

"Get yerself down to the East End and see what's goin' on. 'Ow bad is it, what state are the 'ouses in, 'ow many people about? That sort of thing."

"Why can't you go?"

"Coz a man wandering around would look funny. You won't be suspicious. Just another nosy boy seein' what's 'appened. Get yerself off as soon as you've finished yer breakfast. 'Ere's a bob, pay for the bus and get yerself some grub."

"What 'appens if there's an air raid?" asked Doris.

"Too bad, 'e'll 'ave to take 'is chance like the rest of us."

"I might get killed."

"No yer won't. If I know you, yer'll get outta the way in time. Now bugger off."

"Take care Patrick," said his mother who was quietly impressed with George taking the initiative for once and this time it seemed like a good idea.

Patrick still wasn't keen, but he could see that further argument was pointless so he stood up and set off. The journey started well. The buses seemed to be running and, with a couple of changes, he reached London Bridge. On the bus, everyone was talking about the air raids. Estimates from the number of dead ranged from five hundred to five thousand. Evidence of the raids was all too clear. He sat on the top deck of the bus heading down Grays Inn Road towards the river. From his birds-eye view he could see fires still raging all along the south bank of the Thames towards the east as far as the eye could see. A thick pall of smoke seemed to cling to the sky.

As he crossed the river, Patrick could also see that the Surrey Docks were being completely reduced to ash by the fires and the West India Dock further down river seemed to be suffering the same fate. Reaching the south bank, he was now in the thick of it. Scores of firemen were still struggling to bring the infernos under control. Unlike his father, the boy had some guts and he cautiously picked his way east along the south bank of the Thames. He was turned back several times by police officers who, too busy to ask what he was doing there, told him to steer clear of certain locations due to the danger from UXBs. He asked the first policeman to stop him what a UXB was. Unexploded bombs, the officer told him.

Every part of the docks seemed to have been hit. Timber yards, gas holders, warehouses, oil terminals, factories, schools and houses had collapsed into a pile of twisted steel, broken glass, brick and ash. He walked inland and saw rows and rows of tiny terraced houses with windows blown out, roofs and doors missing, and walls collapsed. Some houses were just a pile of bricks and dust. In others the missing walls allowed a peek into people's deserted bedrooms with beds and wardrobes precariously poised on the edge of the floor. Hundreds of people were scrambling about in the ruins. He asked a boy of about his own age what they were looking for. "Anythin' we can find," he was told, "clothes, money, food, beddin', jewellery, anythin' that we could rescue."

"Just 'round the corner a school where people were shelterin' got 'it. They're still lookin' for the bodies. The ole' Prime Minister Churchill was 'ere not long ago. He promised to drop tens of thousands of tons of shit on the Nazis in Berlin."

To confirm what he'd been told, Patrick watched as stretchers were carried towards ambulances, doctors and nurses tended to the walking wounded, and mobile snack bars were set up to feed the homeless. Patrick decided he was one of those and helped himself to a bowl of vegetable soup and a chunk of bread. He'd seen enough. He was tired and had a long journey home and didn't want to be caught there if the Germans returned in the afternoon. He walked back to London Bridge Station and bought ten Woodbines with some of the money his father had given him. Three buses and a lot of walking later, he reached home at about five. He was relieved that the bombers had stayed away during the afternoon. He walked in and slumped straight into a chair. His father asked him to describe what he'd seen and he was about to begin when Angela walked in.

"Where the 'ell 'ave you bin?" asked Doris.

"Brighton, I told you. I went for a day out with Pam."

"Where did you stay last night?"

"At Pam's 'ouse. She lives over Barnet way. When we got back to Victoria we could see all the smoke and she thought we'd be safer in 'er part of the world."

"We were worried about you," said George.

"No you weren't. You couldn't care less about me. Since I stopped goin' down the 'dilly, you 'aven't paid a scrap of attention to me."

Angela hated being a prostitute and had told her parents last May that she was packing it in. They'd been furious, but nothing they said could force her to change her mind.

"You might 'ave to think again about that," said George. "We're runnin' short of money. It's even better in the West End now. Place is overrun with all them 'andsome fly boys. After a day of givin' 'Itler a bloody nose in the sky, they dyin' for it. Most of 'em are young and they got plenty of dosh."

"For the last time, NO. I ain't ever doin' that again."

George shrugged his shoulders.

"Too bad. Patrick'll 'ave to take yer place. Loads of 'em are bent."

Patrick looked at his father in horror.

"Bugger off, dad," he shouted.

Doris got up from her chair, walked across the room and slapped her son hard on the face.

"You'll do as yer bleedin' well told. Anyway, it mightn't be necessary. Yer dad's got some new ideas. Come on George, let's 'ear 'em."

"Before I start, let's 'ear about what Patrick saw."

Angela wasn't part of this discussion so she sat at the dining table and read The Sunday Pictorial. She kept one ear on what was being said and what she heard hardened her conviction that she needed to get away from this house permanently. Patrick was just a boy. He was growing up into a nasty piece of work, but there was still time to turn things around. He was under the influence of his parents and she regarded both of these as thoroughly evil. She had never really loved them since she realised when she was a little girl that they were both very bad people. She was scared of them. She knew they'd stop at nothing to get what they wanted. She had to get away.

Patrick told his mother and father about his trip to the East End. His father asked a few questions and then came up with his plan.

"If these air raids carry on, there's ways we can make our fortune."

"'Ow?" asked Doris.

"'Ang on. Give me time. Yesterday will have taught everybody a lesson. The next time the Germans come, we'll all know they mean business.

Everyone'll make a mad dash for the shelters, leavin' all them empty 'ouses piled 'igh with goodies."

"Don't be stupid, George. Yer can't break into people's 'ouses during a raid. Yer might get blown up."

"The Germans can't be bombing everywhere at once, but I reckon everybody'll be takin' cover as soon as the siren goes off. They won't know where the Germans are aimin' for. And they'll stop in the shelters till the all-clear. Meanwhile, Wallace and Son will be relievin' 'em of their possessions. It'll just be bad luck if we're caught in a raid, but it's no more risky than sittin' in that shelter."

"Sounds like a nice little earner," said Doris.

"No, a big earner," said George. "Not just 'ouses either. What about shops with their winders blown out? They might as well put up a sign sayin' 'elp yerself."

"You'd better get started down the docks."

"No good there. According to Patrick, there's not much left standin' and, anyway, there's no dosh down there. There'll be richer pickins when the Germans start attackin' other areas."

◆   ◆   ◆

George was right. After a restless Sunday night in the shelter when the Luftwaffe almost polished off what was left of the Docklands, they bombed Holborn late on Monday. The newspapers and radio continued to avoid identifying stricken areas, so that the Luftwaffe wouldn't know whether or not they were hitting their targets, but the gossip amongst Londoners soon spread the word. Everyone was relieved that there were no further daytime raids and the citizens soon settled into a routine of work during the day, then down to the shelters when the siren sounded at eight o'clock. The King and Queen visited the East End and the Prime Minister made a radio broadcast to urge the people to stand firm. This they largely did. Volunteers worked day and night to help the victims and it soon became obvious that London would indeed "stand firm."

Something that concerned everyone over the first few days was the lack of any real defence. Most of the anti-aircraft guns had been deployed to defend the airfields in the south-east. Now they were brought back to defend the capital and the Luftwaffe faced a nightly barrage as searchlights criss-crossed the sky and the AA guns spewed shells at the raiders. This had the effect of forcing the planes higher, making accurate strikes more difficult. More residential areas and shopping centres suffered as the Germans made sure they'd dropped their load for the night before flying back to their bases in France.

All of this suited the Wallaces very nicely. They slept through the morning, did their usual jobs after lunch—pick pocketing and acting as look out for Gibson—then sat at home waiting for Moaning Minnie. Doris and Angela set off for the shelter and the other two waited in their house until the raids were well under way before venturing out. They each carried an empty kit bag. They had to be extra careful. The blackout was nowhere as effective as it had been before flames began to light up the sky. There were uniforms everywhere: police, fire fighters, ambulance staff, ARP wardens and even soldiers. The Wallaces were dressed completely in black. They steered clear of the districts actually under attack but chose areas on the fringe where they could be almost certain that the houses would be invitingly empty.

Three houses in Shoreditch were burgled on their first excursion, before they cautiously made their way home just before the all-clear and dumped their haul in the sitting room. Doris had just returned from the shelter with Angela, who went straight up to bed, as the bags were emptied. They'd done well and had pinched a big pile of clothes, mostly in good condition, a radio, some food and a small amount of jewellery and money.

"Brilliant," Doris said. "Now what we gonna do with it?"

"I thought you were gonna get rid of it like before," George replied.

"I will but I won't be able to shift all this lot at once. We'll 'ave to put it in the shed."

"Yeah, but what 'appens when the coppers come lookin' for it?"

"We'll 'ave to 'ide it."

"'Ow?"

"When you two 'ave 'ad a kip, you can dig a big 'ole in the floor of the shed. Line it with wooden sheets so the stuff won't get damp. I'm sure you'll be able to pick up some timber. You might even 'ave to pay fer it, but we can afford that now. Mind you, I don't expect the stuff to be in there long. Finish it off with an 'idden entrance, so it looks like the rest of the floor."

"Good idea that, Doris."

"I'll get rid of the stuff bit by bit in markets and pubs."

"Right, Patrick. Eat up your breakfast. We'll grab some sleep and then get on with it."

The door opened and Angela walked in. She was dressed ready to go out to work.

"What's all this?" she exclaimed.

"None of yer business. Eat yer breakfast and bugger off to work," replied her mother.

"You've stolen it 'aven't you? While people 'ave been cowerin' in terror in the shelters, you've been ransackin' their empty 'omes. You're worse than rats scavengin' for food."

With this she put on her coat and rushed out the house. She'd have something to eat when she got to work.

◆   ◆   ◆

George and Patrick went further and further afield and plied their filthy trade successfully for the rest of the week. One night they nearly came unstuck when they arrived in Hackney at the end of a raid. A couple of German tail-end charlies were heading for home, but it meant that the Wallaces would find out what it was like to be bombed.

There was the now familiar sound of the boom boom of the AA guns and the deafening explosions as death rained down from the sky. For the first time they were really frightened. A few bombs made a disturbing whistling sound as they raced to earth. They ran, but there was nowhere to go. Almost as soon as they seemed to find a safe spot, a building nearby began to blaze or disintegrate, or both. The Germans dropped their load and moved on, but the bombs stayed. Some were UXBs, others mines with delayed action fuses and most of the rest just blew everything in their path to smithereens. That almost included George and Patrick as one high explosive shell landed in the middle of a street just over two hundred yards from where they were cowering in fear. The impact seemed to suck all the air from their lungs and then they were thrown from their feet, crashing into a garden wall. For a second they lay stunned and then the boy spotted a silver cylinder plummeting to the ground, far too close to them for comfort. He grabbed his father, lifted him to his feet and then dragged him away from the threat as fast as he could. Mesmerised by the menace of the bomb, Patrick watched in fascination as the cylinder broke open, twenty yards above the ground, revealing several smaller missiles which landed harmlessly on roofs, in gardens and in the street. He didn't wait to see what happened next as he helped his father to safety, so he missed the fireworks display ninety seconds later as the tiny missiles burst into flame and started fires raging all over the area. The frantic sounding of bells announced the arrival of two fire engines, the first of which plunged head first into a crater. The flames were leaping from house to house as the second engine began the impossible task of dousing the inferno.

Patrick told his father to get a move on. He noticed that George's trousers were wet. He was so frightened he'd pissed himself.

"You alright dad?"

"I've banged me 'ead and I've got a pain in me chest. You'll 'ave to elp me 'ome."

Poor Patrick had to manhandle his father through the streets. Their direct route home was blocked off by rubble, vehicles and panicking crowds, so they had to take a roundabout route and found themselves outside Finsbury Park tube station just after the all-clear sounded. They were surprised to see a large crowd of people leaving the station, clutching pillows, blankets and bottles. Some of these made their way to one of the mobile snack bars that were doing a roaring trade so George and Patrick joined them.

"What you been up to down there?" George asked a large middle-aged woman with a scarf wrapped around her head.

"Sleepin'. It's safer there."

"I thought the government said people weren't to use the tube for shelterin'. They need to keep the trains runnin'."

"The trains were runnin', but it didn't stop us from havin' our best night's sleep for a bit. We started comin' last week. Just bought a pile of penny 'apenny platform tickets and Bob's yer uncle."

"What did the tube staff say?"

"Nothin'. They've been told to let people in after four. Don't even 'ave to buy a ticket now."

Patrick and George walked home. Doris was waiting for them when they arrived.

"Why are them bags empty?" she asked.

George told her of their near miss.

"So what. Yer still alive ain't yer? You missed a big chance."

"'Ow do yer mean?"

"You wouldn't even 'ave 'ad to break in to those 'ouses. The Germans did it for you. You could just 'ave walked in."

"You weren't there."

"If I 'ad bin, we'd 'ave 'ad two full bags tonight."

Upstairs, Angela could hear everything that was being said. She was almost physically sick with disgust and asked herself how much longer could she put up with this.

George said he hadn't thought straight and promised it wouldn't happen again. He told Doris about the tube station.

"Official now is it?" she asked.

"Seems like it."

"I reckon we can make a bob or two out of that," Doris said, staring towards the window, deep in thought.

CHAPTER NINETEEN

Before George could put his latest plan into action, the Wallace family received another visit from their friendly neighbourhood corrupt policeman Scott. He banged on the door and, as soon as it opened, marched in and made himself at home without invitation from either George or Doris.

"Doin' well I see, George," Scott began, a sneer on his face. "Reckon you must be pocketin' a tidy sum, judgin' by your smart clobber. Suppose you're dinin' like kings an' all."

"Now look 'ere, Mr Scott," Doris responded, trying to appear insulted, "we've scrimped and saved almost every penny we get to give our children a decent life."

"Where's your daughter, by the way?

"Out working. She's at it every hour she can. She brings 'ome all 'er wages and tips and gives everything to 'er mum."

"Rubbish," said Scott. "We're getting' reports of break-ins during air raids and lootin' of bombed 'ouses. I bet that's you and Al Capone Junior there," he said, glancing at Patrick. "I think I'll 'ave a little look round."

Scott marched upstairs and the Wallaces looked at each other with concern. He soon returned.

"Let's 'ave a butchers in that shed."

"Ave you got a warrant?" asked Doris.

"Fancy comin' down the nick? You know me, I could easy get a witness to your criminal activities and keep you there while I apply for the warrant. Now give me the bloody keys."

With a small show of reluctance, Doris handed over the keys and Scott disappeared into the yard. He was soon back.

"Where 'ave you 'idden it all then?"

"Don't know what yer talkin' about, Mr Scott."

"You know full well. Any'ow, that's not the reason I've come 'ere. Mrs Scott would like to 'ave a better life, like the one you're leadin'. So I thought to meself, 'ow can I 'elp 'er? Of course, pal up with them master criminals, the Wallaces."

George and Doris relaxed and waited for Scott to continue.

"Lots of 'em that's well off 'ave left London for the safety of the countryside since the bombing started and all the Jewish refugees 'ave been locked up. All them empty 'ouses just waitin' to be done. Naturally the police 'ave got a list of these properties so we can keep an eye on 'em, but we're too busy for that. So, I'll give you a copy of the list, you do the 'ouses, and we'll split the proceeds fifty-fifty."

"Sounds a good scheme, Mr Scott. When do we start?"

"As soon as I get you the list. Steer clear of this neighbourhood. You don't want to be steppin' on Gibson's toes. I've 'eard 'e's tightenin' 'is grip. Anybody 'oo gets in 'is way he gets topped and his associates sling the body on the rubble after the raids, so they look like victims of the blast."

"Don't worry. We'll steer clear of 'im," Doris said.

"Right. I'll be off. I'll be back with the lists when I get 'em."

◆　　◆　　◆

That afternoon, George decided to put his wife's latest plan into action. It wasn't original and she'd heard somebody talk about it in the pub. Just after three, he set off with Patrick and they bussed and walked their way to Arsenal tube station. Each carried a large, empty suitcase. They reached Arsenal just after three and they found a lengthy queue outside the station. Legitimate passengers were being admitted, but a member of the station staff was stopping anybody from the queue from entering. Everybody had suitcases, bottles, small bags and other paraphernalia and were obviously planning to spend the night underground. George walked up to the man controlling the queue. The master criminal's shoulders were slumped and he dragged his right leg. He was looking even more pathetic than usual. Patrick, looking suitably miserable, was close behind him.

"'Allo guv," George said in a whimper. "Can you 'elp us out?"

"Gates open at four," said the station man. "You'll 'ave to go to the back of the queue."

George hung his head and started to cough.

"Do us a favour guv," he wheezed, "me 'ouse got bombed two days ago and I lost everythin', includin' me wife and daughter. Me leg's done for and me chest is givin' me terrible trouble. 'Ow about lettin' me and the boy in so we can get a nice spot?"

The station man took pity on them and let them in first when the gates opened at four. As soon as they were out of sight of the station man, they raced down to the northbound Piccadilly Line platform and found the best spots. Patrick stretched out on one and George put their suitcases on the other. The platform quickly filled up as families set out blankets, pillows, bottles and food parcels for the night. Small girls clutched their dolls and boys began to play with their Dinky cars. George told Patrick to guard their places with his life then set off along the crowded platform towards the exit. By now the platform was packed to capacity and people were trying to find whatever space they could; on steps, in the tunnels leading to the platforms and even the booking hall, which wouldn't have offered much protection from a direct hit. George spoke to an elderly woman and her grown-up daughter. He told them he'd got a couple of nice spots on the platform which they could have for five bob each. The ladies were surprised and looked at him distastefully, but then swallowed their disgust because they needed shelter. They followed George down to the platform where they found Patrick still guarding the spaces. The women were reluctantly grateful and the mother handed over a ten shilling note and George and Patrick left, clutching their suitcases. They waited until a train arrived and then mingled with the passengers exiting the station in case they were spotted by the Underground staff. They made their way to a cafe where they drank tea, ate some sandwiches and smoked until the siren went off at eight o'clock. Then, with the sound of anti-aircraft guns filling the sky, they walked northwards where they stuffed their suitcases at two large houses opposite Finsbury Park.

They were in bed asleep when the all-clear sounded. Doris and Angela returned from the shelter and grabbed an hour's sleep or so. Patrick slept on so it was just mother, father and daughter who sat down for breakfast.

"'Ow did it go?" asked Doris.

"Brilliant," replied George and he gave a full account of the night's activities.

Angela listened with complete revulsion. She looked at her father and said, "I read in The Daily Mirror they think looters should be 'ung. You'll end up at the end of a rope."

"We won't get caught," said George.

Angela looked at the pair of them smugly eating their breakfast. She hated them, but they were her parents, so she decided to make one last appeal to her father.

"Look dad, it's not too late to pack all this in and do somethin' for the war effort. I'm startin' at the school just down the road from my work tonight. It's a rest centre for people 'oov'e been bombed out. I'll be 'elpin' to make 'em comfortable, bringin' 'em tea and soup and so on."

"Ow much does it pay?" asked Doris.

"Nothin', it's voluntary. Doin' me bit. You could be a fireman or an air raid warden. They're desperate for people to sign up. Saw a sign the other day, "Serve to Save" it said. They're looking for more ARP people."

"That's not a bad idea," said George. "I could just walk into 'ouses all legit then turn 'em over."

Angela stared at him. She was speechless. Tears began to fill her eyes. She knew she'd reached the point of no return. She'd have to find an escape route, and quickly. She put on her coat and walked out of the front door without a word.

◆　　◆　　◆

Father and son repeated their tube scam several times over the next ten days, using different stations, including Highbury and Islington, Old Street, Kings Cross and Liverpool Street. Each night they collected their ten bob and then filled their suitcases in different locations on their way home, amongst them Dalston, Hornsey, Clapton and Harringay. They walked the soles off their shoes, but their new-found wealth meant that they could both afford a smart new pair of hard wearing, working boots.

The papers soon got wind of the distasteful tricks that George and others had got up to on the tube. They were called droppers and there was a public outcry for the government to do something about it. The Home Secretary acted promptly and instituted a ticketing system for sheltering in the Underground station. For George, Patrick and the rest of them, that was that.

Doris meanwhile was disposing of the stolen goods in markets and pubs. Romford seemed to be the best place and she made many tiring trips there on slow buses, frequently diverted because roads, badly affected by the bombing, were closed. Frustrating as these journeys were, they were very rewarding. She bought a sturdy metal cash box and hid it under the shed. The family treated themselves to new clothes and better and more plentiful food. Most purchases came from the black market.

The black market was flourishing, but the war wasn't going well. Essential goods being brought in by sea were frequently destroyed by attacks on what was left of the docklands' warehouses before they could be distributed. Many ships didn't even reach British ports, so successful were the German submarines in sinking them as they crossed the Atlantic. There were massive shortages and the black marketers became rich as they sold their mostly stolen goods to those who desperately needed them. In the area where the Wallaces lived, the black market was controlled by Gibson. The Irish gangster was keeping his eye on the Wallaces and thought they might be getting too big for their boots so he decided to pay them a visit and have a friendly chat. He didn't arrive alone. His companion was a small evil looking man in his forties with greasy black hair and a pencil moustache. He wasn't very tall, but dressed smartly; he had an air of menace about him.

"Come in, Mr Gibson, good to see you," said Doris, a nervous smile on her face. "I see you've brought a friend. 'E's welcome too."

Without a word, both men stepped into the sitting room and sat down. George and Doris were also seated, but there was no room for Patrick, so he lounged against the wall.

"So what can we do for you, Mr Gibson?" asked George.

Gibson looked at the two adults, then at Patrick before returning his icy gaze to Doris and George. He stared at them for what seemed to be an eternity. The man who had come with Gibson pulled out a wicked looking knife and started cleaning his nails. Gibson finally broke the silence.

"You're doing very nicely. New clothes, smart furniture. Win the pools did you?"

There was no satisfactory answer to that so, after a brief pause, Gibson continued.

"I heard you've been dropping at the tube stations. Pity the Home Secretary put a stop to that. I'm guessing that you called into a few empty houses on your way home. How did you do?"

George was staring at his feet and didn't look up as he mumbled an "alright" in reply to Gibson's question.

"Good, but remember, keep off my manor. If I find out you've been in houses round here, my friend Charlie here will have to come round and have a word with you."

Gibson glanced at his companion, whose nose was running. He sniffed several times and then wiped his nose on the sleeve of his jacket. When he finished, he resumed cleaning his nails, though it was a futile task as they were bitten to the core and, on the right hand, his fingers were stained with dark brown nicotine.

"Charlie doesn't say much and, as you can see, lacks certain social niceties, but he's good with that knife. You step out of line and he'll use it to cut off your boy's balls and then use the other tool of his trade to punish you two."

Charlie pulled a razor from his pocket.

"He'd chop your balls off too George, but you haven't got any. So you and Doris will have to make do with having your throats cut."

Doris managed to keep some sort of composure, but George and Patrick were terrified of the gangster and his hit man.

"You can be sure we won't tread on your toes, Mr Gibson. Is there anythin' we can 'elp you with?"

"Now that's the attitude, Doris. As a matter of fact there is. Tell me George, when your thieving from those houses that aren't on my patch, do you ever come across ration books, coupons and identity cards?"

"All the time, but we just leave 'em. We got no use for 'em."

"But I have, so, in future, take them with you and bring them to me. I'll give you a small sum for this service."

"Of course, Mr Gibson," said George. "Glad to be able to 'elp you."

"I could use the boy too, now and then. Being small he can get into places my men can't manage. Places like warehouses where food is kept and employment exchanges where they store coupons and so on. He'd be very handy distracting lorry drivers and give my men a chance to help themselves to the goodies on board."

Patrick looked at him and nodded.

"Good. Now George, there's just one more thing. I've got a few clients who don't much fancy trotting off to confront Hitler. When they're called up, they need some way of, how shall I put it? Opting out. Now I'm sure that a nasty little coward like you George will have a medical certificate that exempts you from serving King and country."

"I 'ave, Mr Gibson. Bad chest."

"And yellow liver no doubt. What my clients need is someone with a medical exemption to represent them at tribunals when they appeal against being called up to do their duty. They're mostly younger than you, so you'll have to make yourself up a bit."

Doris interrupted: "Just a minute, Mr Gibson. That certificate 'as got 'is name on."

"I bet its illegible scribble. I've never met a doctor yet whose writing you can read. Besides, he'll have a nice false identity card. It's a good job they don't put photographs on those. So he should be fine. I'm arranging all this for the poor desperate souls and my fee is £150 of which you'll get 50. Not bad, eh?"

"Yes. Very good, Mr Gibson. We 'ad thought of that, but didn't know any customers. When do I start?"

"When my clients are called up."

Gibson got up to leave, closely followed by Charlie who folded up his knife and returned it to his pocket.

"Good to do business with you George, and you, Doris. I'll be in touch. Oh yes! Another thing. They'll be a small fee for joining my organisation. Shall we say a fiver a week?

The Wallaces saw their unwelcome visitor out and then slumped into their chairs. They sat in silence for a while. Doris was the first to speak.

"Gawd, I 'ate 'im. We're just skivvies as far as 'e's concerned. I suppose we've got no choice but to do as 'e says."

"I don't fancy 'avin' me balls cut off mum."

"It won't come to that, Patrick," said George. "You can learn off someone like 'im. It'll 'elp you to set up your own business later on in life."

"Any'ow," said Doris, "we'll just do as 'e says, keep off 'is manor and bring in the cards and coupons 'e wants. We'll see what 'appens with the other jobs 'e mentioned."

◆   ◆   ◆

The bombing of London continued without any sign of the Germans letting up on their reign of terror. George and Patrick carried on burgling houses. They were doing so well that Doris couldn't shift the stuff fast enough. The hiding place in the shed was full to overflowing so they decided not to go out every night and went to the shelter instead. Angela was usually helping out at the rest centre, but, when all four family members were at home, they went to the shelter together. They hadn't heard from either Scott or Gibson. Angela often sheltered near to the rest centre and spent the weekends with her friend Pam. Having little to do with her family helped her to swallow her mounting dislike, even hatred, of them.

So far they'd been lucky. Bombs had fallen all around them in neighbouring boroughs, but not actually on them. All that changed in mid-October. The four Wallaces were in the shelter together when the raid started. It lasted for more than three hours. They knew little of what was going on outside, but everyone inside felt it was very bad. Bomb after bomb rained down on them. Every time there was an explosion the structure shook violently and those inside began to wonder how long it would remain standing, even without a direct hit. They could hear strange pinging noises outside and machine gun like thuds on the sandbags protecting the shelter. Women cried and children screamed. The heat inside became almost unbearable. One small boy panicked and rushed to escape through the steel door but, as he attempted to push it open, he let out an agonising howl of extreme pain. The door had turned into a kind of giant hot plate on which the skin of the palms of the boy's hands was gently sizzling.

Fortunately the all-clear soon sounded and the still horribly distressed boy and his equally upset mother were first out to rush and seek medical assistance. The rest of them emerged to find that their locality had been changed forever. Fires raged as far as the eye could see and the air was filled with dense black smoke. As they made their way home, not knowing whether their house was still standing, they saw people with torches burrowing in the rubble looking for people and possessions. Firemen were trying to douse the flames and stretcher bearers carefully rushed towards waiting ambulances which then raced away to the nearest hospital.

Their home was still intact. In fact, their area seemed to have escaped the worst of the raid and only a few windows had been blown out. Doris made tea which they drank in silence and then went to bed. The tireless Angela had gone to work when the other three struggled down for a late breakfast. At midday Doris left with a full suitcase. She was gone for just over two hours but, when she came back, she had with her an empty case and a pile of cash and looked a bit excited.

"The Rochester didn't get 'it so I sold everything there. Loads of people 'ad lost stuff in the raid. We got off lightly. Them ugly flats took it on the nose. Evidently, when there's a raid, they all go down in the cellar, but the flats took a direct 'it and the 'ole building collapsed on top of 'em. They're still tryin' to find people in the mess but, by all accounts, they've already come across more than an 'undred bodies. Seems that the gas mains broke and all the water and khazi pipes burst. Them that didn't get killed by fallin' bricks were either gassed or drowned. 'Orrible."

George asked, "It's mostly Jews wot live there, ain't it?

"I think so."

"That's all right then."

"I've kept the only piece of good news till last. Gibson was in the building when it got 'it. 'E's dead."

CHAPTER TWENTY

With Gibson out of the way, Doris and George were keen to expand their activities. They knew that the Irish gangster was so confident in his own powers of leadership and organisation that he didn't need a strong number two. His death left a vacuum amongst the north London criminal fraternity and everyone knew that months of squabbling within his entourage would follow before a new leader emerged. Doris even thought that she might be that person but preferred, for the time being, to take advantage of the decline of Gibson's empire to build her own. Good thing, she thought, George and Patrick wouldn't have to do those jobs that Gibson had lined them up for. Robbing vans and trucks didn't appeal to her and she doubted that her husband would have the guts to carry out tasks like that. On the other hand, making use of George's medical exemption certificate was attractive, but she didn't have any contacts. So she shelved that, though, she told herself, not necessarily permanently.

Meanwhile, Patrick was thinking about his own situation. He was almost seventeen and was starting to worry about his life to come. He was beginning to take an interest in girls and thought he'd prefer to be spending his time in the cinema, at the dance hall or exploring the mysteries of the young girls who'd caught his eye in the attractive darkness of the local park, rather than risking his life night after night dodging the bombs. He had some sympathy with Angela who seemed to be on the verge of breaking away from the family. Perhaps, he thought, he'd do the same. But Angela had a job and some money. He had no work or qualifications and could barely read or write. Besides, to have the kind of life he wanted, he needed money. At the moment he had it and he had bought new clothes and more cigarettes, which considerably enhanced his standing amongst the local tearaways, and he was beginning to attract the girls with these outward signs of prosperity. Patrick was terrified of his mother and shuddered to think what she might do if he chose to opt out of the family business. He decided it was wise to forget about the future, for a while at least.

Doris and George were happy. They had more money than at any time in their lives. The neat new house in the suburbs was no longer a pipe dream, but they had to keep on working to bring it closer to reality. Opportunities dramatically increased when Scott came up with the promised list of empty houses. There were plenty in the Wallaces' own area, no longer off limits thanks to Gibson's demise. But there were many further afield: in Harringay, Tottenham, Hornsey, Wood Green, Kentish Town and even Hampstead. Some of these were some distance away and George was fed up with the unreliability of the buses and the long treks. All three of them recognised that being on foot restricted the amount of goods they could pinch and then fetch back. They needed transport, so Doris suggested they steal a van.

None of them could drive and had no idea how to start a car without keys. Doris, in her travels in the North and East London underworld, knew of a garage in Dalston where they handled stolen vehicles. She went to see the owner, who was a plump red-faced guy called Les, and they did a deal. For fifty pounds, the owner would give George some basic driving lessons, teach him how to hot-wire a vehicle and give it a make-over after it had been stolen. George took the driving lessons. He was hopeless but, after ten days, Les pronounced him fit to take to the roads. He wasn't really ready, but the garage man couldn't care less. If George got killed he wouldn't give a hoot. He'd got his fifty quid. If, on the other hand, George came back with the van, he knew he'd have to complete his end of the bargain. He knew Doris of old and didn't think it sensible to double cross her.

A confident George waited until it was dark and then, one mid-November evening, set off with his son on the number 69 bus to Tottenham. He hoped to get back before the siren. He didn't fancy driving home with bombs dropping all around him. They started on the Tottenham High Road, where Patrick had made his debut as a bicycle thief. They were out of luck. There were one or two cars and a couple of trucks. The cars wouldn't be big enough to get much in and George didn't fancy trying to cope with handling a truck. They tried Lansdowne Road, but there was nothing doing there either. They wandered through the narrow streets between Lansdowne Road and Church Road, trudging the pavements continuously for about half an hour before, at last, they found what they were looking for; a small dark van parked in Argyle Road. Patrick, using the skills he learned outside bookies and brothels, acted as lookout, while his nervous father walked up to the van and smashed the driver's side window with a brick he'd picked up. He reached inside to open the door and slid into the seat. All this went very smoothly but, to Patrick at least, the next part was painfully slow. Eventually the engine spluttered into life and they set off. George was panicking and he forgot all he'd learned during his lessons and the car jumped down the street before eventually stalling at the corner. George had to re-start, expecting shouts of pursuit any minute, but nothing happened, so they set off again. Belatedly, George remembered to put on the lights and then spotted that the fuel gauge was low. He wasn't sure they'd make it home.

It was a cold evening, but he was sweating profusely. The sirens went off as they were approaching Stamford Hill, but the Germans were concentrating their efforts elsewhere and they limped home without further mishap. Doris was waiting for them.

"Got one then? Good stuff."

"It was a bit 'airy and we're nearly out of petrol. Not sure if I can make it to the garage tomorrer."

"Don't worry. Me and the boy'll go down to Les's garage first thing and buy a can. It'll cost a bit, but we can afford it. I'll ask the bloke if we can 'ide the motor in 'is yard. It's not safe 'ere. Some toe-rag might nick it. When we come back with the juice, you can drive it down there."

Then the three of them left for the shelter. There was no sign of Angela.

◆   ◆   ◆

Doris and Patrick set off after breakfast and re-appeared with a can of petrol an hour later. She told her husband that Les had agreed to look after the van for a couple of pounds a week. George drove it to the garage. In the daylight he could see it was dark green. Les said he would spray it black, remove the engine and chassis numbers, fit new number plates and sort out the ignition so they could use a key.

Doris now took over full control of the planning side of the business. She closely examined Scott's list of empty houses and ordered her menfolk to drive to Hampstead where she was sure they'd find rich pickings. She was right. When they returned the van was crammed full of furs, rugs, jewels, a radio and a vacuum cleaner.

"There were some expensive lookin' paintins'," said George, "but I left 'em. I 'aven't got a clue 'ow we'd shift 'em."

"That's fine. Yer right. Now I've bin doin' a bit of askin' round. Seem's the war's caused a shortage of toys and I've found a new place to get rid of decent fresh and tinned food. 'Ouses where people 'ave left London are no good for grub obviously, so you'll 'ave to look out for decent places and do 'em when the siren goes off. Some of 'em shelter in cellars so watch out!"

The bombs kept dropping and the Wallaces kept thieving. Sometimes they stole from empty houses in Hampstead and other wealthy areas, and at other times they restricted themselves to emptying gas and electricity meters nearer to home. They successfully burgled a couple of places where the residents slept in their cellars and Doris filled the suitcases with decent food and set off to the West End with Patrick. George asked her where she'd been.

"Gettin' shot of that food down west. The restaurants are rationed like the rest of us. They pay well for decent food and they're not bothered where it comes from."

Business was booming and they didn't have to put up with lectures from Angela because she was hardly ever at home. She'd either shelter in Wood Green or spend time at Pam's house. She put in an occasional appearance to wash and collect clothes. Nobody spoke to her and she didn't speak to them. This suited all of them fine. They didn't care for her and she didn't care for them. She was, however, a bit worried about her brother. Patrick was slowly turning into a sort of mini version of his mother. He was confident and surly. In direct contrast to the ragamuffin of six months earlier, he was now a smartly dressed and cocky young hooligan. Angela was worried that, if he didn't break away from this existence soon, he'd be condemned to a life of crime and all the misery that came with it.

The van and the death of Gibson meant that George and Doris were having the time of their lives. If they weren't working, they were usually in the pub. The beer may have been watered down and spirits in short supply, but they had cash to burn and they doubled their weekly alcohol intake. Doris switched to Craven A cigarettes and George to Players as further evidence of their new found wealth. The regulars in the pub remarked on their smart clothes. Everybody knew where their money was coming from but an unwritten local law forbade any whispering to the coppers. Besides, they had their very own policeman, Scott, and he made regular visits to their house to collect his cut.

George and the boy continued to make regular visits to the more well-heeled areas but soon their activities, and those of other thieves, put householders on the alert and the returns from their outings became sparser and sparser.

Doris noticed this and suggested a change in strategy.

"Now that Gibson's out the way, it's time we started doin' one or two 'ouses round 'ere."

"Yeah," said Patrick, "and the first place we should 'ave a go at is them bastard Jews round the corner."

"What Jews?" asked George.

Feeling rather sheepish, Patrick told his parents about his run-in with Jonathan and the subsequent loss of his knife.

"What!" exclaimed Doris. "You let a Jew get the better of yer?"

"'E was a big sod and the two with me scarpered as soon as 'e went for us. He knew 'ow to use 'is fists. Anyow I kept a sharp look-out for 'im, so I know where 'e lives."

"Seems like we owe 'em one," said George, "specially as they're Jews. You sure their 'ouse is empty?" he asked his son. Before Patrick could answer, Doris told them both there was only one way to find out and that was to go around and check for themselves.

◆　　◆　　◆

The Wallaces weren't unusual in their dislike of the Jews. Before the war plenty in the East End resented their presence, suggesting that they were taking jobs that should have been for English people. The fact that many Jews had been here since the last century didn't seem to occur to them. Some people also blamed the blitz on the Jews, claiming that Hitler was deliberately targeting the docks because he knew that there were thousands of Jews living there.

◆   ◆   ◆

In late November they decided to pay a visit to the Gerber house. It was in complete blackout darkness and was certainly unoccupied. Benjamin and Jonathan were on the Isle of Man and Ruth was staying with Reg and Mary Martin. The rear fence did not present a problem and the two of them scaled it without difficulty. Patrick broke the back kitchen window and clambered in and then opened the back door to let his father in. They put the blackout curtains back in place and switched their torches on. The kitchen was empty. There was no sign of pots, pans, plates or cutlery. In the other rooms on the ground floor the furniture was covered in dust sheets. It was the same upstairs. There wasn't a single item worth stealing. Bombs were falling about five miles away and the noise was considerable but, in the cellar, all they could hear were muffled thumps.

"That ceilin' must be thick. I can't 'ear a thing down 'ere," whispered George.

"They probably 'aven't been 'ere since the raids started," added Patrick. They went back to the ground floor.

"Let's smash the place up," said Patrick, thinking this would be some kind of revenge on Jonathan.

"'Ang on a bit," replied George. "The fact that's there's nothin' 'ere means they've got plenty of value to 'ide. Yer mother read in The Mirror they're releasin' some of them German Jews. They could be back soon and they'll bring their stuff with 'em. Then we'll do 'em. I bet they'll shelter in their cellar," continued George. "That ceiling's so thick they'll never 'ear us movin' about. While they're down there nice and cosy, we'll be quietly nickin' their stuff."

"What about the wind'er?" asked Patrick. "Won't they know someone's bin in?"

"Naw. They'll think it got blasted out in the raids. Smash a couple more so's it looks like bomb blast."

Patrick did as he was told and they went home and reported to Doris. She said George had shown some common sense for once when he stopped Patrick from breaking the place up. She said that people who'd left their houses were cottoning on to the risk of leaving possessions and valuables there and were taking them with them. Doris suggested a new tactic.

"You two need to be on the spot as soon as the bombs 'ave dropped. Nobody'll know what's goin' on. They'll be too busy rescuin' people and puttin' the fires out to notice you slippin' in."

"Blimey, Doris. We've already nearly been blown up in one raid. I don't fancy this."

"Don't be stupid. See where the raid is and drive there as soon as it's finished. There's always a gap between the droppin' of the last bomb and the all-clear. That's when yer do the business."

This wasn't an original idea from Doris. She'd read about these "bomb chasers" in the newspapers and she wanted a piece of the action. Two nights later, George spotted a big raid in nearby Hackney. They drove to the scene, arriving just after the last German plane had shed its load and headed back across the channel. The emergency services were everywhere and the Wallaces weren't noticed as they made their way through streets full of damaged houses behind Homerton High Street. Doors and windows had been blown in and access was easy. They were rummaging about when a voice disturbed them.

"Oi, what you up to?"

It was pretty dark despite the flames and the light from the unwelcome guest's torch and this enabled George to slip away through the back door into the yard where he jumped over the wall and sprinted down the narrow lane between the rows of houses. Patrick wasn't as lucky. He set off in the same direction as his father, but caught his leg on the remains of a table in the kitchen and fell flat on his face. Immediately he tried to scramble to his feet but he felt a strong hand gripping his neck and he couldn't move.

"Now then yer little bleeder, yer nicked."

Patrick looked up and saw a black tin helmet with POLICE in white letters painted across the front. The officer had him in a vice-like grip and Patrick knew that there was no chance of escape.

George arrived breathless back at his van. His hands were shaking but somehow he managed to unlock the door, turn the key in the ignition, pull out the choke, start the van and get away. He reached home just after the all-clear had sounded.

"Where's Patrick?" asked Doris.

"Coppers got 'im."

Doris couldn't believe what she'd heard. She shouted at her husband.

"And you left 'im there?"

"Look Doris, I know it looks bad, but I thought quick. If I'd been took, I'd 'ave got ten years. You know 'ow the courts are 'ammerin' looters. What would you 'ave done wiv me banged up for ten years? The boy'll probably get off, first offence an all that."

"Where is 'e?"

"Dunno. 'Ackney cop shop I expect."

"As soon as it's light, you can drive me there. Keep out of the way. I'll go in and find out what's goin' on. Yer'd better pray 'e's all right."

The police were too busy dealing with the aftermath of the raid to trouble themselves with Patrick, so they locked him in a cell for the last hour of the night. They told him he'd be in court later in the morning and that most likely he'd be sent to borstal. The boy was really frightened and sat in the cell worrying and waiting. He was given some foul tasting tea just after eight. The policeman who'd arrested him appeared and told him to admit everything to the magistrates, because then he might get a shorter spell in borstal. He'd been caught red handed. There was no point in denying it. He was asked to give his name and address and he tearfully confirmed that they were the same as the details he'd given to the desk sergeant when he'd arrived at the station. He was asked if anyone was with him in the bombed house. He said no. Then he sat and waited.

Meanwhile Doris had arrived. Her husband had made himself scarce. She asked if Patrick was in the station and was told he was. She was refused permission to speak to him, but told to be in the nearby juvenile court at ten. Here, she was informed, she could speak to the court solicitor appointed to look after Patrick's interests.

Doris cut a splendid figure of a woman in the court. She was expensively dressed and had taken some considerable trouble with her appearance. She told the solicitor that Patrick was a fine boy and that this was the first time he'd been in trouble. She blamed the war for him going off the rails. There was a long list of defendants and it wasn't until after twelve that Patrick was ushered into the dock. He looked thoroughly miserable, but was relieved to see his mother. The charge of burglary of a bombed property was read out. Patrick admitted that he'd done it. The solicitor told the magistrates that Patrick was normally a very well behaved boy and the offence was completely out of character. He mentioned that the boy's mother was in court to support him, but that his father was absent as he was engaged on war relief work near to his home.

There were two magistrates, both men. They listened to the solicitor's statement and then retired to consider their verdict. It took them ten minutes. When they returned, one of them, a tall thin man with grey hair and a matching suit who looked like a bank manager, told Patrick to stand up. Patrick looked, and was, petrified, as he got to this feet.

"Patrick Wallace. You've admitted that you've committed a disgusting crime. I should send you to borstal. This is, however, your first offence and you wasted neither the time of the police nor the court in denying the charge. You clearly have strong and loving parental support. Nevertheless, an offence as disgraceful as this cannot go unpunished. You will be taken back to the police station where you will receive six strokes of the birch. If you appear before the court again, you will be sent to borstal for a very long time. Do you understand?"

Patrick smiled inwardly. The birch. That was nothing. "Yes sir. Thank you sir."

He was taken back to the police station. Doris thanked the solicitor and accompanied her son to the station, where she was told to wait for him near the front desk.

Two police officers were waiting for Patrick when he was taken to a room near to the cells. A table stood in the middle of the room. On it was the birch, a collection of thin twigs bound together by what seemed to be a leather handle about a foot long. Patrick wondered how he would be punished and was relieved when he was told to stand at the end of the table, place his chest and stomach on the surface and stretch his arms out in front of him. One officer held him down, taking care to keep his legs together so that his genitals weren't struck during the birching. The other officer struck him hard across the buttocks six times. It hurt Patrick a lot more than he thought it would, but he clenched his teeth and accepted his punishment without sound or tear. He was told to stand up. His backside felt as if it was on fire. He gingerly followed the policeman back to the front of the station where his mother was waiting for him. They left the station in silence.

"You alright?" Doris asked.

"It 'urts a bit. Where we goin'?"

"Yer father's parked the van about five minutes walk away."

"'E scarpered as soon as the copper arrived. Left me right in it."

"I know, but if 'e'd stayed and the two of you 'ad fought the copper off and then got caught, 'e'd 'ave got ten years and you'd 'ave bin sent off to borstal."

Patrick wasn't convinced of this, but he kept quiet as he limped towards where the van was parked, climbed into the back and lay on his stomach to take the pressure off his stinging buttocks. The journey home passed in complete silence.

Patrick stood in the sitting room while his parents sat down and talked about what had happened.

"We'll 'ave to keep our 'eads down for a while" said Doris. They'll be keepin an eye on you, we'll 'ave to think again. I don't want you two locked up. What would I do if that 'appened? We're pretty well off at the minute and there's no sign of the Jerries letting up. There'll be plenty more opportunities to line our pockets."

◆   ◆   ◆

The Germans did provide these opportunities. They continued to attack London every night, except on those rare occasions when thick cloud cover kept them at home. The blitz was the real battle of Britain as the almost defenceless citizens faced death and destruction night after night. The size of the raids varied. Sometimes there were hundreds of planes and at others just a handful. The Luftwaffe now added the Northern and Scottish ports and the industrial cities of the Midlands to its list of targets. Coventry was particularly badly hit.

The battle of the Atlantic was going badly as hundreds of tons of ships laden with food and war materials were sent to the bottom of the sea every day. The Italian dictator Mussolini, always looking for a soft target, sent his army into Greece. Almost every country in Northern and Western Europe was under Nazi control, except neutral countries like Switzerland and Sweden. The outlook looked very bleak indeed, but at least the threat of invasion appeared to have receded for the time being as the winter weather made seaborne landings impossible. Prime Minister Churchill continued to urge Britain to stand firm. And she did.

CHAPTER TWENTY-ONE

The Blitz went on and on. The bombs kept dropping. Houses, factories, warehouses, cinemas, shops, cafés and public buildings were destroyed. Hundreds of civilians were killed and thousands of them were made homeless. Many members of the emergency services died and countless others were injured. German planes were shot down but most escaped the net and poured death and destruction on the Londoners. There was no sign of a let up, but neither was there any sign that morale would collapse. Many chose to ignore the raids altogether. Instead of sheltering in the gloom and damp, dozens seemed indifferent to the threats from above and slept in their own beds. The picture houses were packed, the pubs, cafés and restaurants full and the night clubs busy. The absence of good food and drink didn't make a scrap of difference to the night-lifers who remained steadfast in their determination to wave two fingers at the Luftwaffe.

But the Wallaces were gloomy. Patrick's recent run-in with the law had left him in fear of being caught again because he knew what that would mean. When George went into the West End to resume his pick-pocketing career, he went alone. Sometimes he stayed until well after dark. The blackout and the confusion that accompanied the raids gave him plenty of opportunities to return home each night with his pockets stuffed full of wallets and purses. Doris kept a close eye on the budget and, although she was a long way short of being satisfied with their income, George was keeping it ticking over and they were reasonably comfortably off. This pleased Patrick because he could now follow some kind of risk-free existence without the shadow of borstal hanging over his every move. At the back of his mind, however, he knew this wouldn't last.

The boy spent his days playing football with his friends. There were often girls watching and one of them, pretty with short blonde hair, caught his eye. She was just a little bit younger than him and was called Rose. She lived nearby. Their relationship began with sharing cigarettes and small talk after the football had finished and then developed into trips to the cinema. Those evenings usually began with an old cowboy film, followed by the adverts, the news and the trailers. The main film that followed was sometimes a flag-waving war film and at others a comedy to cheer up the audience. Patrick and Rose couldn't care less what was going on because, by the time the feature started, they were fully engaged with kissing and fondling each other on the back row. On the evenings when they weren't at the pictures, they had fun in the local park. Before the war, parks had closed at dusk, but the railings and fences had been taken away to become tanks or other machinery of war. The two youngsters joined dozens of others in the darkness, behind trees and bushes, where moans of pleasure, slaps and shouted warnings of "don't do that" and "keep yer 'ands to yerself" were frequently heard. Patrick was happy. Could it last?

Angela returned home from time to time. She sometimes slept there overnight or joined the others in the shelter, but was usually gone by morning. Once or twice she stayed longer, usually at weekends, to do her washing, but then she vanished for days on end. When she was there, she had little to say to her parents and they mostly ignored her. Her mother told her that the money might be getting short and her father suggested she went back on the game. She ignored them both and walked out of the house.

The financial pressure on George and Doris was mounting. They were nowhere near the breadline, but they'd got used to a good life and were finding it hard to adapt to their ordinary existence. Things weren't helped by another unwelcome visit from Scott. He arrived one early December morning, made himself at home and told them that he wasn't happy.

"Mrs Scott's still goin' on at me about money."

"Well, we're a bit short ourselves," said Doris.

"Why's that?"

"We've 'ad a bit a bad luck and Patrick was birched."

"I 'eard about that. What difference does that make?"

"'E thinks if it 'appens again, 'e'll get locked up."

"That's the risk yer take in your game. I think it's time to get goin' again."

George was looking fed up and stared at the floor. Doris stared at Scott who moved to the edge of his chair and said to Doris in an angry voice.

"Now look 'ere, you two, I can see to it that word gets to my colleagues that you've been up to no good. Then you'll be right in it."

"What about you?" shouted Doris. "You'll be joinin' us be'ind bars when I've 'ad my say."

"They'll never believe you. A good, honest cop like me on the take? Leave it out, Doris."

Doris thought for a moment and then realised that Scott was probably right. "Drink yer tea, Mr Scott. It'll get cold."

Scott sipped his tea, pulled a face and made a sound of disgust.

"This tea tastes like cat's piss. Where's the sugar?"

"Ain't got any," said Doris. "There's 'ardly any about and what there is costs a fortune on the black market."

"There's yer answer then. Nick a load, flog most of it and keep a bit fer yerself. Everyone's 'appy then, includin' Mrs Scott."

"Where we gonna get it?" asked George, suddenly coming to life.

"There's warehouses full of the stuff and loads more in the railway goods yards. Kings Cross might be a good spot."

Doris could see the sense in this. If they could get hold of a van full of sugar, she could flog most of it to the restaurants in the West End and keep enough for themselves to last a long time.

"All right, Mr Scott, we'll give it a go. George, you'll 'ave to take Patrick."

"'E's useless. Found out that what's between 'is legs isn't just fer peein' out of. 'E's out every night."

"Well, you'll just 'ave to tell 'im to keep is trousers buttoned up fer one evenin'. I'll leave it with yer."

The three of them chatted about the Blitz. Doris said she was glad that the daytime raids had stopped and Scott explained that the Germans were terrified of the Spitfires and Hurricanes, neither of which were effective at night.

◆   ◆   ◆

Patrick was furious when his father told him he had to help steal a van full of sugar. He made it clear that he didn't want anything more to do with thieving. George's response was pretty feeble, but Doris left her son in no doubt that, if he didn't do as he was told, she'd kick him out of the house with just the clothes he stood up in.

Reluctantly, Patrick sat in the passenger seat in the van as his father drove towards Kings Cross just as it was getting dark. They parked up and strolled cautiously around, taking note of the location of the goods yards and buildings, the lack of security and the easy access to the sheds. George made a mental note to bring some tools for dealing with padlocks. They drove home, made their plans and set off the following night to do the job.

George parked the van in York Place. They were walking along the road when the bombers came. Luckily for them, Kings Cross was some distance from the explosions and they were able to scale the fence into the yard without interruption. George smashed the lock on the side door of the largest shed and they stepped inside, torches at the ready. The found themselves in a vast area piled high with boxes and sacks. It took them half an hour to locate the sugar. The sacks were extremely heavy and they began to sweat as they lowered them to the floor.

"God, they weigh a ton," whispered a clearly distressed George.

"We'll only manage two," replied his son.

"It'll 'ave to be enough. Come on."

It was back-breaking stuff and it took them almost half-an-hour, with several stops to rest, to manoeuvre them to the foot of the fence. It would have been quicker if they'd made two trips with one of them at each end of a sack, but neither had the brains to think of that. Patrick stared up at the fence.

"'Ow are we gonna get this lot over that?"

"No bloody idea."

"What about that gate over there."

"Didn't know it was there. I'll go and sort the lock out."

When George returned, Patrick asked him why they hadn't come in that way instead of scrambling over the fence.

"Never saw it."

Another fifteen minutes of struggle ended when they loaded the sacks into the van with a sigh of relief. Apart from the bombing in the distance, it was a quiet night and nobody was about to disturb them. The cafés and shops were shut and the locals were either in the shelters or tucked up behind the blackout curtains in their homes. George drove the van back to north London.

"'Ow much did yer get?" asked Doris when they reached home.

"Couple o' sacks," replied George.

"That's not much."

"If we'd 'ave 'ad Tarzan with us, we could 'ave fetched more."

A resigned look on Doris' face indicated that she accepted this. She went outside to the van and came back and told the two of them to lock it in the shed. She said that the next day she would split it up into smaller bags. She thought she'd need four journeys to the West End to sell it at the restaurants.

"Perhaps you could make another trip," she suggested.

"I ain't goin' again," shouted Patrick.

"I've told yer before, yer ain't got much choice in the matter. Yer'll do as yer bleedin' well told," Doris said, glowering threateningly at her son.

◆   ◆   ◆

Doris made several outings to the West End and made a lot of money from unscrupulous restaurant owners. She steered clear of the bigger establishments. These were already being supplied by organised gangs. Things were looking up again. She didn't keep any sugar for the family, reckoning they didn't need it after making do without. Patrick returned to learning the facts of life and George went back to picking pockets in Piccadilly. He returned one day very excited. Patrick was out but Doris was all ears as he told her about his day.

"Shops 'ave been 'it everywhere; Oxford Street, Regent Street, Bond Street, Piccadilly, just about every street in London. Some's a pile of rubble like John Lewis, but there's plenty standing and most of 'em are still open."

"So?"

"That's the point, they're open. 'Arf of 'em ain't got no doors or winders so, as soon as the staff shut up shop for the night, people'll are wanderin' in and 'elping' 'emselves."

"Pull the other one, George. If people're 'elping themselves, why do they bother openin' the next day? There'll be bugger all left to sell."

This seemed to confuse George and he scratched his head in thought for a few seconds.

"What I mean is, er, they go in there just after the raids, just like we do with the 'ouses."

"Don't sound too promisin' to me but, go on then give it a try. You'll 'ave to take the boy to 'elp you load up the van, but that's no problem. 'E'll do as I tell 'im."

Thoroughly fed up, Patrick joined his father on the first of these outings. When they reached London's shopping streets, they had a big disappointment. Those shops that hadn't been damaged were very secure. The managers of those that had suffered strengthened the security pretty impressively with temporary boarding up and dozens of emergency police patrolled the streets. To top it all, the West End had had a night's respite from the bombing and so there were no newly damaged shops to ransack. They went home empty handed to be received by an irate Doris who ordered them to persist until an opportunity arose.

Their second visit, three days later, looked like proving to be another waste of time. They parked the van in Bloomsbury and made their way to Marble Arch. There were no bombs and plenty of security but then, shortly after ten, the planes came. At first, they seemed to be dropping their loads some distance to the west but then, as Patrick and George made their way towards Oxford Circus, they could hear the roar of enemy engines overhead. The noise was so loud, it even drowned out the constant pounding of the AA guns. They decided to shelter and raced for Oxford Circus Underground but, before they could reach it, there was a terrifying whistle followed by a huge explosion about two hundred yards to the north. The pair of them were knocked off their feet, but they got up relatively unscathed and guessed that the bomb had dropped somewhere near the BBC. The threat from the air was still there and a second, smaller, bomb crashed to earth only about one hundred yards behind them in Soho. Then the planes flew off, leaving only the receding drone of their engines, the ever present anti-aircraft fire and the noise of war; bells, shouts, explosions and the crackle of blazing buildings.

"Come on," said George. "Let's 'ave a butchers."

"It ain't safe," pleaded Patrick.

"Course it is. The Jerries 'ave gone."

"Let's go 'ome, dad."

"In a minute. I wanna see what's 'appened in Soho."

It didn't take them long to find the scene of the second bomb. A three-storey building, not far from the seedy nightclub The Blue Lagoon had taken a direct hit. The ground floor had been occupied by a smart restaurant and night club from which came belching black smoke, bright orange flames and the sounds of moans and screams.

"Please, let's go," said Patrick.

"'Ang on. Keep watch by the door while I pop in and 'ave a look round."

Patrick, feeling that this might be his last day on earth, did as he was told and watched as his father cautiously picked his way in. The smoke was thick but Patrick could get some idea of the scene of devastation inside. Smashed tables were lying on their side and mangled iron chairs littered the floor. There was food all over the room; on the floors, walls, ceilings and covering the diners who were sprawled everywhere. The back of the restaurant was on fire and George carefully avoided the flames as he picked his way across the dead, dying and seriously injured lying on the floor.

In the light created by the fire, Patrick could see the horrendous detail of it all. Some were lying deathly still and were probably dead. Several of the corpses had their heads missing and amongst the mass on the floor there were men and women without limbs. Everyone appeared to be drenched in blood. Patrick watched, transfixed in horror, as his father began to search pockets and handbags. He stuffed wallets, purses, cigarette lighters, gold cigarette cases and compacts, broaches, bracelets and rings, as well as loose cash, into his pockets. Twice George failed to remove tight fitting rings from fingers so he used his knife to cut them off, which he thrust into his pocket.

It became all too much for Patrick. His gorge rose at the sight of his father behaving like an animal and he was violently sick. The smoke swallowed him up and he was fighting for breath as a violent coughing fit seized him. George was also attacked by the smoke and edged his way to the exit where he found his son doubled up with coughing spasms and kneeling in a pool of his own vomit. He picked him up and dragged him back on to Oxford Street. The pair of them coughed their way across Tottenham Court Road back to Bedford Square where they'd left the van. They found it OK, but it was just a twisted heap of smouldering steel.

"What we gonna do now?" screamed Patrick.

"Catch the bus or walk. What else?"

Both of their chests were still suffering from the effects of the smoke, but it gradually eased as they staggered past the British Museum onto Russell Square and then up to Euston Road via Woburn Place. They made it as far as Kings Cross before George decided that they had to rest. They joined hundreds of others crammed into the narrow corridor outside the station toilets. Neither slept. Patrick was trembling from head to toe and George daren't nod off in case anybody tried to rifle his pockets while he was asleep.

The all-clear sounded at six and they emerged into a still dark blazing London, smouldering in the cold December dawn. The buses were doing their best, but there were so many diversions to avoid damaged streets and buildings that it took almost two hours for them to reach home. Doris was horrified when they walked in. Their clothes were filthy and torn, their faces black and George's hair was singed. Her concern turned to delight as George began to empty his pockets.

"My lovely boys," she beamed. "There's enough 'ere to keep us goin' for a bit. You can both 'ave a well-earned rest."

Patrick was stone faced. He didn't show a flicker of emotion.

"Come on, Patrick," said his mother. "You'll soon feel better. I'll make us some breakfast and then we'll go to the matinee at the pictures. There's a cowboy film at the Majestic called *The Dark Command*. John Wayne and Roy Rogers 're in it."

◆   ◆   ◆

The Pathé Newsreel before the main film at the Majestic reported that the war had taken an interesting, if hardly conclusive, turn. The Italians had been given a bloody nose in Greece and were now retreating into Albania, a weak country they'd seized for no apparent reason just before the war. Mussolini's brave soldiers had also begun an offensive in North Africa, pushing towards the Suez Canal, which they wanted to grab.

The newsreel also mocked the Italians and said that they made wonderful ice-cream, cooked fine food and played a good game of football, but they were useless soldiers. Given the choice, the vast majority of them would have preferred to have been enjoying excellent food and wine in their fine temperate country. They poked fun at the blustering, bullying Italian dictator Benito Mussolini who had set his heart on conquest, like a modern-day Roman Emperor, and needed to impress his ally and partner-in-crime, Adolf Hitler. So off to war they went, but their hearts weren't in it and soon thousands of their finest were languishing behind barbed wire in temporary British Prisoner of War camps in the North African desert. It was, at least, some good news for Britain and her Empire. A film clip from the North African desert showed hundreds of Italian prisoners of war being marched off into captivity by a handful of British soldiers.

◆   ◆   ◆

Doris slowly traded in the loot from George's restaurant and night club robbery. The Jewish fence she dealt with drove a hard bargain. Some of the black marketers were Jewish as well and were charging ever-increasing prices for their goods, as shortages began to bite. There were constant mutterings about the Jews in the pubs, mostly about black market prices, but also asking why they weren't in the services. Of course, there were bad Jews as well as bent coppers but the vast majority were honest, hard-working people. But this didn't matter to Doris and George. They hated them and regularly said awful things about them in front of Patrick, who was slowly recovering from his trauma and had taken up, once again, with Rose. Nothing would persuade him to resume his life of crime and his mind was made up that, the next time his father asked him to go thieving with him, he'd refuse.

A couple of weeks into December, Patrick was walking home for his tea before meeting Rose when he spotted a familiar figure walking towards him. It was Jonathan. Immediately, his blood was up as he recalled his humiliation at being disarmed by the German Jew before he'd been sent away with the other German Jewish refugees.

As the two closed in on each other, Jonathan appeared to Patrick to be some kind of giant. He thrust his hands deep into his pockets and stared at his shoes, avoiding eye contact with the German. Jonathan, belatedly recognising Patrick, stared at him with disdain. The two passed each other without incident but Patrick swore to himself that he'd do one last job with his father. He scampered off quickly, taking a brief glance over his shoulder. He saw Jonathan entering the house they'd found empty on their last visit. They'd return here, steal everything in it that could be moved and then wreck the rest of the place, ruining the Jews' lives forever.

PART FIVE

Retribution: December 1940

An eye for an eye and the whole
world would be blind.
KAHIL GIBRAN

Richard and the Gerbers might just have heard a faint siren at six o'clock, but they didn't. The cellar was so well insulated from noise that they slept until some-time past first light.

"We should be safe here," Ruth said when all four of them were awake.

"Unless a bomb drops right on top of us," replied Benjamin.

Richard told them that some people were sleeping in their bedrooms throughout the raids.

"They're doubling the risk. The blast from a bomb hitting an adjacent building could kill them. If the house next door to yours gets hit, you'll be safer in the cellar."

Richard left after breakfast. Benjamin walked down to the High Street to use the public phone box to call the Post Office and let them know that he'd like their telephone re-connected. Ruth and Jonathan unpacked their suitcases and began to prepare the house to be lived-in once again.

Benjamin returned an hour later, accompanied by a small pasty-faced man in working clothes who was introduced as Ken, the local glazier. Ruth made him a cup of tea while he measured up the empty window frames. While he drank his tea, he told them that he was replacing broken windows virtually every hour of every day. He drank up, said he'd be back in two days to fit the glass and then left.

After he'd gone, the three of them sat down to plan their next steps.

"It's going to be difficult," said Ruth, "but we should try to live as normal a life as possible."

"Do you think I should go back to helping Reg?" asked Benjamin.

"Of course," his wife replied, "and as soon as possible."

"I'd like to go back to school, if they'll have me," said Jonathan. "I've almost managed to keep up with my studies. I hope there won't be any problems."

"I'm sure there won't," his father agreed. "You should go down there tomorrow, tell them you're back and ask if and when you can start attending school again. You don't need us to come with you."

"Right," replied Jonathan. "I'll set off first thing in the morning."

"I'll do the shopping," said Ruth. "You two better get used to some unpleasant surprises. While you've been living it up on the Isle of Man, the Germans have been sinking ships in the Atlantic and bombing warehouses to bits. There's not a vast amount of food and what there is won't be what you've been used to for the past five months."

"I'd rather be here with you two eating rotten food than living it up on the Isle of Man, as you put it," said Jonathan.

"The food's not rotten," protested Ruth. "It's just, well, er, ordinary. Anyway, get your coats on. We need to get down to the police station to register and then find out where we can sort out new ration cards."

The rest of the day was spent doing these jobs and, after a modest evening meal, they listened to the radio before returning to the cellar for the night. Jonathan set off for the City first thing. The journey was trickier than in the last summer before the war. He was seeing the ruined landscape of London for the first time. Familiar landmarks had gone, whilst others were damaged almost beyond recognition. Some vast areas had been totally cleared, leaving large open spaces in one of the most densely populated cities on earth. Elsewhere, there were piles of rubble and craters in the road. Whole streets had been cordoned off to keep the citizens away from buildings in danger of collapse and UXBs. Jonathan stared open-mouthed at the devastation, which seemed to get worse the nearer he got to Kings Cross.

His journey suffered from numerous diversions, so he decided to get off at Kings Cross and walk the rest of the way. Unbeknownst to him, he followed much of the route that Patrick had taken in September: down Grays Inn Road to Chancery Lane and Middle Temple Lane, and on to the Embankment. With every step he took, he saw more evidence of the havoc that the Luftwaffe had wreaked on London. Some buildings had gone forever while others, including many dating back hundreds of years, seemed so severely damaged that they might never rise again.

Jonathan was relieved to find the school still standing but then, he thought, it was strangely quiet. There was no sign of life outside in the yard and none of the rooms had lights on, despite the fact that it was a gloomy day. He tried the main door and found it open. A quick glance around told him that most of the rooms were deserted. However, he could hear a faint voice from one of the offices. He approached it cautiously and tapped on the door. For a minute or so there was no response and then a woman's voice invited him to come in. He entered and saw a very efficient-looking elderly lady, her hair tied in a neat grey bun, sitting behind a desk.

"I'm so sorry to have kept you standing outside, but I was speaking on the telephone. How can I help you?"

Jonathan explained who he was, where he'd been and that he wanted to return to the school as soon as possible.

"I'm Miss Allen," she told him. "I'm just here holding the fort for the Headmaster. The school was evacuated to the country in early October and is now sharing with a public boarding school in Wiltshire. Obviously, I'm not in a position to say whether or not you can return to the school."

Jonathan looked crestfallen, but she quickly lifted his spirits.

"I'll telephone the Headmaster now and ask him if he'd like to speak to you."

Jonathan thanked her as she picked up the phone and asked the operator to put her though. Her call was answered at the other end and she asked to be put through to the Headmaster of the London school. The Head was soon on the line.

"Mr Lawton. It's Miss Allen here. I've Jonathan Gerber here with me."

"Good heavens! Please put him on, Miss Allen."

Jonathan took the phone and uttered a tentative "hallo" into the mouthpiece.

"Gerber," said Mr Lawton. "How wonderful to hear from you. How are you?"

Jonathan told him that he was fine and that he had been interned, but was now free. He reported that he had done his best to keep up with his studies and would now like to return to school to complete them as soon as possible.

"Miss Allen will have told you we're down in Wiltshire now. Will that be a problem?

"I don't think so, sir, but I'll have to ask my parents."

"Of course. Make a note of the number and call me back tomorrow. If your parents approve, you can return here after the Christmas holiday. You know, Gerber, they've been very kind to us here, but their boys tend to look down on ours a bit. It would be nice to put one over them on the sports field and your presence would certainly increase that possibility."

Jonathan chuckled. "I'd like to help with that, sir. I'll call you tomorrow."

With his business satisfactorily concluded, Jonathan thanked Miss Allen and left. It was a dry day so he decided to take a long walk. He set off along the Embankment at a decent pace, walked up Villiers Street and then stopped for lunch at the Strand Corner House. Afterwards, he crossed Trafalgar Square, noting with pleasure that Nelson's Column was still intact, and then continued to Oxford Circus via the Haymarket and Regent Street. He jumped on a Piccadilly Line train at Oxford Circus, got off at Kings Cross and then completed the journey by bus.

It was dark by the time he reached home and, as he walked along his road, he spotted someone loitering outside his front door. On closer inspection, he recognised Patrick. The Wallace boy didn't spot Jonathan until it was too late and he had a nasty shock when his nemesis spoke to him from less than ten yards away.

"What do you want?" Jonathan asked.

Patrick was shaken. He couldn't think of anything to say so he muttered "Nothin."

"Well, clear off then."

Patrick needed no second invitation and he set off briskly towards his street, not daring to look back. Yet again, he felt a deep sense of shame and humiliation. Jonathan shrugged his shoulders and walked into his house to tell his parents about his day.

◆   ◆   ◆

Patrick stumbled into the sitting room.

"I've just seen that bastard German. 'E told me to bugger off."

"Where were yer?" asked his mother.

"Outside his 'ouse."

"That's bloody stupid," said his father.

"'E'll think it was you wot broke in a couple of weeks ago and 'e'll guess you're plannin' to do it again."

"Sorry. I was just checkin' to see they're still there and 'aven't cleared off with their stuff like last time."

"Well, it looks like they're 'ere to stay," said Doris.

"When we gonna do 'em then?" asked a frantic Patrick.

"When the time's right," George said. "We'll wait for a big air raid because then they're bound to be in that cellar or else the shelter."

"I bloody 'ate that bloke," said Patrick, his fists clenched. "I can't wait for the next time we get loads of bombs, then we'll wreck is 'ouse."

"'E's really upset you 'asn't 'e?" said his mother. "Let's 'ope the Nazis don't beat you to it."

Patrick had calmed down a bit by the time he met Rose in the park. He gave her a Woodbine and told her about Jonathan. He didn't tell her that they were planning to burgle his house, but he did say that he wanted to put one on him. Rose couldn't really understand why Patrick hated the German so much. She knew her new boyfriend had a reputation in the neighbourhood as a bit of a hard case, but she knew nothing of the humiliation that he'd suffered in front of his mates from Jonathan. She couldn't quite follow what was going on, so she changed the subject and talked about the cinema and the films they hoped to see that weekend. Patrick listened to her and then looked at her and smiled. He put his arms around her neck and kissed her, but she abruptly broke away.

"Everyone round 'ere knows what you've bin up to, Patrick Wallace," Rose said. "If you wanna keep goin' wiv me, you'll 'ave to pack it in. I don't wanna be 'angin' round 'ere, waitin' for you to come out of borstal."

Patrick promised that he wasn't doing any more thieving and would tell his father that when he got home. Rose let him carry on where they'd left off when she'd interrupted him. Half-an-hour later they set off home, after arranging to meet again the following night in the park. He bounced into the house. His parents were slouched in the sitting room enjoying a smoke.

"Allo, 'ere comes love's young dream," said George. "Bin givin' 'er one?"

Patrick flushed and then shouted at his father. "It's none of yer bloody business."

Doris said she agreed with her son, but warned him to be careful.

"I don't wanna be lookin' after yer little bastard. I've got enough on me plate."

At this moment, Angela walked in.

"Just collecting some stuff, then I'll go back to the rest centre." She walked upstairs and the other three resumed their conversation.

"Any'ow," said Patrick, "I've told Rose I'm givin' up thievin'."

"I've told yer before," his mother replied, "you'll do as yer told."

"I don't want to and I ain't gonna do it no more, apart from that German's 'ouse round the corner. That's personal. Then I'll get meself a job."

Doris, recognising some of her own stubbornness and determination in her son, let it drop. Angela heard every word. She was beginning to be proud of Patrick, but didn't like the sound of the one last job.

Christmas was only a little bit more than two weeks away. It would be the first holiday season during the Blitz. The air raids hadn't been too bad in December, apart from one heavy one at the beginning of the month, but, as the festivities approached, the Luftwaffe appeared above the skies of the capital in huge numbers.

"Now's yer chance," said Doris. "Go and do them German Jews."

CHAPTER TWENTY-THREE

Benjamin and Ruth listened to Jonathan's account of his visit to the school. When they heard that the pupils had been evacuated, they were a bit disappointed. The thought of their only son spending a fair amount of his time fifty miles apart from his parents made them a little sad. Jonathan, however, was desperate to complete his studies and, when he promised to work hard to try to complete his Higher School Certificate the following summer, they gave their blessing. They knew how much his exams meant to him and how keen he was to follow this by going to university.

Jonathan said that he would ring Mr Lawton tomorrow. He would ask if he could return home for weekends and whether or not he could take the certificate in the summer. If the Headmaster said that he could, it would mean seven months, minus holidays, when he would be separated from his parents.

That settled, they made their way to the cellar when the siren sounded at eight o'clock. Soon they heard the sound of exploding bombs, sounds that would become all too familiar to them in the months to come. Ruth had already slept through several air raids but, for Benjamin and Jonathan, it was a relatively new experience. They quickly adapted to the noise. Jonathan lay on his back with his hands behind his head thinking of Hilde, something he did often. Despite the dreadful news from the continent, he continued to believe that she was still alive. With this thought, he fell asleep.

◆ ◆ ◆

Just around the corner, not much more than two hundred yards from the Gerber house, George and Patrick were listening to the bombs. Doris was there, having decided that a visit to the shelter wasn't necessary that night. The raid, big as it was, appeared to be focused south-east of them. She decided that if one bomb hit her, that would be that. It was just the luck of the draw, she thought.

George and Patrick were in their burglary kit; rubber-soled boots, trousers, a thick jumper and a woollen hat, all of them black. Each carried a torch and an empty, folded-up kit bag.

"'Ow will yer know if they're in their cellar or the shelter?" asked Doris.

"We won't," replied George.

"Yer'll 'ave to be silent as the grave," his wife warned him. "Assume they're there."

"We'll go in the same way as before," said George. "The boy'll crawl through the back wind'er and then let me in through the door."

Doris protested, "They're bound to 'ear breakin' glass."

"We ain't gonna break it," smiled George, holding up a red handled glass cutter and a plunger, normally used for unblocking the sink.

Doris laughed. "George, I do believe yer startin' to show a bit o' nous after all these years. Start with the upstairs. They definitely won't 'ear yer there."

Half an hour later, the raid seemed to be in full swing and the two thieves set off. Patrick was excited. It was his chance of revenge although he realised that, if there was the slightest chance of the Jews being in the cellar, they'd be asking for trouble if they started smashing the place. Perhaps they'd be in the shelter, he thought, in which case he would totally trash the place and urinate all over the posh carpets. If they were in the cellar, he'd think of some way he could leave his mark as well as stealing all of their cash and valuables, leaving them penniless, he hoped.

Father and son crept cautiously towards the Gerber house. There was no one about. The sky was full of fire, smoke and thunder. The building was in total darkness. They listened at the front door to try to detect any sign of life. Inside it seemed still and silent, but they knew, from their earlier visit, the cellar was almost totally soundproofed.

They went round the back of the house, quickly climbed the fence and George went to work on the window. He sliced right around the outside of the glass. Patrick held on firmly to the plunger and, as soon as the cutting was finished, the two of them carefully detached the window from its frame.

It was heavy, so they took extra care and placed it against the outside wall then the boy squirmed his way through the space, landed safely on the kitchen floor, unbolted the back door and let his father in. The two made their way to the stairs and tip-toed to the first floor. The doors were closed, so they tried one each. Patrick found himself in Jonathan's bedroom which, as far as he could see, contained nothing of value. There were clothes in the wardrobe, some shoes, a pair of football boots and a small chest of drawers which contained shirts, socks and underwear. A full bookcase lined one wall and a cricket bat was leaning against another, with a football resting by its side. Patrick had no idea what any of the books were about and if they were of any value, so he went to find his father.

George was in Benjamin and Ruth's bedroom. His son whispered to him that there didn't seem to be much of value in the other room.

"There's bugger all 'ere either," whispered his father in reply. "There's no wallets, purses or cash, but I've got 'er jewel box. Let's try downstairs."

Jonathan, normally a tidy boy, had left an empty glass on the bannisters at the top of the stairs and George, his torch shining on the stairs, didn't notice it. The sleeve of his coat brushed the glass off its perch and it tumbled down the stairs, bouncing neatly against the wall at the bottom and then breaking into pieces. It wasn't a large glass and it didn't make a lot of noise when it broke, but to the Wallaces it sounded like someone had banged a gong to announce their presence. Throwing caution to the winds, they dashed downstairs, made for the kitchen and opened the back door.

Down below, it was the racing footsteps, not the breaking glass, that woke the Gerbers.

"Dad, there's someone in the house."

He leapt out of bed and ran up the cellar stairs. Feeling a draught from the back of the house, he guessed it came from the kitchen and dashed through, arriving just in time to see the young thief's backside disappearing over the back fence.

"Come here," shouted Jonathan, and Patrick turned briefly towards the house, allowing Jonathan enough time to catch a glimpse of his face. There was just enough glow from the flame lit sky for him to recognise the boy with whom he had had a couple of run-ins. He couldn't give chase. He had bare feet and was still in his pyjamas. He made his way back to the sitting room where he was joined by his mother and father, both still in their night clothes.

"Did you see who it was?" asked Benjamin.

"I recognised the boy. I've seen him hanging around. There was definitely someone with him. I'm sure I could hear two sets of footsteps."

"Let's see what's missing," said Ruth.

They went through the house, room by room, and came to the conclusion that all that was missing was Ruth's jewellery box.

"Nothing's worth much," she said, "but my mother's ruby brooch will have gone. That's rather sad."

"We'll go to the police station in the morning," said Benjamin. "Can you give a full description of the jewellery?"

"I think so."

"Good. On the way back from the police station, we'll call and see Ken, the glazier. In the meantime, Jonathan and I will board up the back window."

◆   ◆   ◆

Doris was furious.

"Is this all yer got? This box of rubbish jewels?"

"Dad knocked a glass over and woke 'em up. We 'ad to get out quick."

"You clumsy bastard, George. Why didn't you stay and do 'em over?"

Before his father could reply, Patrick interrupted, a fierce look on his face. "Coz 'e's a bleedin' coward and I wasn't gonna stay and take on that giant Jew on me own."

"Well, it's done now," his mother replied. "I'll 'ave to get what I can fer this lot, though it won't be much. I quite fancy this ruby brooch for meself."

Doris took the brooch out of the box, pinned it to her washed out green cardigan and took the box containing the remainder of the jewellery to the shed.

◆   ◆   ◆

Benjamin, Ruth and Jonathan were at the police station in the High Street just after nine o'clock on the morning after the robbery. Benjamin gave the desk Sergeant their details and told him that their house had been burgled during the previous night's raid. They'd been sheltering in their cellar when they heard movements in the house above them. Jonathan had disturbed the thieves, who then ran off into the night with just a box of jewellery.

"Please wait here for a moment. I'll go and fetch a detective."

He returned a few minutes later with a rather overweight man dressed in slacks and a worn sports jacket with patches on the elbows. He looked to weigh a lot more than Jonathan, but was at least four inches shorter. What was left of his thin greying hair looked as if it hadn't seen either a comb or a bottle of shampoo for weeks. His mouth hardly opened when he introduced himself as Detective Constable Scott. Benjamin repeated his story to Scott who sighed, turned to them and said, "So little of value was stolen?"

A clearly surprised Benjamin said, "That's not the point officer. Our house has been burgled and we expect the police to do all they can to bring the culprits to justice."

"Of course, sir. We'll do all we can, but I don't hold out too much hope. We're understaffed and terribly stretched with all that's going on with the air raids."

Ruth spoke for the first time. "The items stolen may not have been of any great value, but one piece of jewellery belonged to my mother and I'd like it back."

"Of course, madam. I say again that we'll do all that we can." He turned to Jonathan. "You pursued the two suspects out of the house, I believe. Did you recognise either of them?"

Jonathan gave such an accurate description of Patrick that Scott felt his stomach turning over. This could turn nasty, he thought to himself.

"Thank you. I don't recognise anybody from your description, but my colleagues and I will do our best to identify him. I'll keep you informed of progress."

The Gerbers left the police station, none too impressed with Scott.

"Look," said Jonathan. "I'm the only one who'll recognise him. I think I'll stroll around the area to see if I can spot him and find out where he lives."

"Just a minute, Jonathan," said Ruth. "If you do find him and his address, you're to come straight back here and tell us and then we'll pass the information to Mr Scott. I don't want you trying to beat a confession out of him."

"That never crossed my mind," smiled Jonathan.

They called in to see Ken the glazier and then went home. Jonathan went out shortly after lunch. The Gerbers had had little luck. They'd been persecuted, robbed by the Nazis, left floating on the high seas, interned and now burgled. But now that luck changed because, as Jonathan entered the park, he saw a group of boys playing football. Amongst them, he recognised the person he was looking for. Patrick was far too engrossed throwing his weight around on the football pitch to notice Jonathan, who now took up a position where he could keep an eye on the game and yet not be seen. He waited patiently. After about thirty minutes the game broke up and the boys headed towards where the park entrance had been before the gates and fence had been taken away to make war materials.

Jonathan followed at a distance as, one by one, the boys headed off in different directions toward their houses. Eventually, just two remained. One boy went into a house at the top of the street, leaving just Patrick, who entered a house that Jonathan presumed was his, half way down the street. He waited for a minute and then walked briskly past, making a mental note of the number. He went straight home and told his parents. The three of them then set off to the police station to see Detective Scott.

Scott listened to Jonathan as he made notes.

"That's very helpful. I'll call there as soon as I can and I'll let you know what happens."

Scott waited for about an hour and then told the Sergeant that he was going out to interview a suspect. Ten minutes later, he was banging angrily on the Wallaces' door. Doris answered and he barged in. George and Patrick looked up. They could see that something was seriously wrong.

"You're right in it this time. Someone at the 'ouse that you burgled last night recognised the boy. I 'ave to carry out an investigation."

"Well, we all know you've got nothin' on us, have you Mr Scott?" Doris said, with a smirk on her face. "You'll 'ave to find some way of puttin' 'em off."

"I will, but don't underestimate them. They're like dogs with bones that won't let go. Don't try and shift that stuff. It's too 'ot. And keep yer bloody 'eads down fer a while."

Scott called at the Gerbers' house later that night. He confirmed that he'd spoken to the person identified by Jonathan. He'd been with his family in the shelter all night and Scott had spoken to a number of witnesses who'd corroborated this. Jonathan must have been mistaken, Scott suggested. He had other lines of enquiry to pursue and he would let them know if anything cropped up. Then he left.

Jonathan was furious. He knew he was right. Perhaps it would have been better to have got hold of the boy and forced him to confess? They ate their evening meal in silence and then retired to the cellar for the night.

The following afternoon Ruth went shopping. Rationing was tightening its grip and she had to show a great deal of perseverance to get even a modest amount of reasonable food, but she managed. She set off home with several bags of food from the High Street and struggled all the way to her front door before two slipped from her grasp. She cursed to herself and was in the act of bending down to pick them up, when a voice piped up.

"'Ere, let me give you an 'and."

Ruth looked up and saw the smiling face of a young woman with black, curly hair wearing a royal blue woollen coat.

"Thank you," said Ruth. "I just hope I haven't broken a precious egg. We've had enough problems in the last day or two."

"I'm sorry to hear that."

"It was just a small burglary. Nothing of great value was taken but I rather miss my mother's ruby brooch which was stolen."

At that moment, Benjamin, having seen Ruth struggling with the shopping, joined them on the pavement outside the house, closely followed by Jonathan.

"I dropped some shopping and this young lady was kind enough to help me pick it up."

Benjamin gave her a grateful smile. "Thank you very much Miss, er..?"

"Angela."

"Thank you, Angela," said Ruth.

The Gerbers went into their house and Angela continued on her way home.

Inside, Ruth asked Benjamin, "Have you heard from the police?"

"I telephoned them while you were out, but Scott said he hadn't been able to pick up any new information."

"I don't think he can be bothered," said Ruth. "You and I should go down there now and push for more answers."

An hour later, Benjamin and Ruth were back. Scott had been impatient with them and protested about how difficult it was to solve crimes in the Blitz. Angrily, he told them that their burglary was nowhere near the top of his list of priorities. The Gerbers left the police station annoyed and frustrated and this mood was noticed by Jonathan when they arrived home.

"Now that we know where this boy lives," said Jonathan, "why don't you and I go around and have a word with him?" he added, looking at his father. "The police don't seem to care."

"No, I should do that," replied Benjamin. "I'll go there and ask if they'd return your mother's jewellery and then we'll let the matter drop. We'll tell Scott that it has been recovered and then ask him to leave it at that. You stay here, Jonathan, and look after your mother."

Benjamin stood up, put on his hat and coat and left to confront the Wallaces.

CHAPTER TWENTY-FOUR

A couple of minutes after helping Ruth pick up her shopping, Angela stepped into her sitting room to find the rest of her family smoking and looking glum.

"I've just spoken to a lady and gent round the corner. They said they'd been burgled. I suppose that was you two." Patrick stayed silent, with a guilty look on his face. Her father, with a nasty grin on his lips, denied it was them.

"Any'ow," Doris said, "what's it gotta do with you? You're 'ardly part of this family."

Angela ignored her and then looked at her mother. "I see you've got a new brooch. Suppose that's part of the stuff you nicked from those people round the corner too?"

"I bought it on the black from a bloke in the pub. 'E probably stole it."

"Don't lie to me," Angela said as she left the room.

The Wallaces settled down to feeling glum again when, about ten minutes later, there was a knock on the door.

"Probably Scott again," said Doris, rising from her seat." I'll tell 'im we ain't got nothin' for 'im."

She opened the door and found a middle-aged man, wearing a hat and coat, standing on the pavement.

"My name's Benjamin Gerber. I'd like to speak to your son."

"What for?"

"I don't want to cause any trouble. It'll only take as minute," Benjamin said, easing his way past Doris into the front room.

Turning towards Patrick, Benjamin said, "My son said he saw you leaving our house after it was burgled, the day before yesterday. He was quite certain it was you. There's no point in denying it."

Doris looked at Benjamin. "The police 'ave already asked us about that. 'E was in the shelter. There's witnesses to back 'im up."

"My son doesn't tell lies. If he says it was your son, I believe him. I don't want any fuss. Please return the jewellery and the matter will go no further."

"It's your word against ours. The word of a German Jew against proper English people," Doris said, a sneer on her face.

At that moment, Benjamin saw Ruth's mother's brooch pinned onto her cardigan.

"That belonged to my wife's mother," Benjamin said, pointing at the brooch, his voice growing louder.

"I bought it off a bloke in the pub."

"I don't believe you," an increasingly exasperated Benjamin said. "You've had your chance. I'm going for the police."

At this point, panic set in amongst the Wallaces. Patrick could see the doors of the borstal closing behind him and George heard a cell door in Pentonville prison slamming shut. Doris could see her nest egg disappearing from her life.

Without thinking, Doris shouted, "Grab 'im, George."

George threw Benjamin to the floor. Patrick wasn't sure what to do as he sat and watched the grappling pair. Benjamin wouldn't give up. George punched him on the chin but still Benjamin struggled and was beginning to get the better of things when Doris, her eyes glazed, came from the kitchen clutching a long bladed knife. Angela, hearing the commotion from upstairs, opened the sitting room door just in time to see her mother plunge the knife into Benjamin's throat. Angela screamed and rushed for the front door but her father grabbed her around the waist and threw her to the floor. Doris stepped back and watched as blood poured out of Benjamin. She rushed over to her daughter, lifted her to her feet by her hair and slapped her hard across her face.

"Lock 'er in the shed, George."

Her husband did as he was told and frog marched a screaming Angela into the yard, pushed her into the shed and locked the door as she fell on to the floor. Back in the house, Doris had taken control. She looked at Benjamin.

"'E's dead. Let's clear this mess up." They could hear their daughter's banging and screaming on the shed door. Doris went into the yard, banged on the door herself and told Angela that she'd get the same treatment as their visitor if she didn't shut up. That did the trick and the banging and screaming was replaced by weeping.

Back in the house, Patrick hadn't moved.

"Right," his mother said, "you caused this. That Jew you 'ad a run-in with must 'ave spotted you. Give an 'and clearing this lot up."

Doris picked up the knife which lay on the floor by Benjamin's corpse, took it into the kitchen, wiped the blade on an old rag and dropped it into a drawer.

"George, get upstairs and get them blankets off 'er bed. You two can wrap 'is body in one. I'll take the other into the shed for 'er. Get rid of the body while I clean up 'ere. The boy'll 'elp yer."

George collected the blankets, gave one to Doris to take to the shed and wrapped Benjamin's corpse in the other. Then he summoned a speechless and terrified Patrick to help him dispose of the body. Bombs were falling a couple of miles away and this helped to distract the attention of anybody who otherwise might have wondered why two people were carrying a suspicious-looking bundle through the streets at the dead of night.

They dumped poor Benjamin's body like a pile of garbage behind a bush in the park. George folded up the blanket, tucked it under his arm and the two of them returned to the house. Patrick was totally traumatised and hadn't said a thing since their unwelcome visitor's arrival. When they arrived back at the house, Doris had cleaned up the carpet and, superficially at least, had eradicated all signs of her monstrous deed. Patrick was sent to bed where he lay trembling and sleepless until dawn came. George was dispatched to get rid of the bloody blanket and the rag she's used to wipe the knife on. She told him to burn it. Finding a fire shouldn't be too difficult. Angela continued to cry in the shed. Doris sat down and lit a cigarette. She'd handled that pretty well, she thought to herself.

◆   ◆   ◆

Ruth and Jonathan waited anxiously for Benjamin's return. The night wore on and there was still no sign of him. The planes left at three and the all-clear sounded at six. By this time, they were desperate. Ruth thought that perhaps he'd gone to the police station to leave a message for Scott about whatever evidence he'd found at the house around the corner. Jonathan thought not. Assuming the phones were working, he felt sure that his father would have called them from the police station.

Eating was impossible, but they both managed a cup of tea. By nine o'clock, Ruth could bear the tension no longer.

"You know where that house is, don't you Jonathan?"

"Yes."

"Then let's go round and see if they know where he is."

Less than ten minutes later, they were knocking on the Wallaces' front door. A tough looking woman with black greying curly hair answered. Ruth explained who they were and why they were there. A smiling Doris introduced herself and said she was dreadfully sorry but she couldn't help them.

"I'm so sorry I can't 'elp you dearie, but we've bin in the shelter all night. The bombin' was terrible. If 'e came 'ere, there would've bin no one to answer the door."

Devastated and overwhelmed with worry, Ruth and Jonathan returned home. They'd hoped to find Benjamin waiting for them when they arrived, but they walked into a cold, lonely and empty house. They sat in silence for a while and then Ruth got up.

"Let's go to the police station and report him missing."

Once again, they approached the desk Sergeant. They gave their names, addresses and details of Benjamin's movements of the night before, as well as a description, including the clothes he had been wearing. The Sergeant, who was a kind man, promised to tell all of the beat bobbies to look out for Benjamin. If there was no news by nightfall, he'd inform the detectives. They returned home and sat and waited.

At about five o'clock, there was a knock on the door. Ruth and Jonathan had been dozing in their sitting room after their sleepless night and awoke with a start. An elderly policeman wearing a tin helmet was standing on the door step.

"Mrs Gerber?"

"Yes."

"I'm PC James. I'm so sorry to tell you that we've found a man fitting your husband's description in the park. I have to tell you that I'm afraid he's dead and appears to have been the victim of foul play."

Ruth put her hand to her mouth, let out an anguished cry and fell to the floor. Jonathan came out of the sitting room, saw his mother in a state of collapse and rushed forward to help her. He and PC James carefully took her to the sitting room and sat her down. She quickly came round, glanced at the policeman and Jonathan and began to scream. Her son put an arm around her.

"What is it?"

He got no reply as the screams subsided into an uncontrollable sobbing. The policeman repeated to Jonathan what he'd told his mother. The boy was speechless.

James spoke to him quietly. "I presume you're Jonathan. Look after your mother and I'll go and make us a cup of tea. I'm sure I can find the things."

He returned five minutes later with a tray, poured out three cups and they drank in silence. Eventually, both mother and son seemed to return to life.

"How did he die?" whispered Ruth.

"It looks like he was stabbed in the throat. The body's at the morgue now. The pathologist will determine the cause of death. I expect he'll carry out a post-mortem quite soon, although, as you can imagine, he's pretty busy at the moment."

Ruth nodded.

"There is one other thing, madam. We're pretty sure that the body is that of your husband, from the description you gave us, but I will have to ask you to come to the morgue to identify him. I know that's a terrible thing to ask of you but, until we're certain that it is him, we can't begin to investigate this awful crime."

"I understand, thank you officer. We'll come as soon as you wish," sobbed Ruth.

PC James asked if he could use the telephone, and he called the station to ask for a car to collect them and take them to the morgue. They drank more tea and had sat in almost total silence for forty-five minutes, when they heard a car draw up outside the house. Ruth and Jonathan were helped into the car by PC James and the three of them were driven to the morgue. Jonathan waited outside while his mother was taken away to identify the body. She returned minutes later in floods of tears. She had confirmed that her husband and Jonathan's father was lying dead in the morgue on a stone cold slab. They were driven home. PC James asked if there was anyone who could come and stay with them. Ruth said she would make a telephone call as soon as he had gone.

"A detective will be round to ask you some questions. I know you've had a dreadful shock, but I'm sure you understand that the sooner the investigation is started, the better.

"Of course, officer. Thank you for being so kind and helpful."

As soon as the policeman had left, Jonathan telephoned Richard and, in a voice that alternated between gasps of extreme sorrow and anger, told him what had happened. Richard was stunned. His old friend, a brave man who had survived persecution, imprisonment in a concentration camp and internment, was dead. Then he pulled himself together.

"I'm coming to you. I'll be there as soon as I can, depending on the state of the roads."

Jonathan thanked him, replaced the receiver and returned to comforting his mother.

◆　　◆　　◆

Doris sat looking at her husband. She had just returned from the shed where she'd given some food to an utterly distraught Angela who'd shouted and hurled abuse at her.

"We'll 'ave to do somethin' about 'er, George. With all the row she's makin', one of the neighbours could tell the coppers and then we'd be right in it."

A still terrified Patrick turned on his mother.

"No. You'll be right in it. You killed 'im."

"You and yer father were there. You're accessories. If they can prove we did it, all three of us will swing."

"They won't 'ang me. I'm too young," protested Patrick

"That's as maybe, but they'll lock you up fer the rest of yer life. Fancy that, do yer?"

Patrick didn't reply.

"So, keep yer trap shut and we might just get away with it."

"What about Angela?" asked George.

"I'll 'ave to think about that," replied his wife. "Fer the time being, we'll keep 'er in the shed. Get out there now and tie 'er up and gag 'er. All that racket she's makin's gonna bring us trouble."

George came back from the shed, having left his daughter bound and gagged and with a single blanket to keep out the December cold. The three of them settled in for the night. Husband and wife appeared to be totally unmoved by the devastating events of the past twenty-fours. Patrick, however, was in a dreadful state. He desperately wanted to see Rose but Doris refused to let him out of her sight. George disappeared early the next morning to earn some cash for the weekend, but returned earlier than usual to allow Doris to do some shopping. She'd decided that one or other of them must be in the house at all times to keep an eye on the children.

The next morning there was a knock on the door, soon after breakfast. A pretty girl stood on the pavement. Doris looked at her with a suspicious eye.

"I'm Rose," the girl said, "is Patrick in?"

"He is," said Doris, "but 'e's got a nasty dose of flu. 'E'll be as right as rain in a day or two."

A tall young lady, wearing a red coat, visited later that day. She introduced herself as Angela's friend, Pam.

"She hasn't been to work for two days," Pam said. "I was wondering if anything had happened to her."

"We've 'ad a death in the family," Doris said, putting on a suitably sad face. "'Er granddad's been killed in an air raid in Plaistow, so she's gone down there ter look after 'er gran for a few days."

"Oh, I didn't realise she had any grandparents in Plaistow. She didn't mention anything to me."

"Well, she 'as," replied Doris, "and, for the time being, family duties come before work and 'avin' a good time. I'll make sure she gets in touch with you as soon as she gets back. Now, if you'll excuse me," Doris said, shutting the door in Pam's face.

◆   ◆   ◆

Richard arrived at the North London house at ten o'clock. There was an air raid in progress not too far away, but it hadn't threatened him. Inge had made sandwiches and soup. Neither Ruth nor Jonathan had eaten since their evening meal on the previous day, the last they'd shared with Benjamin.

"I'm staying here until everything's sorted out. I'll be with you when you talk to the police and when the body's released. I'll help you to organise the funeral. You must come and stay with us over Christmas.

"We can't do that Richard," said Ruth. "It'll spoil your Christmas."

"I thought you might say that, so I've brought you a message from Inge and my boys and Reg and his family. If you won't come to us, then we're all coming up here to you. So," he said, with a hint of a smile on his lips, "what's it to be, crammed in here like sardines or comfortable at our place?"

Ruth looked at him and burst into tears. She knew, at that moment, that, however great the tragedy that had overtaken her and Jonathan, life would go on because they were blessed with the best friends that anyone could wish for. She stood up and walked over to where Richard was standing and threw her arms around him. Jonathan followed her and the three of them stood in the centre of the room, embracing in silent tears.

Scott appeared the next morning. He told them that Benjamin had died as the result of a severed artery, caused by a knife-wound to the throat. A post-mortem would be held that afternoon and it was likely that the coroner would then release the body for burial. The detective then asked one or two fatuous questions and then left, promising to keep in touch.

"He's useless and doesn't care," said Richard. "We might have to look into this ourselves. Still, that comes later. Let's assume the body will be released today and organise the funeral."

Benjamin was buried in the Jewish cemetery in North London on Christmas Eve. Inge and her children and Reg, Mary and Roger Martin, joined Ruth, Jonathan and Richard at the service. Then they packed what they could into the two cars and set off to spend Christmas in south west London.

◆   ◆   ◆

There was a kind of unofficial bombing truce over Christmas and families throughout Britain were able to enjoy the festivities as best they could, free from the fear of air raids. Elsewhere in the world, the Italians continued to march backwards through Albania, with the Greeks in hot pursuit. It seemed that, before too long, the Italian army would fall into the Adriatic. Mussolini's armies did little better in North Africa where British troops were in complete control in the desert. The Prime Minister told the public that the RAF were bombing German towns and cities. Despite these snippets of good news, the war was far from being won and it still seemed possible that the Allies might lose.

In north London, the Wallaces sat and waited for the knock on the door that might signal the end of their liberty. Thirty miles away, Ruth and Jonathan's despair at Benjamin's death was turning into a hardened resolve to help find and punish the killer.

CHAPTER TWENTY-FIVE

For most in Great Britain, it was a miserable Christmas. True, they were having a respite from the bombing, but the country felt grey and many of the big cities were in a shocking state. Despite the best efforts of the emergency services, heaps of bricks and thousands of damaged buildings remained. The roads were pock-marked with holes where bombs had dropped. Public transport had been horribly disrupted, especially around London. The railway lines had taken a fierce battering and some of the stations had been hit. Buses had fallen into craters and many normal routes were no longer passable, even with care. Despite all this, those responsible for public transport had done a brilliant job in keeping Britain moving. Rail services ran every day, even on Christmas Day and Boxing Day.

The shops did their best and tried to catch the holiday spirit with decorations, but there was a shortage of toys and few set up Christmas bazaars. Santa Claus made only a tiny number of appearances. In the food shops, there were shortages of everything. Meat was scarce and traditional Christmas extras like nuts and figs were very expensive. Fruit was in short supply and was also very dear. Everything, in fact, cost more than Christmas 1939.

The misery was nowhere more evident than in the Wallace house. They still had some money and Doris put together a reasonable Christmas lunch, mostly following her visits to the black market. The Christmas dinner was a brief interlude in the day-to-day depression in the house. Angela was still trussed up in the shed. Patrick hardly ever spoke. Carol singers came to their front door and were either ignored or sent away with fleas in their ears. Doris and George had no idea what to do with Angela.

In south west London, the Walkers and the Martins did all that they could to help Ruth and Jonathan get over their awful loss. Christmas dinner was frugal but more than adequate. Everyone was determined that they should all have some fun, however trying the circumstances, in this, the first Christmas of the real war. Carols were broadcast from King's College, Cambridge and, after lunch on the twenty-fifth, they listened to the King's speech. Over tea, they followed an adaptation of Dickens' *A Christmas Carol* on Children's Hour and, later in the evening they tuned in to A Christmas Day Variety, starring such favourites as Arthur Askey, Dicky Murdoch, Jack Warner, and Elsie and Doris Waters.

The Christmas Day festivities took place at the Walker home. The following day, there was a full house nearby with Reg and Mary Martin. Ruth missed Benjamin terribly and cried from time to time, not just because of her bereavement but also because she was overwhelmed by the kindness of her friends. Jonathan, quiet at first, slowly realised that life must go on. Paul and Michael Walker were terrific and soon the three of them were inseparable. They played Monopoly and spent hours kicking a football about in the local park.

Roger Martin made a flying visit to see his parents on Boxing Day. His girlfriend Jane, now a Lieutenant in the Pay Corps in the Women's Army, joined them for tea. John Martin, sadly, was too consumed by his hush-hush work to take any holiday leave.

On 28 December, while Jonathan was in the park with his new friends, Ruth and the other four adults sat down for a morning cup of tea.

"I've called the police twice to see if they've anything to report, but they haven't. I'm sure Scott doesn't care," said Richard. "We don't think you should go back to North London, Ruth. It's too dangerous and there are those horrible memories. We all want you to be safe and close to us. Reg and Mary have kindly agreed to let you have John's room until you can find a place of your own around here."

Ruth looked at the three of them and her eyes began to fill with tears. "Thank you all for being so kind, but what about Jonathan?"

"He's off to school on January sixth. Until then, and when he comes home at weekends, he can have a camp bed in Michael's room. They seem to get on famously. I'm sure that neither of them will mind," replied Richard.

"Thank you, but we can't live on top of you for ever. We'll have to find a place of our own, and the sooner the better."

Reg, who'd lived in the town for most of his life, picked up the discussion.

"There are plenty of small houses around here which I'm sure you'll like. I'm certain you'll find something suitable."

Ruth nodded in agreement and told them that they would like to make their permanent home close to their friends. Gradually it began to dawn on her that there would be life after Benjamin, something to look forward to.

"Right," Ruth said in a business like way, "we'll start house hunting tomorrow."

"There's not that much of a hurry," said Richard. "Leave it till the New Year."

Mary, who had sat in silence up to this point, said to Ruth. "We're not doing this out of pity Ruth. We're doing it because we love you and Jonathan and we owe it to Benjamin's memory to see you both get back on track again."

Tears again began to well up in Ruth's eyes but she quickly recovered. "I know that. Nobody ever had better friends than you and your families."

"You know, Ruth, this war has played havoc with my staff. Many of them, even some women, have left to join up. Not that I'm against that, of course, but it has left me a bit short handed. There's a job with me as soon as you're ready. I've offered the same to Inge but she prefers to wait until the boys finish school."

"Thank you, Reg. I'd love that."

"So that's all settled," said Richard. "Ruth, please tell Jonathan about all this when he comes back. He and I will go to North London tomorrow, pile as many of your possessions as we can fit into the car, hassle the police about the investigation and give your notice to the landlord. How long do you have to give?"

"A month."

"Fine. We'll return in the New Year to finish emptying the house. If Scott isn't there tomorrow, we'll stay the night and go back first thing on Monday morning and have it out with him. Then we'll drive back here."

Later, Ruth explained all this to Jonathan. Like her, he wondered what on earth they would have done without their friends. Reg and Richard left for evening parade with their Home Guard unit and the three mothers prepared provisions for the following day. The amount they prepared suggested that Richard and Jonathan were setting out on some kind of expedition requiring mountains of sandwiches. In the morning, they would make flasks of tea, coffee and soup.

Richard had an appointment at Reg's store and so it was after lunch before they set out. The journey was slow. The bombers had returned the previous night, causing more damage. It was dark by the time they pulled up outside the police station. Scott wasn't there and none of the officers had any information about the investigation. He'd be there tomorrow, they were told. Richard said that he'd be back.

◆   ◆   ◆

While Richard and Jonathan were en route for North London, Doris was making a rare excursion from her house to do the shopping, leaving George to keep an eye on their children. George was totally drained. The tension of the past few weeks had taken its toll on him and, soon after Doris had left, he fell asleep in the sitting room. Patrick, keeping a close eye on his father, saw that George had fallen into a deep slumber and was unlikely to wake up for a while. Now was his chance and he put his coat on and quietly slipped out of the front door. He dashed to the park, hoping to see Rose, but she wasn't there and so he doubled back and called at her house. Rose answered the front door. Patrick told her he could only stay for a few minutes. Rose could see that something was troubling him, so she put on her coat and the two strolled back towards the park. As they walked, Rose asked him to tell her what was bothering him. He told her everything; about the burglary, the murder, Angela's imprisonment and how he was being kept at home by his parents. She told him to go to the police, but he thought he couldn't get near the police station, the way his parents were keeping a close watch on him. Patrick asked Rose if she would go to the police, but warned her to keep away from Scott. He explained why and, after hesitating for a moment or two, she agreed to go the following morning. Patrick thanked her, kissed her and then ran home.

His father was snoring deeply allowing Patrick was to sneak back in unnoticed and settle down in his chair just before his mother returned. He sat and waited. Doris had done well with the shopping and began to prepare the food. George woke up and the three sat down to the first decent meal they'd had since Christmas Day. Patrick ate his in silence and, when they'd finished, Doris set about preparing something for Angela. She took the food to the shed, unlocked the door and found her daughter sprawled on the floor, looking dead to the world. She rushed back into the house.

"George, come quick, it's Angela."

With a cigarette in his mouth, George followed Doris to the yard.

"Christ," he said, "she's dead."

Doris knelt down and felt her pulse. "No she's not, she's just passed out. 'Elp me untie 'er and we'll take 'er into the 'ouse."

George pulled off the gag and untied the ropes around her wrists and feet. Carefully, her parents carried her into the sitting room and laid her on the floor.

"What the 'ell we gonna do now?" asked George.

"No idea," replied his wife, "but we'd better bring 'er round or we'll 'ave another corpse on our 'ands."

Doris, reverting to the age-old remedy of a cup of tea, went to the kitchen to boil some water. Patrick, who had been in sullen silence since his sister had been fetched from the shed, started crying and screamed at his father. "You've killed 'er, you bastard," he shouted at George. "'Oo's next? Me?"

George turned his back on Angela and told his son to shut up.

Angela, who had been lying on her stomach, opened her eyes. She hadn't been unconscious at all and the row between her brother and father and her mother's temporary absence gave her a chance. She rolled on her back, got unsteadily to her feet and picked the poker from the grate. George, alerted to movement behind him, turned to face an onrushing Angela who smashed the poker across his face. It hit the bridge of his nose. George screamed as his nose broke and blood began to pour out of it.

"You bleedin' bitch. Now yer done for."

Angela didn't bother to reply. She dropped the poker and rushed out of the front door. Doris rushed back from the kitchen just too late to grab hold of her. She saw her husband standing unsteadily with the lower half of his face covered in blood.

"What's appened?" she bawled.

"The bitch 'it me with the poker."

"You'd better get after 'er."

"Me bleedin' nose is broke."

"I'll sort that out."

Doris came back with a cloth, wiped his face and stuffed cotton wool up both nostrils.

"Patrick, yer goin' with yer dad to bring Angela back. If she gets to the law, yer'll be spendin' the rest of yer life be'ind bars."

A traumatised Patrick put his coat on. His father did the same.

"There ain't many places where she can go," Doris said, with an evil steely glare in her eyes. "When yer find 'er, kill 'er. She knows too much."

CHAPTER TWENTY-SIX

Richard and Jonathan were packing all they could into the three suitcases they'd brought with them. They couldn't manage everything so they agreed to come back early in the New Year to collect the rest. Just after six, the siren sounded. There was a full moon, a bombers' moon. Richard said that the Germans, who had resumed the raids two days previously, might come in force tonight. They decided to eat some sandwiches and then retire to the cellar to sit out the air raid. As they were drinking their tea, the first bombs began to drop. They could tell they weren't right on top of them, but somewhere not too far away to the south. They finished their tea and were just about to set off for the cellar when they heard a frantic banging on the door. Richard looked at Jonathan and then went to answer the knock. On the step, he found a girl in a filthy red dress, gasping for breath.

"'Elp me please," she whispered.

Richard didn't need to think twice. "Come in."

The girl followed Richard into the sitting room. Jonathan was astounded. Standing before him was a young girl, filthy, barefooted and with her face and legs covered in sores. Yet, through all the grime, he recognised her.

"You're the girl who helped my mother with her shopping."

Choking with tears, she replied, "Angela."

"What happened to you?" asked Jonathan.

Before she could answer, Richard stepped in.

"You can tell us later, Angela. What you need now is a hot bath, some clean clothes and something to eat before you pass out."

Taking an arm each, the two men gently led her up the stairs and sat her on Ruth and Benjamin's bed.

"Go and run the bath, Jonathan, while I sort out something for Angela to wear. I think there's enough of your mother's stuff left for her. It'll be on the big side but it'll just have to do."

Jonathan ran the bath and returned a few minutes later to say that it was ready. Richard produced a large towel and led Angela to the bathroom.

"We're going downstairs. I'll be back in about twenty minutes and I'll tap on the door to make sure you haven't fallen asleep. Get dressed and bring down your old clothes. I'm afraid they'll have to go in the bin. When you've had something to eat, you can tell us what this is all about. You seem very upset and maybe frightened, but I can promise you that you're safe with us."

Angela nodded and sobbed a "thank you." She looked at the two of them and realised that her father and Patrick would be no match for these two.

When she reappeared half an hour later, Angela looked a lot better, although she was still very pale and her complexion was further wrecked by the sores on her face. She was wearing a brown, pleated skirt, with matching shoes and a green cardigan over a cream coloured blouse. Not surprisingly, everything was too big for her and there was a ghost of a smile on her lips. She couldn't care less what she looked like. She felt warm and safe for the first time in more than two weeks.

She slowly and methodically ate some sandwiches and drank some soup. Outside, they could hear seemingly endless explosions. Richard and Jonathan patiently waited for her to finish. She put her head in her hands and started to cry.

"Angela," said Richard softly, "we need to know what's going on."

"I know," she breathed in reply.

Angela then gasped out the whole story. Knowing where the Gerbers lived, she'd raced from her house knowing that they'd listen to her. She told them how her father and brother had burgled the house in which they were now sitting and how her mother had murdered Jonathan's father when he'd come to confront her family. Since that night, she said, she had been bound and gagged in their shed and she recounted her escape.

"They'll come for me, I know it. My mother thinks she'll 'ang if I get to the coppers."

"They must have treated you terribly if you're prepared to turn them in," said Jonathan.

"I 'ate them. For a while they even made me work as a prostitute down the dilly. Not the 'ole thing just, you know, er... hand jobs. I loathed it. I still feel 'umiliated."

The full horror of the evil Wallace couple's doings was now coming to light. Even Richard, who had seen one or two shocking things in his time, was stunned by the revelations, but he quickly recovered and said, "You'll have to tell the police as soon as possible before the rest of your family disappears, but we'll stay with you."

"We can't use the one in the 'igh Street," she said and then told them about Scott.

"No wonder he's not trying to solve my father's murder," Jonathan said.

"Where's the next nearest police station?" asked Richard.

"No idea," replied Jonathan. "I'll check in the phone book."

He looked in the book and then said to Angela. "What about Holloway?"

"Probably," she said, "but will they believe me against Scott?"

"I've had a bit to do with the police," said Richard, "and most of them are honest. They'll listen to you, don't worry. What's the number Jonathan?"

He picked up the phone and wasn't all that surprised to find it dead.

"Line's dead. We'll have to go there. We daren't take the car. We'll get in the way of the emergency services with this big raid on and, with all the blocked roads, we might never get there. Do you think you can make it there, Angela?"

"I'll try. 'Ow far is it?"

Jonathan produced a small, pale yellow book: the A-Z map of London's streets. He found the right page and quickly calculated the distance. "About one and a half miles."

"I think I can manage that," said Angela.

"Good. Jonathan, make a note of the route please."

"Alright, but I think I know most of the way. It's near the Arsenal Football ground."

While these discussions were going on, there was bedlam outside and even inside the house the noise was almost deafening, even though the centre of the raid was more than five miles away. They put on hats and coats. Richard shoved some crumpled-up newspaper in Ruth's shoes which were too large for Angela. The full horror of the bombing became evident as they stepped outside. To the south, the whole sky seemed to be ablaze and new fires were starting every second, as the Luftwaffe hurled bombs at the ancient City of London. It was windy but, fortunately for Angela, Richard and Jonathan it was blowing from the west. The poor East End was engulfed with the thick, black smoke that was pouring out of the fires. So intense was the racket, the drone of the bombers was drowned out. The heat, even at their distance from the inferno, was overwhelming, greater than even the warmest of summer days.

"The docks?" asked Jonathan.

"No, the City," replied Richard.

The tell-tale groans of buildings collapsing accompanied them as they set off.

"At least we're not in danger," said Jonathan.

"Let's hope not," said Richard. "It looks like they're using loads of incendiaries, as well as high explosive bombs. This could be the biggest raid so far."

Avoiding Angela's street, they passed the park, crossed Green Lane into Collins Road and Kelross Road, pausing as they reached Highbury Park Road. All of the houses were totally blacked out as the inhabitants huddled together in terror in cellars, public or Anderson shelters. The fire bombs continued to rain down on the City.

"Old London's burning down," sighed Richard. "Buildings that have stood for centuries are being smashed into thousands of tiny pieces and reduced to ash." Still it continued, with a fresh explosion almost every thirty seconds, closely followed by the whoosh and crackle of another fire. Flames spat skywards. Old buildings, constructed of ancient inflammable bricks and timber and full of paper, paint and wood provided easy fuel for the terror from the sky. In great fear, but with grim determination, the three of them continued on their journey.

◆   ◆   ◆

George and Patrick couldn't find Angela anywhere. They searched the streets, looked behind every bush in the park and asked the very few people who were out and about if they'd seen her. No one had. George had a splitting headache from Angela's attack with the poker. They sheepishly returned to face Doris' wrath.

"What d'yer mean yer can't find 'er," shouted an enraged Doris. "She can't just 'ave vanished inter thin air. Ye'd better find 'er or it's the gallows fer us both."

"Where the 'ell d'yer think she is?" asked George.

"The cop shop," said his wife, "but not ours. She'll be too scared of Scott. My guess is 'olloway, so get there before she does and get yer bloody skates on."

They set off at a jog, following the same route as Angela, Richard and Jonathan, although they weren't aware of this. They were too worried about what would happen to them if they didn't find Angela. They padded on in silence, checking every side street and alley as they passed them. They reached Drayton Park Station and there, standing just outside, were two men and a girl.

Neither George nor Patrick expected to find Angela with anyone and her unfamiliar dress meant that, at first, they didn't recognise her. They approached the trio, hoping they might have seen Angela. Suddenly, in the light of the blazing sky, George recognised her. At the same time, Patrick saw she was with Jonathan and another man whom he did not recognise. The Wallaces were rooted to the spot. They couldn't approach her and yet, George knew that, if he let her go, he and the rest of his family were doomed. Angela looked across towards where her brother and father were standing and screamed. "It's them!"

She was barely heard above the din of the raid but now an even more sinister noise became apparent; the drone of a single bomber. It was probably on its way home or had wandered off course. Whatever the reason, the pilot decided to shed the last of his load and the chilling whistling of a high explosive device as it rushed towards them brought about two entirely different sets of actions. Richard grabbed hold of Jonathan and Angela and they ran into the station. As they entered the booking hall, they heard the gigantic explosion. They quickly realised that they were safe from it, but could see that George and Patrick were frozen to the spot. Not even the blast of the bomb could move them and, in the immediate aftermath, George could hear the terrifying pinging of shrapnel flying towards him. He recognised the danger too late and, while most pieces of the deadly metal passed harmlessly by, one tiny fragment hit George in the centre of his eye and passed straight into his brain. He uttered a cry of surprise and then collapsed to the ground. Patrick saw his father lying next to him either dead or dying stood paralysed in fear He hadn't noticed that, to his right, a small stick of incendiaries was quietly fizzing away on top of a pile of rubbish. Jonathan saw it and screamed at Patrick. "Get away, there's a fire bomb."

But it was too late. One of the small shells burst into life, lit the tinder dry rubbish and the flames engulfed Patrick who ran towards the station screaming and flapping his arms. Richard moved to help him but it was a futile gesture. The boy's hair and clothes were fully alight and his skin was melting. Soon, he dropped to the ground and slowly died, with a low moan escaping from him until he was silent.

"Let's get to the police station. The man might still be alive," said Richard. In all the drama, he'd completely forgotten about Angela who stood beside Jonathan with tears streaming down her face.

"I'm sorry, Angela," said Richard. "I'd completely forgotten that it was your father lying there."

"I don't care about 'im, but Patrick needn't 'ave died. 'E could've been all right. It wasn't the Germans who killed 'im, it was me mother and father."

"I understand what you're saying," said Richard, "but, if he's alive, he could act as a witness against your mother."

"'Ed never do that. 'Es terrified of 'er."

Richard walked over to where George lay, bent down and searched for a pulse. He walked back towards them, shaking his head. "He's dead."

The all-clear sounded. Richard looked at his watch. "Good heavens, it's only midnight. They've left for home early."

"Probably nothing left to drop," said Jonathan.

"Or left to destroy," added Richard.

The three of them made their way onto Hornsey Road and, about ten minutes later, walked into Holloway Police Station. There was still Doris to deal with.

CHAPTER TWENTY-SEVEN

Richard took charge as they approached the desk which was manned, as usual, by a sergeant. Such was Richard's coolness and conviction, the policeman stayed silent throughout the long outline of the events that had brought them there. The sergeant took notes and, when Richard had finished, he turned to him and said, "Thank you, sir. I'm sure you understand that this has been a very difficult night. The raid seems to have been the biggest yet and it's a matter of all hands to the pumps and we haven't any officers to spare at the moment. As soon as the phones are working, I'll ask the emergency services to recover the bodies. It would help," he said, looking at Angela, "if you could give us a description."

Angela described her father and told the officer that there wouldn't be much left of Patrick to recognise.

"May I ask you, sir, why you didn't report this to your local police station?" the sergeant asked when he'd finished jotting down the details.

Richard explained about Detective Constable Scott.

"These are very serious allegations, sir. I'm not sure we can handle them here. That would be a matter for Scotland Yard."

"In that case," said Richard, "perhaps you could try to speak to Detective Superintendent Newman. He knows me well from some things we did together in the summer before the war. I'm sure he'll know what to do."

"I'll ring him in the morning, sir, assuming the phones are working."

As Richard and the others were thanking the officer, another uniformed policeman walked in. The sergeant asked him where he was going and was told that he was collecting something from his locker. "Then I'm heading off to the City to lend a hand. It's total chaos there."

"In that case, please drop these three off at their house on your way to the City. It's not far."

The policeman nodded his assent and drove them to Jonathan's home. Periodic explosions and the roar of a thousand fires filled the air as they drove eastwards. It was just before two in the morning when they entered the house. They drank the last of the soup and then went to bed. Angela slept in Jonathan's room and Richard and Jonathan shared Benjamin and Ruth's big double bed. Back in south London, Ruth almost certainly knew about the massive raid and must have been worried sick about Jonathan and Richard. Frustratingly, there was nothing she could do. The phones just weren't working.

All three slept like logs. Richard woke first, shook Jonathan awake and then banged on Angela's door. Angela awoke with a start and, for a moment, couldn't remember where she was. As she shook the remnants of the best night's sleep she'd had in ages from her head, she remembered the horrors of the night before. The phones were back on so Richard rang Inge and told her what had happened. Then Jonathan rang Mary and asked to speak to her mother. He told her he was alright. They'd be back as soon as the police had sorted things out. Jonathan asked Angela if she wanted to speak to anyone and she gladly rang Pam's house. Pam wasn't there so she spoke to her mother who was horrified at the news and insisted that Angela come to stay with them as soon as she could. Angela thanked her and told the others.

A car pulled up outside at ten o'clock. A tall handsome man in his forties introduced himself at Detective Inspector Hawkins. Two others were with him, both in uniform; PC Reece and WPC Dougan. The plain-clothes officer passed Superintendent Newman's best wishes to Richard and then told them briefly about the second Great Fire of London which was still raging in the City. He told them that casualties were fairly light as relatively few people lived in the City. More than a dozen firemen had died and countless buildings had been completely destroyed. The level of the Thames was low and this had made it well-nigh impossible to get sufficient pressure into the hoses. Hawkins then turned to Angela and gently asked her to recount the whole story to him, which she did in a faltering voice. Hawkins stopped her for a moment and asked permission to use the telephone. He spoke to a colleague at the Yard and instructed him to organise, as a matter of urgency, a search warrant for the Wallace house.

He resumed and Angela told him about her family's close ties with Scott.

"Have you any evidence to support this?" the detective asked.

"I over 'eard several chats where Scott give 'em a list of empty 'ouses for them to burgle."

"I'm sure you're telling the truth and, no doubt, they did burgle these houses. But a court of law would say this was hearsay. Can you be a bit more specific about, say, one incident?"

Angela stared at her hands, folded in her lap, and remained silent for more than a minute. Then she looked up.

"There is one thing. I remember my father boastin' to me mother that 'e and Scott had arrested a Jewish couple, telling 'em they were gonna be interned. I think it 'appened in Romford. Then they dumped the Jewish people outside Barkin' Police Station and drove back to collect Patrick. 'E'd been robbin' the 'ouse while they were drivin' over to Barkin'."

"That could be very helpful. Just a minute." He turned to Jonathan and asked if he could use the phone again. Jonathan nodded and Hawkins again spoke to his colleague at the yard, asking him to contact Romford Police Station and check the story which he outlined over the phone. "Call me back on this number, please."

He finished questioning Angela and they all had a cup of tea. As they drank, the phone rang. Jonathan answered and passed it to Hawkins, who listened and then gave out some instructions.

"Thank you, Angela," said Hawkins. "It seems that the couple involved, who are called Abrahams by the way, had already complained to the police about this, before they were interned on the Isle of Man. They're back now and, with every good reason, they're still kicking up a fuss. A warrant has been issued for Scott's arrest. My colleagues at Romford are going to collect the Abrahams and take them to attend an identity parade. If they point the finger at Scott, we've got him."

Richard went out to buy some food for lunch and came back with a modest snack. He also had The Daily Mail with him. The front page of the newspaper had an amazing photograph of St Paul's Cathedral surrounded by smoke and flames during the previous night's raid.

"Well that's one building in the City the Nazis didn't manage to knock down," Richard said, "although Inspector Hawkins told me that more than two dozen bombs had been dropped on it. That picture looks like a symbol of defiance."

"I hope my school's still in one piece," added Jonathan.

While they were admiring the photograph, another car drew up outside. Hawkins went out and greeted his plain-clothes sergeant who was clutching a warrant giving them permission to search the Wallace house. He came back in to thank Angela, Jonathan and Richard. They expressed their gratitude to him.

"Murder's a serious business," he said, "and dishonest policemen need to be weeded out and punished. I'll probably need you, Jonathan, to identify any of your family's possessions we find when we search Mrs Wallace's house. I assume that none of you will be staying here, so I need to take down contact telephone numbers and addresses."

He jotted them down.

"And thank you, Inspector," said Richard, "for acting so promptly."

Hawkins smiled at him. "You seem to have friends in high places, sir."

◆　　◆　　◆

Doris had sat up all night, smoking and drinking tea. She was beside herself. Where was Angela? Had she got to the coppers? What about George and Patrick? Were they alive or dead? She was shaken out of her trance by a sharp knock on the door. She opened it and found four people on the pavement outside; a policeman and police woman, both in uniform, and two men in plain clothes.

"Are you Doris Wallace?" asked the man in uniform.

"Yes."

"I'm PC Reece. I'm afraid I may have some bad news for you. We believe that your husband and son were both killed in last night's air raid. I'm very sorry, but we'll need you to come with us to identify their bodies."

"What about my daughter?" Doris asked in a trembling voice.

"Your daughter's safe and staying with friends. She's unhurt."

Doris knew then that it was all over.

"Do you want me to come now?"

"In just a moment, madam. Detective Inspector Hawkins has something to say to you."

"I have reason to believe that there are stolen goods on these premises and I have a warrant to search your property."

In other circumstances, Hawkins would have felt uncomfortable about turning over the house of a woman who'd just lost her husband and son, but one look at Doris' hard face and the thought of how she'd treated her daughter and the pain brought to the Gerber family was enough to dissolve all sympathy.

The Detective Sergeant and the uniformed policeman headed straight for the yard, broke the lock off the shed door and went inside. Hawkins marched into the kitchen and began rummaging through the drawers. He returned, holding a knife, his fingertips clutching it at the tip of the long blade. WPC Dougan kept a close eye on a trembling Doris. The other two returned from the shed, laden with all kinds of goods. Crucially, this included some jewellery which seemed to match Jonathan's description of his mother's possessions. Hawkins reached forward and detached the ruby brooch from Doris' cardigan. Everything was bagged up. Hawkins nodded to PC Reece who addressed Doris.

"Doris Wallace, I'm arresting you on suspicion of receiving stolen goods." He then cautioned her and told her she would be taken to the police station for further questioning as soon as she'd been to the morgue. From the morgue, Hawkins rang Jonathan and asked him to come to his local police station to try to identify his mother's jewellery. He explained that, if the case came to court, his mother would have to testify. Richard and Angela stayed in the house while Jonathan undertook the short walk to the High Street where he confirmed that the jewellery did belong to his mother and he remembered that the ruby brooch had been his grandmother's.

While Jonathan was walking back home, Doris was charged. Shortly afterwards, Scott appeared for his shift. He was arrested and taken to

Romford Police Station where Mr and Mrs Abrahams identified him from a hastily assembled line-up. The following day Scott and Doris appeared in separate Magistrates' Courts where both were remanded in custody. Doris, whom the police said could be facing more serious charges, was sent to Holloway and Scott to Pentonville.

◆   ◆   ◆

Richard drove Angela to Pam's house in Barnet. He got out of the car with Jonathan and each in turn hugged Angela. Even though they had known each other for a very short space of time, a strong bond had grown between the three of them. Angela walked up the pathway towards the waiting Pam and Richard turned the car towards south-west London.

◆   ◆   ◆

The next day was New Year's Eve. Hawkins had phoned to update them on the results of the court hearings. Celebrations were muted. 1940 had been a dreadful year both for the Gerber family and the country as a whole. Surely 1941 would be better? Ruth and Jonathan had made a pact. Though they would never forget Benjamin, life had to go on and they would not look back with regret, only forward with optimism. Those responsible for the tragedy that had overtaken them had either been killed, or were about to be punished. They had money, their health and the best friends that anybody could wish for.

Jonathan left for school on the following Monday and was welcomed back with both sympathy and delight. Everyone, teachers and fellow pupils, seemed pleased to see him. It was all rather cramped, with two schools sharing facilities designed for just one, but they managed. Soon the boys and staff recognised that Jonathan was keen to move on. He immediately began to study hard for his Higher School Certificate and returned to the playing fields and made a telling impact. He began to feel happy again, with only the uncertainty about Hilde clouding his mood.

Ruth went to work at Reg's store. She went house-hunting with Inge at weekends and soon found a delightful two-bedroomed terraced property less that half-a-mile from Inge's home. Negotiations on the sale proceeded quickly and Ruth arranged to move in at the beginning of February. She gave her notice to her landlord in North London and told him she would return there at the end of the month to collect their remaining possessions.

◆   ◆   ◆

Scott pleaded guilty at the Old Bailey and was sent to prison for seven years. He'd already been sacked from the Police Force. Doris was exhaustively questioned by Hawkins about the murder. He told her he had her fingerprints on the knife, which he was sure was the murder weapon. There were also traces of blood on the blade which corresponded to Benjamin's blood group. He had eye witness testimony from Angela and further evidence from Patrick's girlfriend who called and repeated to the police what Patrick had told her. Doris was returned to the Magistrates' Court, charged with murder and returned to Holloway. Hawkins visited Ruth and told her what had happened.

"But," he said, "I'm not sure we can get a conviction."

"Why on earth not?" Ruth asked, with a hint of frustration in her voice.

"To start with, the traces of blood on the knife are Benjamin's blood group, but it's a common one. The shape of the fatal wound suggests that her knife might have made it, but we can't be sure. Then there's Angela's testimony."

"Don't you believe her?"

"I do, but judges and juries don't like family members testifying against one another. They always believe there's some other motive for them coming forward. And how will Angela stand up to cross-examination by the defence? Patrick's girlfriend's testimony is just hearsay. It'll never make it into court."

Ruth looked at him with a resigned look on her face.

"I've got another option, however. She doesn't know of some of the question marks about the evidence. I could tell her that we've got enough evidence to secure a conviction and that would probably mean she would hang. If she would confess, I'd tell her the judge would almost certainly give her life imprisonment. We don't hang many women in this country."

"I don't want her to be executed. I don't believe in that 'eye for an eye' nonsense, but she should be punished," Ruth said.

"I'll see what I can do."

Hawkins met Doris in the interview room at Holloway on the following afternoon. He told her that pleading guilty would probably mean that she would escape the rope. She stared ahead, not looking at him. She remained totally silent. He asked her to think about his offer. He'd be back the following morning for her answer.

Doris was taken back to her cell. She ate her evening meal and then lay on her bed and thought about what Hawkins had said and what the rest of her life might hold for her. She had no money, no family and would probably die in prison. She wouldn't give them the satisfaction of hanging her. She'd go out on her own terms. She took off her thick, rough prison dress and sat on her bed in her underwear. It was cold, but her mind was set and she didn't notice the chill in her cell. She picked at the seams of her dress and then began to tear it into thin strips. She then painstakingly wound the strips together to make a strong rope. Doris hanged herself just before midnight and was long dead when her cell door was opened at six on the following morning. Hawkins was told what had happened when he arrived to interview Doris. He returned to Scotland Yard and telephoned both Ruth and Angela, but there was no reply from either.

It was late that night when Angela found out that her mother was dead. She told Pam who put her arms around her. It was never mentioned again. The two girls continued to work at the A.B.C. Tea Rooms during the day and at rest centres on some evenings. At weekends, they went dancing. They met two soldiers who promised to look them up when they were next home on leave.

◆　　◆　　◆

Ruth received the news of the death of her husband's murderer with a kind of grim satisfaction, but she too was determined to move on. She told the others, but not Jonathan who was, in any case, due home at the end of the week to help with the house move.

The war spluttered on. The Italians continued to retreat in the Balkans and North Africa. They left Ethiopia and the Emperor was returned to his throne. Churchill's constant badgering of President Roosevelt began to show signs of success as the Americans began to consider a Lend-Lease Bill which would give Britain weapons and ammunition, food and money to boost our war effort. The Blitz continued and cities all over the country suffered death and injury and destroyed homes and other buildings. The Battle of the Atlantic continued to go badly as more ships, carrying vital supplies, were lost. The Swastika flew over most of Europe. The Germans seemed indomitable. The free world watched, waited and hoped that things would change in 1941.

Jonathan briefly returned home at the end of the month. He was in a good mood. On the day before, his school had played the public boarding school, who were their temporary hosts, at rugby. Rugby was the public school's main game, not football which they regarded as a working-class sport. They expected to win comfortably but reckoned without Jonathan who caught, passed, tackled, ran and fell on the ball like a man possessed. Seeing this, the rest of the team raised their game to new heights and they edged a thrilling match by 18 points to 16.

Richard drove Jonathan and Ruth to North London to help them to clear the house. Briefly, bad memories surfaced when they arrived, but these were quickly dismissed as they set about packing everything into the car. They were in the sitting room, congratulating themselves on a job well done, when there was a knock on the door. Ruth answered it. A post man stood outside.

"Is there a Jonathan Gerber here?"

"Yes." Ruth called Jonathan to the door.

"Sign here please, sir."

Jonathan did as he was asked and was handed a large white envelope with his name and address typed on the front. He walked back into the sitting room and looked at Richard and his mother.

"Perhaps you've been called up," Ruth said.

Richard laughed. "You're not citizens, not yet anyway."

Jonathan nervously opened the envelope. Inside was a typewritten sheet and another envelope which had clearly been opened and re-sealed and had "censored" and other things stamped on it. He dropped the sheet of paper on the floor and stared in disbelief at the envelope. He recognised the writing. In a fever pitch of excitement, he tore open the envelope and took out the letter. The others stood in total silence as he read it. He looked up at his mother and his friend, his eyes filling with tears. Gradually a huge smile spread across his face.

"It's from Hilde," he said. "She's alive. She's living with her family in Switzerland."

Two Families at War is a work of fiction, built around real events. The only real liberty which I took was to invent a restaurant and night club bombing based on the destruction of the Café de Paris in an air raid in March 1941.

The vast majority of the characters are fictitious and several appear in my previous novel *The Blue Pencil* (Sacristy Press, 2012). However, an Italian-born swimmer who had represented Great Britain in the 1936 Olympic Games in Berlin was interned on the Isle of Man in 1940. Harry makes his second appearance in these stories. This was my choice of pseudonym for a real person who had been the press attaché in the German Embassy in London in the early 1930s.

The most important real character in *Two Families at War* is Gustav Schröder, Captain of the *MS St Louis*. After the passengers of the *St Louis* left for their various destinations, he took the ship back to Hamburg before crossing the Atlantic once again for a series of North American and Caribbean cruises. The ship was caught in the ocean at the outbreak of war and Schröeder cautiously steered her home to Hamburg via Murmansk, reaching her home port on New Year's Day 1940. Schröder then took a desk job and never returned to sea. The *St Louis* remained in Hamburg Harbour where it was badly damaged in the extensive air raids on the port. After the war, it was repaired and served as a floating hotel before being scrapped in 1950.

Schröder himself suffered, like so many Germans, in the immediate aftermath of the war. Unable to find work, he tried, unsuccessfully, to start a second career as a writer. Some of the former passengers of the *St Louis* sent food and clothing to help him through the harsh post-war times. Like so many Germans who had played some part in the war, he was arrested as part of the denazification process but was quickly acquitted following testimony from former passengers of the May and June 1939 voyage of the *St Louis*.

Schröder was honoured with the order of merit in 1959 by the Government of the Federal Republic of Germany for saving the lives of the passengers of the *St Louis*. In 1993, the Yad Vashem of the state of Israel, the Jewish living memorial to the holocaust, posthumously recognised the former *St Louis* captain as a righteous gentile among the nations. He died in 1959 at the age of 74.

A vast majority of the *St Louis* passengers who went to England survived the war. Most of those who settled in France, the Netherlands and Belgium were rounded up and sent to their deaths in the extermination camps of Eastern Europe.

Dame Joanna Cruickshank had founded the RAF Nursing Service in 1918 and became Matron-in-Chief in the 1920s. She retired in 1930 and was soon after created a Dame of the British Empire. She was brought out of retirement in the summer of 1940 to become Commandant of the Women's Camp on the Isle of Man. She went back into retirement at the end of the war and died in 1958.

NOTES ON SOURCES

Amongst the many books which I consulted were:

Connery Chappell, *Island of Barbed Wire: The Remarkable Story of World War Two Internment on the Isle of Man* (Robert Hale, 2005).

Edward Smithies, *Crime in Wartime: A Social History if Crime in World War II* (Allen & Unwin, 1982).

Juliet Gardiner, *The Blitz: The British Under Attack* (HarperPress, 2010).

Juliet Gardiner, *Wartime: Britain 1939–1945* (Headline Review, 2005).

Peter Gay, *My German Question: Growing Up in Nazi Berlin* (Yale University Press, 2000).

Richard J. Evans, *The Third Reich in Power: How the Nazis Won Over the Hearts and Minds of a Nation* (Penguin, 2006).

Yvonne M. Cresswell (ed.), *Living with the Wire: Civilian Internment in the Isle of Man During the Two World Wars* (Manx National Heritage, 2010).

I visited most of the locations for the novel and spoke to eyewitnesses of the Blitz in Stoke Newington, London, as well as others around the country who remember the dark and dangerous period from September 1940 to May 1941. My own expansive collection of documentary film of the period again served me well.

ACKNOWLEDGEMENTS

I would like to thank my publishers Richard Hilton and Thomas Ball of Sacristy Press. It was they who published my first novel, *The Blue Pencil*, in November 2012. Had it not been for them, I would still be doing the interminable round of emails and telephone calls to literary agents.

My friend Brian Cooper did a quite fantastic job in proofreading this novel. The first read by him produced so many mistakes from me that I sometimes wondered if I was literate. He then did a second read and came up with more suggestions, all of which I adopted. Thank you very much Brian.